"Blackie..."

Catherine said his name tentatively, uncertain how to phrase her apology. "It's none of my business how you live your life. It's just that...I suppose I care about what's good for you," she finished lamely.

Blackie turned around quickly, surprise and pleasure on his face. He caught her shoulders and, as his gaze met hers, his smile faded.

"Cat'rine...." His fingers tightened on her arms, and his voice sank to a husky whisper. "A man could drown in your eyes. Did you know?" He pulled her forward and took her mouth with his.

This time the kiss was different. His lips, hot, moist, moved over hers with a fierce hunger that hinted at the banked heat within him. His mouth tasted like dark wine, and when his tongue invaded her mouth, she felt the breath go out of her body.

Out of her depth, Catherine felt as if she were drowning in some forbidden bayou.

ABOUT THE AUTHOR

Sisters Judith Linsley and Ellen Rienstra share more than close family ties—both are passionate about their Cajun roots. In fact, the pair has also penned a historical romance based on their forbears' past. Natives of Beaumont, Texas, Judith and Ellen chose to honor their hometown with their contemporary romance pen name. *Catherine's Song* is their first novel.

Catherine's Song

MARIE BEAUMONT

Harlequin Books

TORONTO • NEW YORK • LONDON
AMSTERDAM • PARIS • SYDNEY • HAMBURG
STOCKHOLM • ATHENS • TOKYO • MILAN

For the Condors—
Becky, "K", Keith, Lis—
for Pat, who began it all;
and for Maureen Walters
and Nancy Roher.

Published February 1990

First printing December 1989

ISBN 0-373-70391-0

CHAPTER ONE

LAISSEZ LES BON TEMPS ROULER, the overhead banner read. The Cajun motto. *Let the good times roll.*

If only she could, things would be so much easier.

Catherine Nolan walked beneath the banner and slowly moved across the broad expanse of lawn. Before her stood the white Victorian frame house that served as the headquarters of the Society for the Preservation of Louisiana's Past. Since she was employed as a restoration architect for the organization and had lived in New Iberia for the past two months, the headquarters were a familiar sight. But tonight everything looked different. Tonight was the big fundraiser.

The grounds had been decorated for a party—a *fais-do-do,* the Cajuns called it—and it promised to be a big one. The crowd was already gathering, some sitting at the cloth-draped picnic tables that had been set out beneath the enormous oak trees, others chatting in little groups in the fading daylight, still others moving across the wide front porch and through the leaded-glass front doors of the house. A few of these people she knew, most she did not. She hadn't done much socializing since she had come to New Iberia, less even than she had done in Atlanta. She certainly couldn't say the same for the people here; they seemed to seize any excuse for a party. And judging from the general laughter, everyone was having a good time.

Everyone but herself. This wasn't the kind of evening she enjoyed. Right up to the last minute she had planned to stay away, using her work load as an excuse. It was Gussie, her assistant, who had talked her into going. "You can't work all the time, Catherine," she had scolded. "Besides, the restoration architect is *expected* to be there."

That hadn't made it any easier, but finally Catherine gave in. Gave up, was more like it. Gussie was hard to resist. She had dismissed Catherine's protest that she didn't have the right clothes with an airy, "Just wear something casual, Catherine. You worry too much."

Undoubtedly she did worry too much, Catherine thought, but her tailored ivory linen dress was definitely not casual. Her limited budget had been spent on clothes suited to an Atlanta office. She looked around at the men in shirtsleeves and women in brightly colored cottons, living reminders that she was as different from the Cajun people as bouillabaisse from gumbo. *Maybe I can just say hello and then slip away...*

"Catherine?" someone called. She looked around. Gussie was waving to her from one of the far tables. Resigned, Catherine threaded her way through the talking, laughing crowd to where Gussie was sitting with her latest love interest, a young dentist from Lafayette.

Christened Augustine Espasie Marie LeBlanc, she had always been known as Gussie to her friends and her Cajun relatives—in other words, practically the entire population of New Iberia. Tonight, her bright red cotton dress created a vivid foil to her brunette beauty. Her face was even more animated than usual, and her dark eyes snapped with energy and *joie de vivre.*

"Catherine, I'd like you to know Alain Voisin," she said. "Alain—my boss, Catherine Nolan."

Alain, a slender, dark-haired young man who appeared to be in his late twenties, rose and shook hands.

"I'm glad to meet you, Alain. I've heard such nice things about you." Catherine gave Gussie a meaningful look.

"Not from me, she hasn't." Gussie sounded like her usual impudent self, but Catherine could see that her cheeks were turning a bright, becoming pink. "Hush, Catherine. He'll get the big head."

Alain grinned, looking anything but conceited. Catherine laughed. "You hide it beautifully."

"Nobody can keep a big head around Gussie," Alain remarked. "She's good at setting people straight."

"You're absolutely right." Catherine remembered all the times Gussie had volunteered her well-intentioned but extremely candid advice. Catherine was almost used to it now, this forthrightness that seemed to be a common trait here, but at first it had required quite an adjustment.

"If you're finished talking about me, Alain," Gussie said, "you could at least get Catherine something to eat."

"I'll take you up on it." Catherine sniffed appreciatively. Mingling with the smell of new-mown grass in the humid air was a sharp, spicy aroma.

"Glad to." Alain pulled out a chair for Catherine. "I'll be right back."

Catherine sat, relaxed a little. In the eddies of small talk that ebbed and flowed around her, she picked up almost as much of the liquid syllables of Cajun French as of English. Since their exile from their native Acadia, in what was now Nova Scotia, over two hundred years ago, the Acadians—Cajuns, they called themselves—were heirs to a culture that, until the past few generations, had remained virtually unchanged. Even now they retained many of their old customs, and sometimes Catherine felt as though she was living in a foreign country.

"There's a good crowd tonight," she remarked to Gussie.

"Oh, everybody turns out for these things. We can raise a lot more money when we give people a good time for it." Gussie watched people milling around, talking, laughing, carrying plates of food to tables. "Tonight should cover a lot of expenses for Bonne Journée. If we're lucky, there'll be some left to apply to the Arceneaux house."

Bonne Journée and the Arceneaux house. The names struck very different chords. Catherine was already in the throes of the work at Bonne Journée, the 1834 mansion she had been hired to restore, and the job was a joy, the kind of project every restoration architect dreamed about. But the Arceneaux house would be something else again. *If* she decided to do it, that was.

Just then Alain emerged from the house, precariously balancing a plate, a bowl and a plastic cup in his hands. With a sigh of relief, he set them in front of Catherine.

"I can't possibly eat all this," she protested. The plate was hopelessly overloaded, and the bowl was filled to the brim with gumbo. Even the beer was in a giant-sized cup. "What is this?" She pointed to what appeared to be shrimp. "It looks wonderful."

"Crawfish *etouffé*. It *is* wonderful."

Crawfish. Or, as they had called them in her high school biology class, crayfish. What else had she heard them called here? Mud bugs? *Crustaceans,* she reminded herself sternly. She'd been working too hard to eat out much, so she had not tasted them, but she didn't tell Gussie that—Gussie thought she worked too much as it was. Catherine swallowed hard. When in Rome, she decided, and gingerly took a bite. It was delicious, as was everything else.

"What's the schedule tonight, Gussie?" she asked.

Gussie looked at her watch. "It's almost time for the *fais-do-do* to start."

"Good." Alain grinned. "It's almost time for my nap, especially if I eat all this food."

Gussie glanced at him scornfully. "Oh, you. You'd better wake up—you and I are going to dance all night long."

Alain groaned. "She's always like this when Blackie plays."

"Blackie?" Catherine asked.

"Blackie Broussard. Don't tell me you've never heard of him." Gussie shook her head. "See? I told you you needed to get out more. Blackie's got the best Cajun band anywhere around. They were lucky to get him for tonight."

Alain laughed. "Lucky, my foot. You just wouldn't let him say no. He didn't have a chance."

"Well, I helped a little," Gussie confessed. "But he's booked up so far ahead, even that doesn't always work."

Catherine was mildly curious. "He must be good."

"He's the best," Gussie affirmed. "He and his band play all over the state."

Just then fragments of music drifted out. Catherine turned to look. Mikes had been set up on the wide back porch, and a wooden pallet had been laid on the grass for dancing. Some musicians were setting up. She could see a guitar, a mandolin, a fiddle, a triangle and an accordion. An accordion. She looked at the man holding the small, square instrument. She didn't have to ask which one was Blackie Broussard. She knew.

No more than medium height, he was powerfully built, with heavily muscled shoulders tapering to a narrow waist and hips. Glossy black hair curled crisply across his wide forehead and along the collar of his blue chambray work shirt. His features—well-defined black brows, a strong aquiline nose and a square jaw—proved his Cajun heritage. As Catherine watched, he threw back his head at someone's remark. His face split wide with laughter, his white, white teeth making a startling contrast to his olive skin.

Then she saw his eyes. A dark, molten brown—black, really—they flashed magnificently with amusement. It occurred to Catherine that they could probably flash the same way in anger. Even across the expanse between them, he seemed to be larger than life.

The aura this man exuded was—what? Purely physical, Catherine decided, for want of a better word. So much raw energy. She was reminded of her father, laughing as if he hadn't a care in the world.

"*Allons*, boys," Blackie called out, and the fingers of his right hand moved on the keys of the accordion, sending out a rippling cascade of sound that poured through the scattered patches of small talk. The crowd hushed a little, and Catherine heard Blackie's rapid, "*Un, deux, trois, quat'*..." The band swung into a fast two-step. The violin sang a wailing obligato, and the guitar throbbed with a strident rhythm, and over and above it all, weaving a continuous thread of sound that beckoned like a magic spell, was the shrill, high, *chank-a-chank* sound of the accordion. Catherine felt herself being pulled bodily along with the music. Her toes began tapping of their own accord. The crowd, less inhibited, clapped, cheered and stomped.

Blackie was an act. His fingers flew over the buttons of the accordion, and his powerful arms guided the bellows in a quick push-pull motion. His whole body responded to the music. His face animated, his eyes glinting in the light from the spotlights on the porch, he stepped to the mike and began to sing in a clear tenor voice. In spite of her six years of school French, Catherine couldn't really understand the words.

"Tu m'as dit, jolie fille, tu voulais plus t'en rev'nir..." As he sang, he threw back his head and closed his eyes in the most blatant, sensuous display of pleasure Catherine had ever seen. Watching him, she felt as if she was intruding, and yet she couldn't seem to keep her eyes off him.

Couples began to move onto the board pallet to dance, stepping to the insistent rhythm. All were caught up in the music; even those who weren't dancing patted their feet or hands or moved in their chairs to keep time.

"Excuse us, please, Catherine?" Without ceremony, Gussie got up and pulled a grinning Alain to his feet and began to push him toward the dance floor, her feet moving the whole way in a funny little step to the music.

Laughing, one part of her wishing she could join in, Catherine turned to watch the band again. The other musicians seemed to be enjoying themselves every bit as much as Blackie was—all, that was, except the fiddle player, a wiry, bowlegged old man with a long, sorrowful face. His heavy eyebrows met in chronic dismay over black eyes that looked dolefully on the world, and two deep lines went from nose to mouth on either side of his lean, wrinkled face. Never smiling, he sawed away on his fiddle, filling the air with its high, wailing sound.

Here's one Cajun who doesn't have much *joie de vivre*, Catherine thought. But then the old man suddenly tilted his head and closed his eyes. *That's pure ecstasy,* she realized in amazement. But why did he look so sad?

The band finished its tune and swung immediately into a stately Cajun waltz. Alain and Gussie stayed to dance, as they did for the next two or three numbers. In fact, the wooden floor never emptied of dancers, becoming more and more crowded as other couples joined in. Catherine thought of her father, something she usually tried not to do. He would have loved this party, just as he had loved any gathering where there was entertainment, food and drink. Particularly drink. She could see him now, surrounded by appreciative listeners, particularly the female variety, the weakness in his handsome face hidden behind his engaging smile. And her mother's face, tight, disapproving...

Finally, after one particularly long, fast two-step, Catherine saw Alain throw up his hands in protest and head for the table, Gussie following reluctantly.

"Hooee!" Alain remarked, sitting heavily in his chair. "I can't dance like I used to."

"I don't see how anyone dances at all after such a huge meal," Catherine said.

"Blackie always plays one song right after another," Gussie said. "He says it's good exercise." She sat back in her chair and settled to watch the band.

They were playing another waltz. Blackie began to sing again. *"Si j'aurais cinq jours dans ma vie, j'en donnerais trois dans les cinq pour passer les deux autres avec toi..."* Catherine couldn't understand all the words, but, watching him, she realized with a little shock that his eyes were bright with tears. He lifted his face and closed his eyes, and the tears spilled over, making silver tracks down his cheeks in the light from the spots. She looked around. The expressions on the faces of the listeners reflected the melancholy mood of the song, but no one seemed surprised that he wept. She turned to Gussie, who sat totally absorbed.

"Gussie." She had to call her twice to get her attention. "Gussie—he's crying."

"Of course he's crying," Gussie answered in surprise. "It's a sad song. It's about a man who lost his sweetheart—it says that if he had five days left to live, he'd give three of them to spend the other two with her. Blackie lost his wife about three years ago. He's probably thinking about her."

"He must have loved her very much," Catherine remarked. *To cry in public like that,* she left unsaid.

"Oh, he did. He goes on." Gussie shrugged. "Life goes on." She turned to watch Blackie.

"Chèr Papa..." Blackie sang, and this time Catherine understood the words well enough to know what he was singing about. Another sad song, something about a young girl and her father... To her horror, Catherine felt her own tears well up, and a large lump constricted her throat. What was wrong with her?

Catherine looked away, tried to shut her ears. Suddenly, the music, the crowd, the strangeness of the whole scene had exhausted her. She was relieved when the song was over at last and the musicians took a break. She stood up to stretch, trying to bring herself into focus.

"Ready to do the two-step?" a voice behind her said. She turned around to see Clarence DuBois.

Clarence, a tall man with salt-and-pepper hair, an aquiline nose and a thin moustache, was a successful businessman and the current president of the Preservation Society board. He was also a courtly, old-fashioned gentleman who reminded Catherine of people she had known growing up in Atlanta. Since her arrival in New Iberia, he had helped her greatly, making contacts, finding dependable workers, locating materials. His lively interest in every phase of the Bonne Journée restoration project never failed to brighten Catherine's day, no matter how badly things might be going.

"I don't think I have the stamina," she answered. "How's my big boss?"

"Very well indeed, *ma belle*. You look beautiful, as always. Such wonderful green eyes—here, we don't see them so often." Instead of shaking her hand, he brought it to his lips. "It's good to see you enjoying yourself tonight—you've done nothing but work since you've been here."

"That should be praise for my dedication." Catherine eyed him quizzically. "Why do I get the feeling it isn't?"

"Dedication is one thing, fanaticism is something else entirely," Clarence declared. "I learned long ago that play is just as important as work."

"Maybe you're right. Your habits have obviously agreed with you."

He chuckled, "Actually, *chère*, so have yours."

"It's a standoff." She laughed.

"Hello, Catherine, Clarence." Toni MacDonald, the executive director of the society and Catherine's immediate boss, came up to them. With her was her husband, Doug, a good-natured, craggy-featured Scot who worked for the local office of the Corps of Engineers.

"Hi, MacDonalds," Catherine said. "Toni, you've done a wonderful job tonight."

Smiling, Toni shrugged. "It's all in getting the right volunteers."

Catherine nodded, not fooled for a minute. Toni was a marvel of organization and execution. And gorgeous, besides. Her dark hair was arranged tonight in a sleek, trendy hairstyle, and she managed to look sophisticated even in her bright country print dress.

"It's wonderful, Toni." Clarence echoed the compliment.

"Thanks, Clarence." Toni turned to Catherine. "By the way, I hate to mix business with pleasure, but I'm afraid I'll forget to ask. Did Gussie give you the report on the Arceneaux house?"

The Arceneaux house again. Catherine had been afraid Toni would bring it up. It was an Acadian cottage, and all she knew about Acadian architecture, or the Acadian culture, for that matter, was that there hadn't been much written about it.

"She gave it to me this afternoon, but I haven't had a chance to read it," Catherine answered. It was true, although she could have made time if she had tried, she supposed.

Toni's tone sharpened. "Is there something wrong? You don't sound too enthusiastic."

Catherine shook her head. "Not really," she hedged. "It's just that from what I've heard so far, it's going to be a difficult job, and I'm not sure what you're going to have when you finish."

"A symbol." Toni spoke gently. "In the past generation the Cajun culture has almost died out, but lately there's been a movement to save it. The Arceneaux house is a perfect example of early Cajun architecture. Do you know anything about it?"

"I'm embarrassed to say that I don't," Catherine said. "I guess that's part of the problem. I don't feel really confident about doing the job."

"Mais jamais," Clarence exclaimed. "We already know you can handle the technical end, and we'll be here to teach you the rest. If anybody can do it, you can. You can learn what you need to know."

"Thanks, Clarence." She smiled at him. Leave it to Clarence to make her feel good. "I'll think about it."

Someone called his name from the porch, and he raised his hand in a wave. "Save me a dance, *chère*." He kissed his hand to her as he moved away.

Uh-oh, she thought. Across the dance floor she spotted Gussie coming toward her, unashamedly towing Blackie Broussard by the hand. Catherine had seen him bare his soul, now she was going to meet him. Somehow, it should be the other way around. She braced herself.

"Catherine," Gussie announced proudly as they came up, "meet Blackie Broussard, the best musician in South Louisiana. Blackie, this is Catherine Nolan, the restoration architect who's working on Bonne Journée."

Their eyes met, and the length of his stare over-stepped good manners. Catherine was the first to look away. "I'm glad to know you, Mr. Broussard." She made herself extend her hand, almost afraid to touch the source of so much raw energy, yet strangely want-ing the contact. His hand, warm, square, enveloped hers, and the black eyes seemed to engulf her.

Then his mouth split into that joyous grin, showing his even white teeth. "Welcome, *chère*," he said. His voice was deeper than his singing had led her to be-lieve, and oh, my, its musical cadence held two hundred years of Cajun laughter—and tears. The warm sound of it swirled around her, enveloped her. She knew she should retrieve her hand, but somehow she didn't want to.

"Thank you," she said faintly. "Do you know Toni and Doug?"

"Sure." He at last relinquished her hand to reach for Doug's.

"Hello, Blackie," Doug said cordially. "Good to see you." They shook hands. "Say, while I'm think-ing of it, I've been meaning to talk with you about something. Mind if I give you a call?"

"Oh, not at all—not at all. But I can't think how I could help you." Blackie shrugged, smiling ingen-uously. "You know me, I'm too busy with my mu-sic."

"Yes, I see that." Doug was smiling, too, but Catherine could tell that more was being exchanged than just niceties. What could Blackie Broussard pos-sibly do for Douglas MacDonald?

"Your band sounds better every time I hear them, Blackie," Toni said.

"Ah, Toni, you know how to make me happy." To Catherine's amazement, he seized Toni's hands, kissed them soundly and clasped them to his powerful chest. Toni, dignified Toni, not only didn't seem to mind, she actually looked pleased.

"Of course, you're right." Blackie eyed Toni soulfully. "We do get better all the time."

Laughing, Toni pushed him away. "Someday I'll learn to save my compliments for someone who needs them," she said fondly. "Doug says it's his bedtime. Good night, Blackie. Catherine, Gussie, I'll probably see you tomorrow."

"Blackie—I'll call you." Doug MacDonald eyed Blackie directly.

"*Mais* sho', Doug. Any time," Blackie called after him.

"Now, where did Alain go?" There was purpose in Gussie's face that boded ill for Alain. "I hope he doesn't think I'm through dancing. Excuse me a minute." Like a small, vivacious butterfly, she was off through the crowd. Catherine had a strong suspicion that Gussie's departure had been planned. She was alone with Blackie, wishing she was somewhere else.

Blackie didn't seem to mind a bit. "Where are you from, Miss Nolan?" he asked politely.

"Atlanta."

"You're a long way from home," he commented.

"Yes." *In more ways than one,* she thought. Why couldn't she think of anything else to say? He was genuinely interested, or seemed to be, and all she could do was give him a one-word answer. She could feel herself drawing back, pulling her reserve around her like a shield.

"How do you like Louisiana so far?"

"I...like it, but I haven't really seen much of it. Except for Bonne Journée and my apartment, that is." She smiled feebly at him. There. She had said two whole sentences.

"No?" He looked genuinely shocked. "That's terrible. Do they chain you to your desk?"

"Not at all. I just don't want to fall behind schedule." She sounded stiff and punctilious, even to herself.

"How long will you be with us?" He must not have noticed. She hoped he hadn't...but now she could see a definite glint in his eyes.

"Probably another year, at least until I finish Bonne Journée. Then it will depend on whether the society decides to restore the Acadian house."

"I see." Apparently he *had* noticed. His grin grew more pronounced, and the glint in his eyes began to appear positively piratical. "But, *chère*, you don't have to call us *Acadians*." He drew out the word elaborately, and Catherine noticed that his Cajun accent was suddenly as thick as oyster gumbo. His tone became intimate. "You can call us Cajuns, *non*?"

What a warm, laughing, *teasing* voice. But she deserved to be kidded. She had sounded pompous and condescending. The sad part was, she knew very well that hardly anyone around here used anything but the term Cajun. But this man seemed to bring out every bit of stiffness in her.

"Cajun, then," she amended, hoping her red cheeks didn't show in the dark.

Gussie came back then, hauling an unprotesting Alain with her. But before they could speak, a dark, lean man walked up to them and slapped Blackie on the shoulder. Blackie turned. "Raymond," he said in surprise, gripping the man's hand. "*Comment ça va,* man?"

"*Ça va*, Ti-neg," the man answered, using the French diminutive for Blackie's name. "I just thought I'd see how the other half lived, me." He was near Blackie's height, but wiry rather than stocky. His hair was slicked down and he was dressed neatly, but unlike the other guests, he didn't look as though he was having any fun.

"Gussie, Alain, you already know Raymond," Blackie said. "Miss Nolan, this is Raymond Hebert. He and I grew up together. Raymond, this is Catherine Nolan, from Atlanta. She's going to show us how to fix up our old houses, her. Maybe even do the old Arceneaux place."

"Is that a fact?" The man's voice held neither enthusiasm nor approval. In fact, on second glance, Catherine thought she saw dislike in his eyes.

"So you think you know about Cajuns, *hein*?" This time the rudeness was unmistakable.

Catherine stiffened. "Not at all, Mr. Hebert. But I intend to learn."

He laughed, an abrupt, harsh sound. "Well, that's just fine. Maybe you'll do as good a job as the corps did on the swamp." His voice was heavy with sarcasm. "Everybody wants to help the Cajuns. Ain't that nice? See you, Ti-neg." After one more insolent stare at Catherine, he turned and left.

A few moments into the shocked silence, Catherine said quietly, "Is this the Cajun hospitality I've heard so much about?"

"Of all the things to say," Gussie exploded. "What's wrong with him, Blackie?"

"Oh, don't pay any attention to him." Blackie waved his hand dismissively, but Catherine could see the concern on his face. "He's just mad at the world. A few years ago the Corps of Engineers' drainage project dried up his trapping grounds in the Atchafalaya Swamp. Then his wife left him, couldn't put up with his temper any more, but he made that the fault of the corps, too. Now it looks like he's decided all outsiders are bad..." His words trailed off and he turned to Catherine. "I'm truly sorry, Miss Nolan. He had no call to act like that." Completely gone was the teasing tone; the French accent was hardly discernible. Now she heard a concern—gentle, genuine—that, strangely, made her want to cry.

A few vagrant notes began to filter through the silence. The band was on the porch. Suddenly, the sounds fell magically together, and the band led off with a fast two-step. In a flash, Blackie was transformed. His face lit up with his jaw-cracking grin. "My band didn't wait for me," he said. "They don't need me anyway. Come on, *chère*, dance with me." He held out his arms to Catherine, his eyes warm with entreaty.

Involuntarily she took a step back. "Oh, no, I couldn't," she protested. "I don't know the steps."

"No problem. I'll teach you," he coaxed.

"I...should go home now, really," she improvised, knowing she sounded phony. "I've got to be at work early tomorrow." To her amazement, she found herself wanting to say yes, to let him hold her, teach her how to move to that driving, compelling beat.

"That's too bad." His grin abated not a whit, making Catherine doubt any real disappointment on his part. "Now, Gussie, here—" He turned to her. "You'll dance with old Blackie, won't you, sweetheart?"

"Sure, Blackie." Gussie gazed worshipfully into his face.

Blackie turned to Alain. "I'll bring her right back," he said.

"Okay, Blackie," Alain said genially.

Blackie threw his arm around Gussie's shoulders and moved away with her. He looked at Catherine, his black eyes full of mischief. "Nice to have met you. See you soon—*chère*."

"Nice to have met you," Catherine murmured automatically. For a moment she watched them dance. Blackie held Gussie in the circle of his arm, and they turned gracefully, both lost in the sensuous, compelling beat of the music.

From nowhere, an old memory materialized in her mind—herself, in an exquisite party dress, afraid to move for fear of ruining it. Watching, while other children played happily. Suddenly she had had enough. Forgetting her half-promised dance with Clarence, she turned and fled into the shadows.

CHAPTER TWO

CATHERINE ARRIVED at Bonne Journée the next morning just after sunrise, well before the workers got there. She made instant coffee in her makeshift office in the pantry of the old mansion, then went to sit under the shaded loggia at the back of the house. Slipping off her shoes, she rubbed her toes on the cool brick floor and watched the muddy waters of the Bayou Teche move sluggishly by. The air was cool, and the house and garden were still in shadow. Except for the chirping of frogs, the silence was absolute.

In Atlanta the pace had been much faster. Even Catherine, who thrived on hard work, had sometimes felt pressured. Here things were more relaxed, and she had moments to reflect. Remembering the comments from the night before about her schedule, she smiled. People thought she was a workaholic, and maybe she was, but she gave herself time off. It was just that what she did for pleasure was usually related to her work in one way or another.

She relaxed, allowed her thoughts to drift to the original occupants of Bonne Journée: Joshua Millard, the South Carolina planter who had built it, and his wife, Eleanor, a Charleston belle who had come with her husband to the bayou country in the 1830s. Catherine had done so much research on them that they had gradually come alive for her, and now they seemed as real as her own family. At this rare, quiet time, the old house fairly stirred with ancient ghosts, and she could imagine Joshua and Eleanor and their children living, loving and dying here.

She drew strength from them. They had lived their lives in their assigned niches. Unlike her, they had never been caught between two life-styles, born to one, by necessity thrust into another, at ease in neither one. And their problems, real enough at the time, she supposed had been buried with them.

Her job was to guarantee their immortality. She could assure their places in history, preserve their home, their possessions and their name. In a way, it somehow alleviated the helplessness she had always felt at her own family's slow slide into poverty. Until the day they had had to sell it, she had dreamed of restoring the Nolan family home. Now, she hoped someday to buy and restore an old home of her own. In the meantime, restoring the old houses gave her a stability—a feeling of rightness—she had never known as a child.

She sipped her coffee, savoring the pungent flavor, and stared thoughtfully at the flowering honeysuckle covering the far bank of the bayou. If it hadn't been for Gerrard, she wouldn't be doing any of it. For as long as she could remember, she had wanted to work with the old houses she loved, and Gerrard Nolan, her father's first cousin and a national name in restoration architecture, had become her mentor. At thirty, she was one of the most promising young restoration architects in the South. When she finished the job on Bonne Journée, perhaps the timing would be right to take the next available job around Atlanta—if she didn't have to take the job on the Arceneaux house.

At the thought of the Arceneaux house, all her carefully nurtured self-confidence threatened to dissolve. She was as well-trained as any architect could be, but this project wasn't anything that was in the book. She might not be able to maintain the high standards she had always set. And Gerrard wasn't there to give advice. She had come to depend on him too much, she realized now.

There were so many reasons for her not to take the job—her unfamiliarity with the restoration, her wanting to go back to Atlanta—but the reasons that she should—the security of another job, the people, such as Gussie, Toni, and Clarence—weighed just as strongly.

Catherine stirred restlessly. Suddenly, unwanted and unbidden, an image of Blackie Broussard thrust itself into her mind in sharp relief—head thrown back in song, black eyes shining with tears. And then, the whole night came tumbling into her consciousness— the warm, friendly Cajun people, the insistent, compelling music, the man Hebert with his palpable hostility. An overwhelming mixture of pleasure and unpleasantness. She pushed futilely at the unruly memory, then, to banish it, rose and headed quickly for her office.

"OKAY, *MON AMI*, let's try this," Blackie urged, his head bent over the battered worktable. In one hand he held a delicate pair of tongs, clamped around a tiny wooden sound post. With the other he steadied a violin on the tabletop.

Carefully he inserted the sound post into the left F-hole of the violin, then gradually wedged it between the top and the back of the instrument. Removing the tongs, he held the instrument to his ear and plucked the strings.

He shook his head and moved the sound post just a fraction. This time, after he plucked the strings, he picked up a bow and drew it across them. The mellow sound filled the room, and Blackie sat back in satisfaction.

"You're a pretty one, you," he said aloud, admiring the subtle tiger-striped shadings on the maple back before he laid the violin lovingly in its case. He pulled a bandanna from his pocket and wiped the perspiration from his forehead, then stretched, working the kinks out of his back.

He glanced at his watch. He should have plenty of time to look at that accordion. One of his in-laws—a cousin of his wife, Angéline—had brought it in yesterday. It had been unused for years. It was dusty, and the bellows might be cracked, or perhaps some reeds were broken.

Blackie pulled the instrument from the shelf and set it on the table in front of him, running his fingers idly over the grimy buttons. He knew this accordion well. He used to borrow it when he was very young, during the years he was trying to prove he could play with the

best of the old-timers. One of them had been Angéline's father, his future father-in-law, and it had been
he who had lent it to Blackie.

Angéline. His hands stilled, and he stared unseeingly at the old instrument. He could recall her face
quite clearly, but the raw pain of grief had faded into
a poignant memory, to be recalled unexpectedly by
dark eyes, a love song—an old accordion. Sorrow was
unavoidable in life; he understood that. One grieved,
one recovered, one went on. It was only that sometimes—and it was usually when he played or sang—the
pain would rise up and take him; he would think of the
waste of such beauty and joy, and he would weep.

As always, he felt the dregs of a bitter anger. He
could accept Angéline's death, but not the reasons for
it. If she hadn't been so insistent on going to see about
Raymond's child—if they had only let him off work
to go with her—if the Corps of Engineers hadn't
ruined the drainage in the first place—if only the
damned outsiders had stayed out . . .

If, if, if. He ran a hand through his crisp curls and
smiled ruefully at himself. He was beginning to sound
like Raymond.

The thought of Raymond Hebert brought a tiny
frown to Blackie's brow. Raymond had been more
than rude; he had been downright hostile. And, while
Blackie had defended him, his real inclination had
been to defend Catherine Nolan. The problem was,
the impulse had come from more than good manners.

Catherine Nolan. Her slender, graceful image kept
disturbing his concentration. He had stared at her for
too long last night. She wasn't really his type, he

thought, remembering Angéline's generous curves, ebony hair and dimpled smile. But she had taken his breath away.

Catherine Nolan. She hadn't had much to say, had in fact seemed almost unfriendly. But he had seen plenty of emotion hidden in the bottomless green depths of her eyes. She had been unsure of herself, uneasy with the music, with the uninhibited crowd and especially with him. Actually, she had hidden it well; probably no one but Blackie had noticed it. There was really no way to compare her with Angéline, yet he had seen a child peering out from behind the adult in both of them. With Angéline, it had been her wish to be loved, petted, indulged. With Catherine, it was—what? Fear? He wasn't sure. But the urge to find out was irresistible.

Blackie chuckled softly at his own folly. It was no secret; he enjoyed women. He always had. And since Angéline's death, there had been women who had been willing to help him forget her. He had flirted with them, danced with them, sung for them and many times taken them to bed. Why, with all the cooperative women in the world, was he attracted to Catherine Nolan, who really didn't even seem to like him? At age thirty-six, he should know better. He shrugged, picked up a bottle of solvent and a cleaning rag and began lovingly to rub the dirt from the buttons of the old accordion.

"CAREFUL—CAREFUL," Catherine called. "It's very brittle." She stood in the large second-floor bedroom of Bonne Journée with her contractor, Frank

LeBoeuf, a burly, grizzled Cajun somewhere around middle age. With an air of expectation, they watched two of the carpenters gingerly lift an ancient pine plank out of the floor and lay it down. Catherine bent over it, studying it closely.

"See, Frank?" Turning it over, she indicated some barely discernible marks on the back. "The floor-boards were pit sawn."

"Pit sawn?" Frank scratched his chin.

"Yes. The logs were too heavy to lift, so they dug a pit and rolled the logs across it so they could saw them into planks."

"Yeah." Frank snapped his fingers. "I remember now. Folks back in the swamp used to cut logs that way when I was a kid. *Mais jamais*, I had forgot, me." He grinned at her. "Do those little marks really tell you that?"

Catherine smiled, enjoying his teasing. "Of course," she said. "All the old houses tell a story. You just have to know what to look for. We'll have to re-place some of the flooring," she went on. "But we'll do it the way it was done originally. The new flooring will be hand sawn, and hand planed, too."

Frank finally broke the pregnant silence. "But Cat'rine . . . nobody knows how to do that anymore."

"When the time comes, I'll show you how." Restoration carpentry had been part of her training. "We don't have to dig a pit, we'll just use the same tools they did."

"Catherine." Gussie poked her head into the room. "I hate to interrupt you, but Clarence is on the phone."

"All right, I'm coming." Catherine listened with amusement to the low murmur of voices behind her. Occasionally it was necessary to grandstand like that, to show the men she knew what she was talking about.

"By the way," Gussie said as they walked down the wide, curving staircase, "I still haven't found anyone to hand carve that segment of acanthus molding in the dining room, but there's a shop in Lafayette that can machine reproduce it for a lot cheaper."

"Gussie..."

Gussie threw up her hands. "I know, I know. Do it the way it was done before." She laughed. "I just thought I'd ask."

Catherine had the grace to smile ruefully. "I'm sorry I'm such a purist, but it would be a moral crime to put something machine made in this house."

"We'd probably be struck by lightning if we did," Gussie agreed. "I hate to sound picky, but aren't you afraid we'll run over budget if we keep doing things the slow, expensive way?"

"Not if we're careful," Catherine answered. "There are other ways to save on costs that won't compromise the integrity of the project."

She walked into her office and picked up the phone. "Catherine?" Clarence's cheerful voice rang in her ear. "How are you, *chère*? Did you have a good time last night?"

"Yes, I did." It was partially true; she had enjoyed most of the evening.

"Oh, me, those old songs brought back my courtin' days. That Blackie Broussard—he'll break your heart with his music, eh?"

And his voice, and his touch, Catherine thought.

"I've got something for the Arceneaux house." In Clarence's voice was an undercurrent of excitement. "Somebody's donated an old violin. It's supposed to have come down with the Cajuns from l'Acadie, in the Grand Dérangement of 1755. It's a wonderful gift, but we have to make sure it's real."

"Did the Cajuns bring anything with them when they were evicted?"

"A few small things—clothes, household goods, Bibles, that kind of thing. We haven't yet found a violin, but it's always a possibility. For a long time, they were the only musical instruments the Cajuns had. It's not likely they'd leave their music behind."

"I see." And Catherine, thinking of last night, was beginning to. She also saw that authenticating this violin meant a great deal to Clarence. "It would be wonderful if it's real, Clarence," she said. "But I don't know anything about musical instruments. You need an expert."

"Oh, that's no problem—Blackie can do it."

"Blackie?" Blackie Broussard?

Clarence laughed. "Blackie repairs all kinds of musical instruments and he knows about the old ones. Give him a call. His office is in Morgan City."

After Clarence had given her Blackie's number, Catherine hung up and stared thoughtfully at the papers on her desk. It was hard to imagine anyone who looked less like an expert on authenticating musical instruments than the man she had seen and heard last night. She thought of Blackie, in faded jeans and work shirt, lecturing on old violins before a dignified group of museum officials in business suits, and giggled.

Gussie stopped by her door. "What's so funny?"

"Nothing. How did Blackie Broussard get to be an expert on musical instruments?" Catherine asked.

Gussie shrugged. "I guess there was nobody else around here to do it. He had to learn to fix the ones he played. But how did you know?"

Catherine told her about Clarence's call. "I want to do this right, for Clarence's sake," she ended. "Isn't there anyone in New Orleans who does this?"

"Yes, but Blackie's better. They send people to him, lots of times. Why don't you want to use him?" Gussie asked bluntly.

"It's not that." But it was. She could deny it all she liked; she would have hesitated even if she had held his credentials in her hand. All too vivid were her memories of the night before, of retreating from Blackie's deep voice and brilliant smile even as part of her was drawn irresistibly to him. "I just like to be sure."

"Okay. You heard it from Clarence and me—that ought to be enough." Gussie laughed. "And when you call Blackie, he'll tell you. He's not shy."

"No, he's not," Catherine replied weakly, then caught a speculative gleam in Gussie's eye. She decided it was time to change the subject. "I'll call him in a minute. First I want to look over the Arceneaux house report. I've put it off long enough."

"Have fun," Gussie caroled, and left, her heels clicking energetically on the ancient pine floor.

Catherine tried to relax. She touched her moist brow with the back of her hand. It was only April, and the weather was already sticky. What would it be like here in the summer? Finally, she couldn't put it off any longer. She reached for the brown paper packet labeled Arceneaux House: Proposed Restoration, took a deep breath and began to read.

A very few pages into the report, she realized with growing dismay that the Arceneaux house job was going to be even harder than she had thought. The wood frame dwelling was to be moved from its present location to a spot on the Teche right next to Bonne Journée, where it would be restored and opened to the public.

How simple the project sounded, but completing it would be a monumental task. It would require the full scope of her training and then some. For much of it she would have no guidelines, no clear-cut plan that she could organize down to the last detail, and for her that was a particularly unpleasant prospect. Already in doubt of her ability to do a restoration in Cajun architecture, Catherine could feel her uncertainty growing by leaps and bounds. She needed the job, she needed the money, but she wouldn't take it if she didn't think she could earn it.

I can't do it, she thought. *I can't.* Maybe the society would let her continue to work on Bonne Journée and hire somebody else to work on the Arceneaux house. And maybe there would soon be an opening for a job closer to home. The trouble was, she couldn't count on either eventuality.

THIRTY MINUTES LATER, Gussie stuck her head around the door. "You haven't thrown anything yet," she remarked.

"I'm too numb," Catherine responded glumly. "Gussie, do you have any idea how much work this is going to be?"

"I know. I glanced at the report. But Catherine, you work us all under the table anyway."

"I don't mind working hard, but this is ridiculous."

"At least the Arceneaux house is in pretty good shape for its age. It's made of cypress, and you know cypress lasts forever."

Catherine frowned. "The structure, maybe. But the rest of it needs so much work—especially compared to this." She gestured around her at Bonne Journée.

"The Arceneaux house is older than this one," Gussie said quietly. "It was built in 1790, and I've seen the craftsmanship. It's beautiful."

Catherine picked up the faint defensive note in the younger woman's voice and was instantly contrite. "I'm sorry, Gussie," she said quickly. "I didn't mean to belittle the Arceneaux house." She regarded Gussie thoughtfully, wondering at the troubled look in her assistant's normally cheerful face. Was it really that important to her? In that moment, Catherine felt compelled to do something she very seldom did. She let down her reserve. But she trusted Gussie, and wanted there to be no misunderstanding between them.

"Gussie," she declared, "I'll tell you the truth—I'm scared. I've never done anything like the Arceneaux

house before, and I would hate to . . . do a poor job."
She couldn't quite bring herself to say *fail*.

"You couldn't do anything less than the best,"
Gussie asserted. "But you've got all of us, and we'll
help you any way we can."

Catherine knew it was true. Gussie, Clarence, Toni,
Frank—she wasn't in competition with these people.
She didn't have to prove herself to them; she could
depend on them. The realization brought an enormous relief.

"Thanks, Gussie." She looked at her fondly. "I
appreciate the offer, more than you know. I'm going
to take this report home with me tonight and do some
hard thinking. But if I decide to take the job, I promise to make the Arceneaux house as fine a restoration
as Bonne Journée."

Gussie's brow cleared, and she gave Catherine her
bright smile. "Oh, I know that," she said. "No need
even to mention it." She dismissed the subject with a
wave. "I'm going to the courthouse to check on those
deed records, then I'm going home. Need me any
more today?"

"I don't think so, but thanks. See you tomorrow."

Catherine looked again at the Arceneaux house report, hoping to read a little farther before she went
home, but Blackie's number, written on a small note-
pad, caught her eye instead. *I can't put it off any
longer.* She straightened in her chair and very deliberately dialed the number.

"Hello?" Blackie's smooth baritone came over the
wire, putting small holes in her composure.

"Mr. Broussard?"

There was a pause. Then, "Cat'rine, *chère. Comment ça va?*" His voice had grown even silkier.

"Very well, thank you," she replied, knowing she sounded hopelessly, ridiculously formal. "And you?"

"Fine, just fine. Except—" his tone grew plaintive "—I wish you'd call me Blackie."

Call him Blackie? At that moment it would have been easier for her to leap flatfooted over Bonne Journée. "Yes, of course," she said, not saying his name at all. "Clarence DuBois just called me. Someone has donated a violin to the society. It's supposed to be old enough to have come from Nova Scotia, but he wants to make sure. He'd like for you to authenticate it."

"I'll be glad to." Apparently, he was going to let her omission slide. "Where is it?"

"At the society headquarters." She was relieved to have gotten off so easily—she wouldn't have put it past him to insist on her saying his name, just to tease her. "Of course, if it would be more convenient for you, I can bring it to your office."

"Certainly not." She could hear the undercurrent of laughter in his voice. He was mocking her formality—but gently. "I wouldn't think of putting you out. I have to be in New Iberia tomorrow evening to play a dance. Can you meet me there around four o'clock?"

"That'll be fine. Thank you very much."

"Not at all. I'll see you then."

When Catherine hung up, she was surprised to find her hands were shaking. No one had ever affected her this way. In fact, it didn't take but a few minutes of reading for her to realize her concentration was gone.

Catherine picked up the report and the rest of her things and walked out of her office, sidestepping sawhorses, paint cans and other clutter in blind annoyance. As she walked through the stately rooms of the old home, however, she felt her nerves begin to settle, her mood to calm.

She stepped into the parlor, where work had not yet begun. In their accustomed places on the end wall hung the oil paintings, done in New Orleans so long ago, of Joshua and Eleanor Millard. The portrait of Joshua showed a stern, serious man with a stubborn jaw and light gray, penetrating eyes. He had succeeded in hacking a sugarcane plantation out of the swamps of South Louisiana.

Catherine looked at the portrait of Eleanor, whose blue eyes serenely regarded her from her nineteenth-century world. With her classic features, porcelain complexion and artfully arranged black hair, she was a striking beauty. Although she had been considerably younger than her husband, she had survived the rigors of the Louisiana wilderness to make an elegant home for him and their children. Catherine had come to feel a special kinship with Eleanor Millard.

She headed toward the front door and cast a last fond glance around her. *Bonne Journée.* A good day, the words meant—and a good day's work. What an appropriate name for this house. Appropriate for her, too. Before she was done here, she would have put in many a long, hard day's work. Far from daunting her, the prospect filled her with anticipation. For this restoration, at least, she was entirely confident of her ability. And for her, accomplishment satisfied the soul as nothing else did.

She locked the massive front doors of the old house behind her, crossed the spacious veranda and stepped out under the ancient, moss-draped live oaks that grew in the front yard. As she reached the edge of the property, she glanced back, unable as always to resist a last glimpse. In the late afternoon sunlight, huge white Tuscan columns lining the porch threw diagonal shadows across the grass. The ancient handmade bricks glowed a dusky coral against the dark trunks and the glossy leaves of the towering live oaks beyond. Catherine could feel the heat lessening ever so slightly. The tiniest of breezes fanned her cheeks, bringing with it the heavy fragrance of honeysuckle. Gratefully, she lifted her face as something pleasant stirred inside her. She reminded herself that she was lucky, after all. Bonne Journée was the kind of project she had been trained to do, was born to do—loved to do.

She drove home slowly in the lengthening shadows.

CHAPTER THREE

CATHERINE UNLOCKED THE DOOR to her apartment, a suite of rooms in a nineteenth-century house just down the street from Bonne Journée, and scooped her mail from the floor. Quickly, she glanced through it. A cream-colored envelope lay at the bottom of the pile. An Atlanta postmark—and her mother's writing.

Muttering something under her breath that ten generations of her forebears would have deplored, Catherine took the letter and settled on the sofa. She tore open the envelope, carefully smoothed the few monogrammed pages and began to read, sure already of the contents.

Dearest Catherine,
I hope this finds you well. I had hoped to feel better by now, but I've been very tired lately. I saw Dr. Wallace again last week—the visit was unproductive, to say the least. He prescribed something for my nerves, but it's simply not working. I'm just not sure he understands my case.

Catherine sighed and leaned her forehead against her palm. That would make three doctors in the past year.

Thanks very much for the check—you're always so thoughtful. By the way, Stella Carrington's giving a little coffee next week, and Virginia Woodward was just showing me the new outfit she's bought to wear. You know how having something new gives one's spirits a lift.

Translated, that meant send money. To Mother, economy meant patronizing the second most expensive dress shop in Atlanta.

I truly wish you were home with me, where you belong. After all, we've always been such good friends, and I'm not getting any younger...

News about mutual friends followed, but there was nothing of import. The letter was signed, "All my love, Mother."

Catherine put the letter down and tiredly pressed her fingers to the bridge of her nose. More of the same. Mother gently complaining, pressuring her to come back to Atlanta, tastefully hinting for more money. But then, everything Mother did was tasteful. Not useful, not productive, not even positive—just tasteful. Catherine sighed, half in amusement, half in exasperation. She had known for a long time that her mother was simply not built to take care of herself, and when Catherine's father died, she, the only child, had inherited the job.

If only he hadn't wasted the money, she thought for the thousandth time, feeling a surge of the familiar impotent hostility. There had been plenty, both from his family and her mother's side. But the truth was, John Lamar Nolan had been a charming, irresponsible wastrel who hadn't been built to take care of himself, much less anyone else. Gambling in all its forms, drinking, women—he had loved them all. In the end, he had ruined his health with alcohol and his marriage with one affair after another. The last one, a sordid liaison with a much younger woman, had almost become public knowledge when he had died in her apartment. Catherine could still remember her sick humiliation.

But fortunately for her and her mother, Gerrard Nolan had come to the rescue. Cousin Gerrard had quietly hushed the scandal—how or for what amount of money Catherine never knew. Then, when her father's will was probated and it became clear that he had left them nothing but a staggering pile of debts, Gerrard had paid off the majority of them and delayed payment on the rest. He had spotted Catherine's talent early, had made sure she had received the proper education. And when he had taken her under his professional wing, it was tacitly assumed by everyone, including Gerrard and Catherine, that she would eventually enter into partnership with him.

It was he who had found her the job at Bonne Journée. In fact, Catherine had been a bit miffed when, instead of making more of an effort to find her a job somewhere in Georgia, he had so readily sent her to the wilds of Louisiana.

"It's good experience for you, Catherine," he had said in his precise, unhurried way. "There aren't any houses quite like Bonne Journée being restored in the

Atlanta area right now. You'll do well, of course. And what you learn will be very useful when you come back.''

To me or to you? Catherine thought, but she held no illusions about Gerrard. He wanted a top-notch assistant, one who could further his career as a restoration architect of national—make that *international*—note. And, not so incidentally, one who could help him redeem the Nolan family name in the eyes of Atlanta, and of the world. Family standing was important to Gerrard. A tiny part of her had resented being used, but she'd said nothing. Gerrard had never been one to hide his aspirations.

And even though he didn't need the money, Catherine wanted to repay him, at least for those of her father's debts he had paid. That particular obligation would continue to haunt her until she had fulfilled it. At the same time, she wanted to make her mark in restoration architecture.

So, even though she hadn't wanted to leave Atlanta, she had welcomed this test of her abilities. For the first time, she would be well and truly on her own, entirely responsible for her own success or failure. And until the job offer on the Arceneaux house had come up, she hadn't really doubted that she could succeed.

Catherine looked at her mother's letter. The only thing it had accomplished was to remind her that she needed to work. It was a matter of elementary economics. She glanced at it again. No matter how she felt about it, she was going to have to accept anything the Louisiana Preservation Society offered her—at least until something opened up in Atlanta.

Feeling a bit like Scarlett O'Hara, she decided to defer most things until tomorrow. For the rest of the evening, she dutifully studied the Arceneaux house report until, exhausted, she went to bed, only to face a restless night of broken sleep and troubled dreams.

EARLY THE NEXT MORNING, Catherine stood in the doorway of Toni MacDonald's office in the Preservation Society headquarters.

"Toni," she said without preamble, "I'll take the job on the Arceneaux house—that is, if you haven't found anyone else to do it by now."

"Of course we haven't." Toni broke into a broad smile, almost a grin, and Catherine was reminded inexplicably of Gussie. "I'm glad," Toni said simply. "I didn't want to hire anyone else."

"I'm glad to be doing it." It wasn't completely untrue. She knew how lucky she was to be working with people like Toni and Gussie. "What kind of schedule do you have in mind?"

"The board's just approved the project," Toni said. "It'll be a few weeks before we actually begin. Moving it will be the trickiest part—we're going to need some engineering help."

"Yes, we are," Catherine agreed. "In the meantime, I've got my work cut out for me."

"What's that?"

"Research," Catherine said. "Before I start work, I have to lay my own foundation. I'm going to read everything I can find on Acadian history, culture, the works."

Toni smiled. "There speaks the Catherine I know. For a while you'll have to be working on both restorations at once. Will that be a problem?"

"I don't think so. I'll develop two separate schedules and commute from one place to the other, which will be fairly easy after the Arceneaux house is moved. It'll be hectic, but I think it'll work out." Catherine tried to sound confident. If she failed, it wouldn't be for lack of effort.

"I'm not worried at all," Toni said. "I'll give Clarence the good news, and we'll start work as soon as possible. By the way, did he tell you about the old violin?"

Catherine nodded. "I called Blackie Broussard yesterday." She grimaced at the memory. "I'm to meet him here this afternoon so he can look at it."

"Good. See? You've already done your first bit for the Arceneaux house."

As Catherine drove to Bonne Journée, she found herself hoping fervently that their trust in her was not misplaced.

WHEN CATHERINE ARRIVED at the society headquarters that afternoon, everyone was gone, and she had to let herself in with the key. She retrieved the violin from the storage room, then set it on a table in the broad entryway.

Before she had time to sit down, a knock sounded on the front door. Trying to quiet her jumping pulse, she opened it. Blackie stood outside, grin in place. His hair was as dark, and crisply curly, his eyes as warm and laughing as they had been at the *fais-do-do*.

She stepped back. "Come in." In spite of herself, she felt the familiar stiffening inside her, formality underscoring her words.

"Thank you," he responded punctiliously, inclining his head with an old-world courtliness that reminded her of Clarence DuBois. His light-blue chambray work shirt was rolled up at the sleeves, exposing powerful forearms, and his faded jeans fitted his muscled thighs. As he entered, she caught a whiff of tangy after-shave.

She led him to the table and switched on the lamp. "Here's the violin. Clarence DuBois—you know Clarence, don't you?"

"Sure, I've known Clarence since I was a *bébé*." The sound of his warm, deep voice in the large entrance hall made it suddenly seem smaller, more intimate.

"Clarence says the person donating it claims it's over two hundred years old. It would have to be if it's going into the Arceneaux house, because the house is being restored to the year 1790."

Blackie took the instrument from its worn case, held it under the light and examined it carefully, front and back. The violin *looked* old, she supposed. The surface of the wood was dull, the edges scratched, the strings frayed. Otherwise, it looked just like any other violin she'd ever seen. She caught herself watching Blackie's hands. They were square, brown, capable. All business, he turned the violin to the light and took a quick look inside.

"What you've got here is a fake." The words were almost casual.

"What?" she said blankly.

He grinned. "That came out wrong, didn't it? What I mean is, it's a real violin, but it was mass-produced in Germany in the nineteenth century. Violins like these are as common as a Sears Roebuck shovel." He ran his thumb absently over the worn strings. "It's only seventy-five or a hundred years old. It couldn't have come from Acadia with anybody."

"What makes you so sure?" Unaccountably, she was feeling defensive.

"Several things." He was intent again, absorbed in what he was saying. "The plain back, for one. But the main thing is the Antonius Stradivarius label inside." He pointed. "They were put there to show they were modeled after the original Stradivarius instruments, and they confuse everybody. I wish I had a nickel for every time somebody's come to me with a violin they swear is a real Strad." He chuckled. "Most of the time, they won't believe me. I have to send them to New Orleans—or New York, if they want to go that far."

Catherine realized that, when the conversation had taken a technical turn, Blackie had lost most of his Cajun accent. She also realized he probably turned it on and off at will.

"Clarence will be disappointed," she mused aloud. "He had his heart set on this violin for the Arceneaux house."

"It's nice of you to worry about Clarence's feelings," Blackie remarked, and it hurt that he sounded a little surprised.

"Why wouldn't I worry about Clarence?" she retorted. "He's one of the nicest people I've met here."

Blackie chuckled. "Yes, he is," he agreed blandly.

"Are there any violins around that actually came from Acadia during the Grand Dérangement?" she asked, still thinking of Clarence.

"Oh, maybe one or two," he said vaguely.

"Well, if you hear of any, let me know," she said, relieved that the interview was almost over. "I appreciate your help. Do you charge for your appraisals?"

"No, I don't." For once Blackie appeared taken aback. "Certainly not for something like this."

"Then you approve of restoring the Arceneaux house?"

"Yes." The answer was firm, positive. He hesitated a long moment, as if choosing his words carefully. "When I was growing up, it was considered shameful to be Cajun." His voice hardened. "Our teachers—most of them Anglos from the outside—tried to make us stop talking French, stop doing anything the way we were taught a home. When I finished high school, they told me I had to leave to make something of myself, so I did. After a few years, I realized I'd be happier at home. So I came back, and I've never regretted it. Now I'm glad my people are looking for their roots. We should be proud of our heritage."

Catherine sighed. She was beginning to see that, for many people, restoring the Arceneaux house was going to be a personal crusade for the Cajun culture. She wondered if any of them really understood how much work was involved. "I'm sure you are..." She almost said his first name, hesitated and saw his mouth quirk in amusement. "But it's going to be an enormous job."

"I've heard you can do it...Catherine." He used her first name smoothly. Deliberately.

"I hope so. And I also hope it's going to be worth all the work when it's done."

For a moment Blackie didn't reply. "It will be," he finally said. Had his tone cooled a little? "It may not be a big fancy mansion that's a carbon copy of every plantation house in the South, but it'll be a perfect example of early Cajun architecture. Even if the house is plain, the Cajun culture is unique, and it's worth preserving. But you seem doubtful of that."

"I'm sure it is. I just don't know much about it yet." He was offended, but she wasn't sure why.

He sighed. "Not many people do, if they weren't born here. When outsiders come in, it's usually a problem."

That hurt. Catherine had been feeling noble about her decision to do her best, and now he was attacking her—unjustly. She couldn't imagine why. "Mr. Broussard." This time she didn't deplore her formality. "I may be an outsider, but the Preservation Society liked my qualifications, and I assure you I'll learn all I need to know. Hiring someone to do this job just because he or she is a Cajun, without any restoration training, could be a disaster."

"Not necessarily." He was still being polite, but now his voice was edged with anger. "In the case of this restoration, I'd consider personal attitudes to be more important."

His words struck uncomfortably close to home. "I never let my personal feelings affect my efforts. I always do my best." In fact, she did have a personal interest in the project; she was doing it for Clarence. And Gussie and Toni. But she wasn't about to tell him that.

"I'm sure you do," he said tightly. "But that kind of thing happens a lot here. People come in, give something their best effort and leave things more screwed up than when they came." Catherine wondered at the undercurrent of bitterness in his voice. "For instance, a few years ago, the Corps of Engineers tried to fix up the Atchafalaya River Basin, to keep it from flooding. Well, they dried up half the swamp. People couldn't trap or hunt or fish any more, and a heavy rain still brings floods. That's what well-meaning outsiders will do for you." His speech had lost his formality, resuming its French cadences.

"I see you share your friend Hebert's views. I'm sorry you feel that way." Catherine's lips were stiff with hurt and anger. She still didn't have the remotest idea how she had offended him. "Fortunately the Preservation Society doesn't. All I can say is that I'll work just as hard on the Arceneaux house as I'm already working on Bonne Journée. And until the society terminates my contract, I'll stay on the job." She put the violin carefully in its case, straightened and met his eyes. "Now, if you'll please excuse me, I have work to do. Research. On Cajun architecture." She held his gaze. She knew she was being rude, but at this point, she didn't care.

He stood silent a moment, an expression in his eyes that, had she not known better, she would have taken for chagrin. He cleared his throat. "Goodbye, Miss Nolan." He turned and walked out the door.

The door slammed, and the noise echoed in the dark hall. For a few minutes, Catherine stood numbly, pressing her hands against her flushed face. It had all happened so quickly that she couldn't begin to explain it. It hadn't been her fault, she thought. All she knew was that, from the moment she had met him, Blackie Broussard had done nothing but throw her off balance—in one way or another. She resolved that in future she would stay as far away from him as she could.

CHAPTER FOUR

"Move the glass a little to your right, please."

Catherine knelt in front of the door to the main parlor in Bonne Journée, Gussie and Frank LeBoeuf hovering intently just above her. Gussie obediently moved the magnifying glass, while Frank trained a flashlight on the doorway.

"That's it!" Catherine, a scalpel poised in her right hand, examined the woodwork through the glass. "Now, if I can just—" She made a tiny, careful slice with the scalpel along the back of the door facing, then looked again. "Here's the *faux-bois* graining," she said triumphantly, "under the sixth layer of paint. I think we'll be able to uncover and restore most of it. Where it's too damaged, we'll simply have to repaint." She rose. "Frank, I'll talk to the painter tomorrow. Can he handle the job?"

"Yeah, he's the best one I know," Frank replied. "Oh, I almos' forgot. One of the men told me somebody's tearing down an old, old barn—he said it was built around 1845. I t'ink I'll see, me—maybe we can use some of the lumber for repairs here."

"Good," Catherine said. "We can use it on the slave cabins, too, and maybe even on the Arceneaux house." Gathering up scalpel and magnifying glass, she headed for her office and settled herself at her desk. She had just picked up a stack of bills from the Millard papers for the year 1837 when Gussie's head appeared in the doorway. Catherine glanced up inquiringly.

"How did the session with Blackie go yesterday?" Gussie asked.

"The violin's a fake," Catherine said briefly. She stared at the bills again.

"Ah ... Catherine ..."

"Yes?"

"Is there a problem? With Blackie, I mean?"

"Of course not. He's the expert. I took his word for it." She bent her head to the papers once more, but raised it again almost immediately. "But he also told me, in so many words, that he doesn't think I should work on the Arceneaux house."

"What in the world happened?" Gussie looked totally bewildered.

"He thinks that because I'm an outsider, I'll do a poor job. He said I didn't act as though I wanted to do it."

"Oh, I'm sure he didn't mean it."

"I think he meant every word," Catherine retorted, "and I plan to stay away from him."

"But you may have to consult him later," Gussie protested.

"I'll try to find someone else."

Gussie put up her hands. "You're the boss." She slipped out the door.

Catherine forced her attention to the stack of bills. "New Orleans, June 15, 1837," she read. "Bought by

Joshua Millard, from the firm of Bogart and Hoops, one dozen mahogany dining chairs, at two dollars each.'' That was undoubtedly the set that was now in the house, but there were only eight. Maybe the other four could still be located.

On her clipboard, Catherine made a note to begin a search. She wondered if Eleanor Millard had been excited to get the chairs. How strange to think that when this bill was written, Eleanor Millard knew nothing of the events looming for her: six children born, two little daughters to die in infancy and two sons in young adulthood, one in battle at Shiloh and the other in New Orleans of typhoid fever. Two surviving children, a son who inherited Bonne Journée and passed it on to his own progeny, and a daughter who seemed to have dropped off the face of the earth. In spite of her affluence, life had been hard for Eleanor Millard.

She thought of the Arceneaux house. Who were the Arceneaux? Unlike the Millards, they were total strangers to her. She had absolutely no idea, not even a fragment of insight, about the kind of people they might have been. Ahead lay a great deal of research, and Catherine had the uneasy feeling that the Arceneaux family would prove to be much more difficult to trace than the socially prominent Millards. Another note went onto the clipboard: *Check courthouse for Arceneaux records.*

The Arceneaux shared a heritage with Blackie Broussard. In researching them, would she find out more about him? But she didn't want to do that, she reminded herself, making a mighty effort to dispel his image from her consciousness. She was so absorbed that she didn't hear the knock at the door.

"Catherine." Something in Gussie's voice put Catherine on the alert. She glanced up—right into Blackie Broussard's face. Her heart lurched painfully. She glared at Gussie, who was looking apprehensive. "I'd like to see you for a minute, Catherine," he said. "I've...got something I want to say to you."

Catherine choked back her reply and waited in silence, her eyes on her work, until Gussie hastily disappeared.

"I owe you an apology."

Surprise jerked Catherine's head up. There was not a vestige of hidden merriment in the black eyes.

"It's not necessary," she said, desperately barricading herself behind her cool dignity. She lowered her eyes to the invoices again, and didn't see a single word.

"It's necessary for me," he said. Catherine could hear an irresistibly persuasive note in his voice but didn't dare look at him. She could already feel her resolve ebbing away.

"I'm most sincerely sorry for yesterday. I had no call to act like that."

Intrigued, Catherine forgot and looked him in the eye again. Too late, she realized her mistake. She was defenseless. *S'il vous plait?* He looked so contrite that she burst out laughing. An answering twinkle gleamed in his eyes, but he asked seriously, "Does that mean I'm forgiven?"

"How can I resist when you're so humble about it?" She took his proffered hand. Hard, callused, warm, it slid along her skin and enveloped her hand like a glove. She had to fight to keep her breath from coming faster.

"Apology accepted. And I owe you one, too. I . . . I sometimes say things very poorly."

He inclined his head conciliatingly, a quaint, courtly gesture. "Then shall we start from scratch? And make it Blackie and Catherine again?" A little devil lurked behind his eyes as he carefully articulated every syllable of her name.

"All right, but at least admit that you were deliberately trying to provoke me the other time you asked me to call you that."

"How can you say that?" He looked hurt. "I never deliberately provoke people." The tiny devil came to the fore again. "It just happens naturally."

"If that's true, it's a wonder you've survived until now—*Blackie*." She said his name more easily than she had expected.

"See? You didn't choke on it." His grin came out in all its blinding force, and he squeezed her hand, which somehow he still held. Catherine caught herself watching his mouth. It was so beautifully formed . . .

"Now I have a peace offering," Blackie said, "as proof of my good intentions."

"What's that?" she asked warily.

"I'd like to take you on a field trip."

"What kind of a field trip?"

"I'll take you to see a real Cajun. As long as you're in charge of this restoration, you might as well learn as much as you can about Cajuns. And I'll teach you. There's nobody better—*chère*."

Did the man ever doubt himself? "Do you know something, Mr. Broussard? You're outrageous."

"I know, I know." He tried to look modest. "Come on." He tugged at her hand. "We can't waste such a pretty afternoon."

"But I've got responsibilities, things to do. I...I can't just walk off the job," Catherine protested.

"Sure you can." He waved a hand. "All you have to do is tell Gussie you'll be gone for a couple of hours for a lesson in Cajun culture." He smiled provocatively.

Catherine thought a moment. She couldn't find a better teacher, she knew that. She also knew she was rationalizing. But she was tired of worrying about it. "Gussie's going to think I've run completely mad," she said ruefully, capitulating.

"No, she won't, not when she finds out you're going with me," he reassured her.

Catherine didn't even attempt a reply. Hand in hand with Blackie Broussard, she went to look for Gussie.

SITTING IN THE FRONT SEAT of Blackie's Chevrolet truck, riding down the main street of New Iberia, Catherine wondered if the man had cast a spell over everyone he knew. Gussie, after her first look of thunderstruck amazement at the two of them, had indeed done just as Blackie had predicted; she had smiled and said only that she hoped they would have a wonderful afternoon. To Catherine's protestations that it was a business trip, Gussie had replied, "Of course it is. And I'm sure you're going to learn a lot, too."

"Oh, she will, *chère*, she will," he had said. Gussie had smothered a giggle, and the look Catherine had shot Blackie had not affected his unflappable good humor.

She glanced out the window. Town was changing rapidly to country. Fields of sugarcane, spiky leaves sparkling emerald in the April sunlight, crowded right up to the old road. It occurred to Catherine that, if the highway was left unattended for very long, the lush, verdant cane would claim it.

As they drove, Blackie talked. And as he talked, Catherine began to gain a better picture of his land, his people and their way of life. When he spoke of the well-meaning attempts of outsiders to integrate the Cajun culture into mainstream Louisiana life, Catherine was shocked. She couldn't imagine a deliberate attempt to destroy a culture. It went against everything she believed in. "They made you turn your back on two hundred years of your heritage, just like that?" she finally said. She felt a sadness that went bone deep. It seemed that she was learning a little more about Blackie Broussard, too.

Blackie nodded. "By the time we realized we should be proud to be Cajun, a lot of our culture had been lost. That's why it's so important now for everything to be done right."

"But I will do it right," Catherine said, a little indignantly. "The first rule of restoring any building is that you never touch the first board until you've steeped yourself in its history."

"I'm not talking about reading books, Catherine," Blackie said mildly. "I'm talking about real understanding—feeling, maybe I should say. You've got to fall in love with the Arceneaux house, the way you did with Bonne Journée. Instead, when anyone mentions it, you look as though you dread it, but you're going to do if it kills you."

"It's not that I don't want to do it," Catherine said. "I just don't feel that I know the people who built the Arceneaux house the way I know the Millards."

Blackie shrugged. "That's natural, the Millards were more like the people you grew up with. The Arceneaux family were just farmers."

Catherine raised her eyebrows. "And what do you consider plantation owners, may I ask?" She glanced at him, and her gaze lingered. Funny—she hadn't noticed before, but there were a few flecks of gray dusting the coal-black hair at his temple. With difficulty, she pulled her mind back to the subject at hand.

He chuckled. "Farmers, maybe. But there are farmers and farmers, and I don't see you having much in common with people who plowed their own fields."

"That's totally irrelevant," she retorted. "As I told you yesterday, I'm a professional."

"Oops, sorry," he said, grinning. He reached down, squeezed her hand. "Come on, Catherine," he coaxed. "Relax. I didn't mean to offend you."

Of course he didn't. Why was she being so touchy? *How musically he speaks,* she thought irrelevantly. She could listen to him all day.

"I take it all back," he said breezily. "All I want to do is make you love Cajun country."

"And?"

"And Cajuns, too, *chère*." He smiled. "I'm going to take you to see my Uncle Bat Charpiot."

"Bat? Is his first name English?"

"Mon Dieu Seigneur!" He looked faintly horrified. "No, he's Cajun through and through. Bat is short for Jean Baptiste. It's his *ti-nom*—his nickname," Blackie explained. "He's my *grandmère's* brother. He knows all the history, all the stories, everything about the Cajuns. He lives on Lake Palourde, down below Morgan City."

He pointed down the road they were traveling. "This is the old highway—the cattle trail. It follows the Teche until we get to Morgan City. There are little towns, old ones, all up and down the Teche. If you go the other way, past New Iberia—" he jerked a thumb over his shoulder "—you come to St. Martinville— Evangeline country. That's where my family lives."

"Evangeline as in Longfellow's poem?"

"That's right. I'll take you there sometime," Blackie promised.

"I'd like that." She found herself hoping it wasn't an idle promise. She settled herself comfortably so she could look out the left side of the car as they drove southeast along the Teche. Here were the oldest homes, because in times past, the bayous served as highways—the only links with the outside world. She saw several homes as big as Bonne Journée, and many smaller ones of various sizes and historical periods. But the atmosphere was all-pervasive: giant, moss-draped live oaks, perennial shadows, a land that was half earth and half water—rivers, bays, bayous, swamps. And moist, humid air that by turns oppressed or caressed. This really was a mystical land.

Catherine soon realized that her position gave her another advantage—while she looked at the scenery, she could surreptitiously study Blackie, whose strong features were silhouetted against the lush green of his Teche country. They were kept from harshness, she decided, by the well-developed laugh lines at his mouth and the corners of his eyes, and by the variety of expressions that crossed his mobile face as he talked. For the first time it occurred to her that this man might be someone she would like very much to know better.

They rounded a sharp bend, and Catherine caught a glimpse of a house that stopped her heart where she sat. "Stop—oh, please stop," she pleaded, grabbing Blackie's arm before she thought. Blackie glanced at her in surprise. "I've got to see that house," she explained hurriedly.

Blackie pulled over and braked. Catherine jumped out of the car and gazed in wonder.

It was a simple raised Creole cottage, a plantation house in miniature, perched on the far bank of the Teche among a grove of ancient, gnarled oaks. It was old, older than Bonne Journée—it probably dated from around the turn of the nineteenth century. It sat on high brick piers the soft coral pink of Teche clay, and a wide gallery with six square wooden columns spanned the front. Three small dormers protruded from the high-pitched, shingled roof. It was exquisitely beautiful.

Behind her a car door slammed, and Blackie came to stand beside her. They stood a moment in silence. "It's perfect," Catherine said reverently. "It has the fine craftsmanship of all the plantation homes, but it's small enough to be livable. Do you know anything about it?"

"A little. When I was a kid, I visited here sometimes. It's named Petit Coeur—Little Heart. It was built—oh, around 1813, I think—by a Creole planter named Jules DeArmas. It's had several owners since then, and it's been vacant for about a year. It's going down fast," he said sadly.

"I could spend the rest of my life in a place like that," Catherine said with a sigh.

"It would suit you," Blackie said gently as he helped her into the car.

What a gallant thing to say, Catherine thought, feeling warm all over. And what a beautiful place. For one crazy moment, the idea of buying Petit Coeur crossed her mind, then she discarded it. She couldn't make a living here. Besides, she didn't belong to this world. She was a foreigner. Even this man—especially this man—had said so. When these jobs were finished she would head back to her own world. But somehow, today, the thought held less appeal for her.

They passed more old homes as they drove along the old trail to Morgan City, but Catherine saw none that compared with Petit Coeur. Blackie maintained a running commentary on their surroundings, and Catherine, amazed at the extent of his knowledge, decided that she really was in the right hands after all. She glanced involuntarily at those hands, strong, brown, effortlessly steering the car along the curving highway, and something stirred within her.

"We're crossing the Atchafalaya," Blackie told her as they started up the incline of a huge, high bridge. "You can see the bottom of the river basin from here. Morgan City is on the other side."

When they reached the top of the bridge, Blackie pointed and Catherine looked. To the north stretched the rusty waters of the Atchafalaya. The river looked angry, turbulent—and barely confined. As they approached the other side, she could see between the river and the town of Morgan City the huge levees that enclosed the basin and protected the town. "It looks as though it wouldn't take much to send it out of its banks," she said.

"It doesn't," Blackie replied. "A whole hell of a lot of water from all over the eastern half of the United States flows right here under this bridge, especially during floods." He pointed. "When it rains way up in Peoria, Illinois, the water comes right through here. The Corps of Engineers has put in emergency outlets, but whether they're enough in a real pinch is questionable." Hearing the skepticism in his voice, Catherine remembered his criticism of the corps.

"It sounds like a dangerous situation," she remarked.

"It's a *very* dangerous situation," Blackie confirmed. "Look at any map. Morgan City is right at the bottom of the sock—it gets all the water. There was a flood a few years back that nearly wiped out the town. We were all laying sandbags and plugging leaks in the levees."

"But I thought the whole purpose of these levees was to prevent flooding," Catherine remarked in surprise.

"Not entirely. Their purpose is also to regulate the entire drainage system of South Louisiana, and particularly New Orleans. For years the Mississippi has been trying to change its course to flow down the Atchafalaya, but enough water still has to go down the Mississippi to keep New Orleans alive, yet not wash it away."

"So the Corps of Engineers is actually changing the course of nature," Catherine mused.

"They've tried," Blackie said shortly. "All they've really succeeded in doing is screwing things up."

"You admit something had to be done," Catherine said thoughtfully. "So why are you so bitter?" She had the feeling there was something he wasn't telling her.

He shrugged. "Maybe changes—and mistakes—are just easier to accept when they're brought about by nature, rather than people." He raised a hand, then let it drop again. "It's a complex problem," he said, "and maybe it doesn't have a solution. Actually, I can see everybody's point—even the corps'. But the fact remains that the people here, instead of being let alone to work out their problems, have been set against one another by a bunch of outsiders who thought they knew best for us."

Catherine raised an eyebrow. "Is this where I came in?" she asked softly.

He hesitated a moment, then he gave his rich, deep chuckle, sending a shiver of pleasure down her spine. "You're right," he said. "You told me before that I sound like Raymond Hebert, and everybody's tired of his griping. Anyway, I promised you a tour, not a tirade." He pointed toward the east. "We're headed that way," he said. "Uncle Bat lives on a little bayou off Lake Palourde."

Catherine looked. She could see that the level of land dropped perceptibly, and everywhere land and water mingled more and more. Huge stands of cypress trees and impenetrable swamp vegetation obscured her vision.

"Is Uncle Bat all the family you have?" she asked curiously.

"Not quite." Blackie laughed outright. "Besides my mother and father, there are seven of us kids."

"Seven!"

"Why, seven's not so many. Just two girls and five boys. I'm the oldest. Then there's *grandmère*, and my aunts and uncles, not to mention *parrain* and *nainaine* . . ."

"Who?"

"My godparents. And of course all my cousins."

"Do they all live down here?"

"No. Most of them live in St. Martinville. Uncle Bat used to live in the swamp, up around Gibson, until the fishing and trapping got so bad. Now he lives down here, he says it's the next best thing."

"That much family—it's incredible." Catherine shook her head.

"Around here, it's normal," Blackie explained.

"Not to me, it isn't," she said, unable to conceive of living so close, either physically or emotionally, to so many people.

"Oh? What size families do Atlantans have?"

"Very funny. I don't know about other Atlantans, but my father died the year I finished college," she explained. "Now there's just my mother and me. And Gerrard, of course."

"Who's Gerrard?"

"My father's first cousin. He helped us out after Dad died. He's a restoration architect—the real reason I'm in that line. Besides Mother, he's all I've got."

"That's it?"

"That's it." She smiled faintly. How ironic that she, who was related to half the old families in Atlanta and could trace her roots back at least two hundred years on either side, had so few flesh-and-blood relatives to call her own.

"Well, that's okay, *chère*, my family will adopt you," Blackie promised expansively. "We've never had a blonde before. A *jolie blonde*." He reached over and squeezed her hand. The warmth of the simple gesture made her feel vulnerable, somehow hungry inside, and she couldn't seem to pull away. Only when Blackie moved his hand back to the wheel was the spell broken. Catherine forced her attention to her view of the swampy terrain.

It occurred to her then that, for an accordion player, Blackie Broussard knew a great deal about a great many things.

CHAPTER FIVE

THEY HAD TURNED OFF the main highway onto a narrow dirt road. On either side grew a solid wall of vegetation—rank, green, trackless. The road curved and disappeared a very short distance ahead. Even to Catherine's unaccustomed eye, the land was changing, growing steadily lower, marshier. Everywhere through the tangle of trees, vines and underbrush, she could glimpse the sheen of swamp water.

After several minutes of driving, they came to a small clearing, really just a widening of the road. Blackie pulled over and parked the car. "We walk from here," he said cheerfully, gesturing toward the jungle in front of them.

"Where?" For the life of her, Catherine could see no opening, no place to go. She got out of the car. Though the sun was warm, she shivered at the idea of plunging into that morass of plant life.

Blackie stopped his rummaging through the glove compartment. "That way," he said, waving toward a spot in front of the car that looked just as thick as the rest.

"I don't see any place to walk. What's that in your hand?"

"A flashlight." He held it up. "We may need it coming out. I always bring one along."

"Somehow, that doesn't make me feel better."

"Don't you trust me?" His voice was plaintive.

"I'm not going to answer that."

He laughed. "Come on, then." Catching her hand, he led her directly into the thicket. Sure enough, there was a trail, twisting and turning like a green tunnel, following the high ground. The trees and undergrowth leaned in, catching her clothes with occasional outstretched limbs.

As the trail narrowed, she released Blackie's hand and slipped behind him, glad at least that she had worn her comfortable shoes. From this vantage point, she could also enjoy watching his broad shoulders as he strode down the trail.

"You know, ladies really should go first," he remarked, glancing at her.

"That's quite all right. I'll follow you so you can spot all the snakes."

"Sure. They'll see me first, then they'll be ready to bite just about the time you walk by."

With an exclamation, Catherine scooted up so that she was only a step or two behind Blackie, and before she thought, she slipped her hand in his again. He turned to look at her, and she caught something on his face she couldn't define. Her heart began to hammer, hard, against her ribs.

He flashed her his piratical grin. "If I'd known you were going to do that," he said, "I'd have brought along a few snakes."

"I don't doubt it for a minute." Her hand securely in his, she forgot to be afraid.

They came finally to a tiny bayou, little more than an inlet. At the far end Catherine could see a frame cabin perched on tall piers, its unpainted siding weathered to a soft gray. Its front porch extended over the water.

"This is it," Blackie said.

"It's charming," Catherine said. "But doesn't your uncle get lonely out here? And where's his car? Where's the road, for that matter?"

Blackie's laugh filled the clearing. "His car is sitting in the bayou, tied to his front porch," he replied.

"I'm sure it is. Now will you tell me the truth?"

"That is the truth. Uncle Bat doesn't own a car— can't even drive," he explained, still chuckling. "He uses his boat to run down the bayou to the bridge. There's a grocery store there, and a gas station. Anything else he needs, he hitches a ride into Morgan City with one of his buddies or tells someone to call me. But mostly he stays right here."

As they approached the rear of the house, a voice seemed to come from under the front porch, down the steep bank near the water.

"Come on, ma sweet li'l engine. Come on and make da noise for *Nonc*." The roar of an engine echoed in the air, followed by a coughing sputter. Then silence.

"Come on, you son-a-ma-guns, *Nonc* gonna bash you, heem, if you don't behave..."

"Hey, *Nonc* Bat," Blackie yelled hastily. "It's Blackie. I brought you some company, so you got to watch your language." He grinned at Catherine.

"Ti-neg," came the stentorian reply. "Where you at, you?"

"Right here—where else?" Blackie answered, laughing.

A little old man climbed over the bank and walked toward them on bowed legs, and, with surprise, Catherine recognized the ancient fiddle player from the fund-raising party. *"Pardon,"* he begged of them. "But my boat, she is bus'."

"Comment ça va, Nonc?" Blackie hugged him unashamedly, enveloping the smaller man with his muscular arms, and in his exuberance lifting him right off the ground. Finally he put him down again and gestured to Catherine. *"Nonc*, it's my pleasure to present Catherine Nolan, from Atlanta," he said formally. "She's working in New Iberia."

"I'm happy to meet you." Catherine smiled, extending her hand.

"C'est mon plaisir de vous rencontrer, mamselle." He took her hand, regarding her solemnly from his unblinking black eyes. Courtly though his manner was, Catherine knew that she was being closely scrutinized. *"Bien jolie,"* he pronounced at length, his deeply etched features never changing their sorrowful expression. "You plenty pretty. Dat Blackie, he got some eye for da women," he added conspiratorially.

Catherine choked on a laugh. "Thank you, sir," she said. "So I've heard." She turned innocent green eyes on the subject of their discussion.

"Et toi, Catherine?" Looking wounded, Blackie put a hand to his heart.

With immense dignity, Uncle Bat gestured to his open door. "Pass yourself into ma house," he said.

"I'd love to." Catherine led the way. Inside, the room was bare but very, very clean. From an old wood stove in the corner, the pungent smell of French coffee issued from a blue enamel pot.

"Sit yourself, *mamselle*." Another grand gesture. They sat around the little table near the stove, and over steaming mugs of the chicory coffee, which Catherine privately thought could be used as paint stripper, Blackie explained her work on the Arceneaux house to Uncle Bat in a fascinating mixture of French and English.

"*Beaucoup bien*—a ver' good t'ing," he said. "Now ever'body understan' about da Cajun people."

"That's why we played the *fais-do-do* last week, *Nonc*, remember?" Blackie explained. "To make money for the project."

"Dat was not a real *fais-do-do*." Uncle Bat's voice was scornful. "Someday you come to a real *fais-do-do*," he said to Catherine. "You like it better, *non*?"

"Thank you, Mr. Charpiot. I'd love to."

Uncle Bat's perennially accusing expression softened a little. He patted her hand. "I play you a French love song, me. But you mus' call me *Nonc* Bat, *chère*."

I should have known that was coming, Catherine thought. From the corner of her eye she saw Blackie grinning. "All right...Uncle Bat," she replied, clasping the old man's hand.

"Ah, *Nonc*, you're always stealing my girls," Blackie complained.

"You jus' don' know how to treat dem, *mon fils*," the old man said loftily.

Catherine glanced involuntarily at Blackie, then reminded herself she couldn't be his girl. She was an outsider. But a small part of her cherished the idea.

Resigned, Blackie spread his arms. "Okay, *Nonc*, she's yours. So now you can help us. Since she's from Atlanta, she doesn't know much about Cajuns. Will you tell her about us?"

Uncle Bat's chest seemed to swell. "*Bien sûr*, I tell her, me. We begin at da beginning," he announced, as generations of pain and suffering settled into his already dolorous expression. "Ma family was dere, in l'Acadie, when da curse' English t'rew us out. We lef' our homes and board' dere curse' ships. Many of dem die from da smallpox..."

He was off and running. While Catherine sat spellbound and the shadows lengthened unnoticed outside the little cabin, Uncle Bat's musical voice wove its tale. He told how, in 1755, the British evicted the Acadian people from their homes for refusing to swear allegiance to the English king. Then, after a decade of wandering, privation and suffering, a band of Acadians under their leader, Joseph Beausoliel Broussard—da six-time-back *p'père* of Ti-neg, Uncle Bat explained—came to the swamps and bayous of South Louisiana. There, they finally found their promised land. It was a sad, sad story, but, like silver threads among his somber narrative, ran the magic gifts of Cajun music—and Cajun laughter.

Catherine was so absorbed that she jumped a little when Blackie spoke.

"Show her, *Nonc*, what you have that came with the family."

Uncle Bat nodded solemnly and rose. He walked to the corner of the room. A small wooden chair stood next to his narrow cot, its once-rough edges smoothed and polished by generations of loving hands. It stood in mute testimony to a people's exodus from one world to another, and Catherine touched it reverently.

"*Nonc*, you want to show her your real prize, *hein*?" Since their arrival, Catherine had noticed that Blackie had unconsciously been slipping more and more into French.

"*Oui*." Uncle Bat knelt by the bed and pulled out an oblong box, laid it gently on the bed and with reverent hands opened the lid.

Catherine held her breath. There lay an old violin. As little as she knew about them, she realized that this one was different from the one Clarence had brought. It was more simply made, but its rich, dark wood gleamed softly with centuries of loving care. Uncle Bat reverently lifted it out.

"Dis came wit' my family from l'Acadie," he said softly. "My *p'père* hide it under hees coat when dey board' da boat. He couldn' leave it behind, heem."

Catherine was almost afraid to touch the instrument, but Uncle Bat held it out to her. She gently stroked the smooth old back. "It's beautiful," she said, awed. "Thank you for showing it to me. Did you play it the other night?"

"Mais non, chère." Uncle Bat made a dismissing motion with his hands. "I got anudder fiddle for dat. Dis one only for da special occasion, heem." He indicated the violin. "I got no chil'ren. When I die, he go to Blackie."

Here was the perfect instrument for the Arceneaux house, Catherine realized. It would make Clarence so happy. But she didn't want Uncle Bat to think anyone was trying to take it away from him. "If you like, Uncle Bat, you can leave it to the Preservation Society," she said gently. "Then it can go to the Arceneaux house, and be there for all time, for everyone to enjoy."

"Give away *mon beau violon*?" Uncle Bat said in horror. "*Mais jamais*—never!"

"Don't worry, *Nonc*," Blackie said quickly. "Nobody's going to take anything from you." His words were soothing, but Catherine could hear the tiny note of hostility in his voice.

Uncle Bat looked at Catherine, and his face seemed to grow longer, his black eyes more sorrowful. He took her hand. "Cat'rine, *chère*," he said gently, "*Mon violon*, he got to stay in dis family. My *p'père*, he tol' me, heem."

Realization dawned on Catherine, flooding her with shame. She had insulted this lovely old man, who had shared with her his priceless family treasures. Somehow, "recommended procedures" of acquiring restoration pieces were all wrong for this situation. Hot tears sprang to her eyes.

"Uncle Bat, I'm so sorry." Her voice shook. "It was wrong of me to ask. Please forgive me," she said simply.

Seconds ticked by. Uncle Bat's expression didn't change, but his callused hand tightened on hers, and she saw the warmth—and forgiveness—in his eyes.

"Certainement, chère," he finally said, all the graciousness in the world in his voice.

Beside her, she sensed Blackie relax. "Well, *Nonc*, we got to take ourselves home," he finally said. "It's getting dark."

Startled, Catherine looked out the window. She hadn't realized it was quite so late. Gussie must have shut down work at Bonne Journée and gone home long ago.

Uncle Bat struck a match and lit a kerosene lantern sitting on the table. The room sprang to life in its soft glow. He walked with them to the door.

Catherine took his hand, wanting somehow to convey to him how deeply she treasured the visit, how much she regretted even momentarily causing him distress. "Uncle Bat, this has meant more to me than you can ever know," she said quietly. "Thank you from the bottom of my heart. And please let me know when I can hear you play the violin."

"Mais sho', *mignonne.* Ti-neg, you bring her, *hein?"*

"It'll be my pleasure."

"Beaucoup bien. Ti-neg..."

"Oui?"

"Dis one fine, *belle jeune fille*. You treat her nice, you." Catherine knew then that she was truly forgiven.

"Oui, Nonc," Blackie answered meekly.

"Cat'rine," Uncle Bat said, a caressing tone in his voice, "you watch you'self wit' dis *canaille*. Don't let heem get too beeg for hees breetch'."

That word, at least, she recognized from standard French. *Rascal.* "I won't, Uncle Bat." Behind her, she heard Blackie's stifled chuckle but didn't dare look at him. "Goodbye—and thanks for everything."

"Bonne nuit, chère."

Blackie and Catherine walked in silence. By the time they arrived at the car, a full moon had risen over the tops of the giant cypresses, although the path was so shadowed that Blackie's flashlight came in handy. Bullfrogs and crickets sang their nocturnal songs from the banks of the bayou, and the air smelled pleasantly of moist earth. While she watched the path closely, Catherine was not nearly as uneasy as she had been on the way in.

Although Blackie was solicitous in helping her over the rough ground, his touch lacked its early warmth. As he helped her into the car, she glanced at his face, but it was in shadow. She was surprised to find herself a little apprehensive. *One step forward, two steps back?* she wondered.

He started the car and swung it around.

"Blackie."

"Yes?"

"Thank you for sharing him with me. He's a very special man."

"I'm glad you enjoyed it," he said politely.

"Blackie? Are you angry?"

"No. Just a little . . . disappointed."

Suddenly, she had to try to make him understand. "I didn't mean to offend Uncle Bat. You've got to believe that was the last thing on my mind. It was just that Clarence wanted the other violin so badly, I thought this would make him happy. But I see now that it was a rude, insensitive thing to ask."

He said nothing, only stared straight ahead, but Catherine thought she saw his expression soften a little.

She felt the tears well up again, she who never cried. "Sometimes I'm . . . not very good at this kind of thing," she said past the lump in her throat, and laid a hand on his arm. The muscles were knotted between her fingers. "Please bear with me?"

She felt him relax then. *"Mais* sho', *chère,"* he said gently. His voice radiated warmth, and she basked in it like a sun-starved sophomore. He covered her hand with his, and the contact sent waves of pleasure skittering up her arm. Blackie turned his gaze from the road, giving her a smile that held more than simple warmth. Something in her expression must have pleased him, for as he faced front and put his hand on the wheel, the smile widened to a grin.

As BLACKIE PULLED into the driveway of her apartment building, Catherine glanced at her watch. "It's late," she said.

"As they say at the *fais-do-do*, it's just the shank of the evening," Blackie said genially, coming around to open her door for her. They mounted the stairs to her apartment. He unlocked the door with the key she gave him and held it open for her.

"It's been a wonderful day," she told him. "I can't thank you enough."

He looked at her speculatively. "Um...you couldn't possibly spare a cup of coffee for a tired driver, could you?"

Surprised, Catherine hesitated.

"S'il vous plaît?" He inclined his head, irresistibly appealing.

"There you go again."

"It worked the first time, didn't it?" His look was all spurious innocence.

"Maybe so," she conceded. "But I warn you, the coffee's instant."

He looked so horrified that she burst out laughing. "Take it or leave it," she warned.

"I'll have to take it," he said in a martyred tone, holding his hand over his heart. "Anything for a few more minutes in your company."

"Uncle Bat does it better." Catherine headed toward the kitchen.

"He's had more practice," Blackie called after her. He let his gaze wander around the flawlessly decorated little apartment. *Antiques,* he thought, *and good ones.* The place was much like its occupant: cool, elegant and understated. But he knew now that, underneath that aristocratic exterior, Catherine was vulnerable—even more than he had suspected.

Actually, he had been angry with her for asking *Nonc* about the violin. But she had been so genuinely sorry. She was finally beginning to relax a little with him. And *Nonc*, a shrewd judge of character, had obviously seen something he liked. After his first distress, he hadn't even held it against her that she had asked for the violin. On the other hand, *Nonc* was still a soft touch for a pretty face—and there was no denying that Catherine had that.

He watched her as she came into the room, wondering how her hair would look free of its confining knot, how it would feel between his fingers. He shook his head at his own desire for her.

Catherine set down the tray she was carrying and looked at him inquiringly.

"Very nice," he said, indicating the apartment. "I don't know much about antiques, but some of these look to be very fine. This one, for instance." His blunt fingers stroked the wood of an exquisite little walnut secretary.

"Thank you," she replied. "That belonged to my grandmother. It's one of my favorite pieces."

"Did you inherit all these things?"

"Some I inherited, some I've just bought over the years." Catherine was secretly proud of the way she had blended in her own possessions with a few wise purchases made from time to time. It had taken a long while, and skillful budgeting, to pay for the antiques. By the time she was able to buy the house she wanted, wherever it might be, she would be able to furnish it correctly. She congratulated herself that, even though she'd only been here a little over a month, the place had a pulled-together look about it. And she was unaccountably glad Blackie was noticing.

She handed him his coffee and sat on the sofa with her own. "I made it as strong as I could—I hope it won't be too bad."

His square hand dwarfed the fragile cup as he took a sip and grimaced. "It's okay," he said nobly, drinking some more.

"I can tell. Would you have preferred decaffeinated?"

"Quelle horreur!" He protested. "My toes would curl up if you did that. Have a little mercy, this is enough for one night."

"I could take it back, you know," Catherine threatened, reaching for his cup.

He chuckled. "No, no, I'll manage." He picked up a photograph in a silver frame on the Hepplewhite table by the sofa. "Your father?" he asked.

"Yes."

"You look like him."

"So I've been told." Her tone invited no further comment.

He shrugged, picked up a snapshot.

"My mother and Gerrard," she explained at his inquiring look, her voice relaxing. "It was taken two years ago Christmas."

"You said Gerrard had helped you out after your father died. Do you mean he's been like a father to you?"

For a moment Catherine had to consider. She'd never really thought about it before. "No, not like a father," she said slowly. "I can't imagine Gerrard being anyone's father—he's not very paternal." To her amusement, Blackie looked askance at the photograph, as if he wasn't sure what kind of species Gerrard really was. "But he's been good to us," she went on, "and I'm very fond of him. In fact, I owe my whole career to him. He's one of the best restoration architects in the country, and he's helped me every step of the way."

"Out of the goodness of his heart?" Blackie cocked an eyebrow.

"No, not entirely," she answered truthfully. "If I'm going to be his assistant someday, he wants me to be the best, too."

"And that's what you plan to do?"

"Yes. As soon as I've finished my work here, I'll be heading to Atlanta, or thereabouts. By then, there should be some restoration projects getting under way there."

"I see." He dropped his gaze to the picture again. "Your mother looks like a—formidable lady," he commented.

"Oh, Mother's quite the *grande dame*," Catherine answered dryly. "On that particular occasion, she was unhappy because the caterer didn't prepare the oyster dressing exactly right for the Christmas dinner." Blackie looked at her incredulously, but his only response was a noncommittal grunt.

In spite of his complaints about the coffee, he drained his cup, then rose to go. Catherine followed him into the little hallway.

"A Cajun's got to have his coffee," he explained, "and it's got to be made right. It's got to be drip, dark roast. It's also got to be *noir comme le diable, chaud comme l'enfer, pur comme une ange, et doux comme l'amour*," he recited.

"Let's see—black as the devil, hot as hell . . . what else?" Her textbook French still wasn't quite equal to his Cajun pronunciation.

"Pure as an angel . . ." He reached for her, pulled her slowly toward him. "And sweet as love." His gaze dropped to her mouth.

Unable to move, she watched his lips descend deliberately to hers.

Warm, surprisingly soft, they moved over hers in an almost leisurely way, exploring, caressing—giving. His hands came up to the middle of her back, stroking, holding her to him. She drew a sobbing breath, and his piquant scent filled her nostrils. She felt a strange, delicious warmth begin inside her, felt herself sag against him. She didn't know her body could behave that way, and it made her half afraid. In all her life, no man had ever made her feel like this.

At his urging, she parted her lips, and he took the kiss deeper, making a first gentle foray with his tongue. His breath came fast, warm, against her cheek. He pulled her closer, wrapping his arms around her and enveloping her in an aura of caring and tenderness. She could feel the pounding of his heart and the hardness of his body against hers. Involuntarily, her fingers explored the corded muscles of his chest.

Suddenly a giant need uncurled inside her that was more than physical; she found herself yearning for all the love and caring that she had never sensed the lack of until this moment. She felt her defenses vanish, and uncontrollable laughter bubbled up inside her—or was it tears? She leaned hungrily into his body.

It was Blackie who broke the embrace. But his lips lingered on hers, then returned for a brief farewell touch—hardly even a kiss, but done with such tenderness that the tears stung her eyes.

He cupped her face with his hands and scanned it for a long moment. "Cat'rine..." His thumb came up to brush lightly across the plane of her cheek. "Go to bed, *ma belle*, and get some rest."

"Blackie..."

The thumb came down to her lips, gently silencing her. "*Bonne nuit*. And thanks for a beautiful day." He left her then, quietly closing the door behind him.

Catherine stared after him for a moment, then carefully, deliberately locked the door.

For a long time afterward, she sat in her living room and stared blankly at a wall, hopelessly awash in a sea of conflicting emotions.

CHAPTER SIX

A WEEK LATER, CATHERINE, in newly purchased jeans and tennis shoes, stood with Clarence DuBois on the grassy lot adjacent to Bonne Journée. The tall chimneys and high-pitched roof of the mansion were just visible above the overgrown hedge separating the properties.

"We'll put the Arceneaux house right about here." Clarence walked to a spot halfway between the road and the Bayou Teche. "Then we can operate it and Bonne Journée together."

Catherine looked around her. The ground where they stood was fairly high, on a level with Bonne Journée, but just beyond them it sloped steeply toward the bayou—too steeply, she realized.

"Clarence," she asked, "what's this soil like?"

"Slippery, I'm afraid. It's gumbo—heavy clay," he added at her look of confusion, "and it slides around. We'll have to have a professional stabilize the foundation, else, come the first heavy rain, the Arceneaux house will slide right into the Teche."

Catherine thought of the months of hard work ahead and hoped that if the house was going to slide into the bayou, it would at least have the consideration to do it before they began the restoration. "Just how are we going to get it up that steep bank?'' she asked.

''Magic.'' Clarence chuckled. ''Well, maybe magic and a little house-moving expertise. It's been done before, more often than you might think.''

''I still can't believe we'll be moving it by water,'' she said. ''Why not the highway?''

''It's a lot easier by water. The house is right on the bank of the bayou, about seven miles downstream. We'll just ease her onto a barge, float her up and unload her.'' His expansive gestures explained more eloquently than words. ''That way we don't have to cross any highways or go under any utility wires.''

''It's a shame you couldn't leave it in its original location.''

''I know, the woods are beautiful there. But the site's too isolated. Better for the house to be here next to Bonne Journée, where everyone can enjoy both restorations.''

Catherine had only seen the Arceneaux house once, but the image was still clear in her mind—a square, plain house with a mud chimney and a wide front porch, sitting dilapidated and forlorn in the midst of an overgrown clearing. That memory alone was enough to discourage her all over again.

When she had talked to Gerrard last week, he had sounded faintly horrified. ''It's not worthy of your talents,'' he had said flatly. ''Besides, I'm investigating a new restoration in Athens. Maybe we can work together on it.'' Meaning, she supposed, that he might soon order her back to Georgia. If the summons came before she finished the Arceneaux house, that would present another problem, one she would just have to deal with when it arose.

"Well, they won't enjoy this one if it ends up in the Teche," she told Clarence. "Do you know an engineer we can call?"

"Why, sure," he replied. "Call Blackie Broussard."

I don't believe this, Catherine thought as the sense of déjà vu washed over her. "Why?" she asked, a bit tartly. "Is he an authority on engineers, too?"

"No, Catherine," Clarence answered in surprise. "Blackie *is* an engineer. Didn't you know?"

Blackie an engineer? A professional man? For a moment Catherine couldn't speak. No wonder he had known so much about the Atchafalaya flood-control system.

"As a matter of fact, I didn't," she finally said. "I thought he was just a musician."

Clarence looked at her in mock horror. "Don't say it like that, *chère*," he said. "After all, anybody can study to be an engineer. It takes a special gift to make people happy with music, the way Blackie does. If you were to ask me, I'd say that Blackie's just an *engineer*."

"*Touché*". Catherine smiled weakly. She should have known. Here everyone would attach far more importance to Blackie's musical talents than to his profession. "Is he qualified?"

"*Bien sûr*, he's qualified. He got his degree in civil engineering from LSU and worked in Natchez for several years," Clarence explained. "He's even worked around here for the Corps of Engineers. Now he has his own office in Morgan City. Blackie's plenty good."

"Did you say he worked with the corps?" She thought she hadn't heard right. "I thought Blackie didn't like the corps because of what they did to the Atchafalaya Swamp."

"He doesn't, now, for—" Clarence hesitated briefly. "For several reasons. That's why he quit. Life's too short to do something you don't want to do."

"All right, I'll call him," she promised, but she couldn't help silently speculating about what Clarence had said.

Clarence waved at someone coming up behind her, and Catherine turned to see Toni MacDonald, looking as usual like something straight out of a fashion magazine, walking carefully through the high grass toward them.

"Sorry I'm late." She ran a careless hand through shiny brown hair. "Well, what have you two decided? Can the house be put here?"

"Yes, but look at the angle of that slope," Catherine replied, pointing. "We think we have a problem."

"Don't look at me." Toni laughed. "I may be the wife of an engineer, but about all I can do is recommend that you have one look at it."

Doug, Catherine thought. Of course! Doug was an engineer; maybe he could help them. In spite of—or perhaps because of—what had happened the last time she had been with Blackie, she wasn't particularly eager to contact him. She still hadn't sorted out her feelings, and the fact that he hadn't contacted her since didn't help.

"Maybe we can talk to Doug," she said hopefully.

Toni shook her head. "Doug thinks that the best people to do local work are local people," she said. "A lot of people around here still resent corps operations, even noncontroversial ones. I'm sure he'd tell you to call Blackie Broussard."

Catherine took a deep, resigned breath. Everyone had known about Blackie's profession but her. "Blackie must be good," she said dryly. "Everyone seems to sing his praises."

"Oh, yes. In fact, Doug's been trying to talk him into coming back to work for the corps, but he won't have any part of it."

"Oh, Blackie would rather be his own boss," Clarence said, but Catherine didn't miss the hint of evasion.

"I know," Toni answered quietly, "but I wish he'd change his mind. He could be a valuable liaison between the corps and the local people. There's been too much conflict over the years."

"There sure has been. Let's hope it's over." Clarence swatted idly at a mosquito. "Well, *mesdames*, I've got to go. Are we agreed on our first step?"

"Yes, I'll call Blackie first thing tomorrow morning," Catherine replied. *Whether I want to or not,* she added to herself.

"Good." Clarence beamed. "See you both later." With a wave, he headed toward his car.

As Catherine watched him make his way across the uneven ground, she wondered why Blackie wouldn't help his people by working with the corps, even on an unofficial basis. In fact, from what she knew of him so far, she couldn't imagine his *not* helping them. She was puzzled and intrigued, yet still couldn't bring herself to betray undue interest in him by asking anyone.

"Well, Catherine, how's the research going on the Arceneaux house?" Toni asked.

"I'm boning up on everything as fast as I can, and just lately I took a crash course in Cajun culture."

"Crash course?" Toni looked perplexed. "Where? From whom?"

"From the world's foremost authority on everything Cajun." Catherine smiled wryly. "Blackie Broussard."

Toni laughed. "Has he taken it upon himself to teach you?"

"He thinks I need more than I can get from books. And I hate to admit it, but he's probably right." She glanced away, not wanting Toni to read her thoughts. "As a first lesson, he took me to Morgan City to meet his Uncle Bat Charpiot."

"Uncle Bat's quite a character. Did you enjoy the trip?"

"More than anything. Uncle Bat's a wonderful old man. He showed me a violin that came down in 1755 with the Acadians—with his family. It's beautiful, and seeing it was a priceless experience. I'm afraid I overstepped myself when I asked him if he would like to donate it to the society, but he was gracious enough to accept my apology."

"I'm not surprised he wouldn't part with it," Toni said. "I just hope nothing ever happens to him, or his violin, for that matter, all alone out in the swamp."

"Blackie wouldn't let anything happen to him," Catherine said, remembering how protective he had been of Uncle Bat. A yearning query brushed her mind: how would it feel to have someone care that much for her?

"No, I'm sure he wouldn't." Toni glanced at her watch. "I suppose I should get back to headquarters. Where's Gussie? I thought she'd be out here where the action is."

"She wanted to be, but I sent her to the courthouse for information on the Arceneaux house. I'm sure she'll get her fill of the site before we're finished."

After Toni drove away, Catherine walked to Bonne Journée, speculating about Blackie. Certainly Clarence and Toni knew more than they had let on. Suddenly Catherine realized she knew someone who was not only a fountain of information but who, she felt sure, wouldn't keep anything from her.

"Gussie?" she called as she entered the office and laid her clipboard on her desk. When there was no answer, she peeked into Gussie's alcove. It was empty, and the only sound in the house was an occasional thump from the workers on the second floor. Gussie must still be at the courthouse, Catherine concluded, disappointed that she'd have to wait for her answers.

She sat down and picked up a sheet of paper from a stack on her desk. It was the bid from the wood-worker on the acanthus molding. At first glance, the quote looked reasonable. She made a note on her clipboard to get a sample of the man's work and was looking at the next item on the stack when she heard the old floor outside her office door creak softly.

"Gussie?" she called, not looking up. No one answered. Out of the corner of her eye, she saw a figure appear in the doorway. Startled, she looked up to see a man standing there. Raymond Hebert.

"Yes?" She willed herself to remain calm.

"Don' you remember me?" He looked at her insolently.

Catherine returned his stare, though her hand crept up to her throat. "Yes, of course. You're Mr. Broussard's friend."

He laughed, and the harsh sound grated on Catherine's ears. "Mr. Broussard's friend," he mocked. "I t'ink *you're* Mr. Broussard's friend now. I got no friends, me. Everybody t'inks I'm *fou*—crazy." He watched her steadily, and she could see the hatred in his eyes. "And maybe I am."

Her unease grew, making it difficult to breathe. "Is there anything I can do for you, Mr. Hebert?" She attempted to keep her voice even. It was an idiotic thing to say, but she felt that she had to try, at least, to make some attempt at normal conversation. She glanced pointedly at her watch. "If not, I have an appointment in a few minutes." Maybe he'd leave if he thought someone else was coming.

"Well, I got an appointment, too. I got to go find some nice, dry sticks and some gasoline." For the first time, Catherine's scalp prickled with real fear.

Hebert picked up the Arceneaux house report from her desk and thumbed through it, then threw it down.

"You're so damn proud of that Cajun house," he snarled, "but it ain't nothin' but old, dry wood. It sho' would burn easy. Then you don't have no job, do you?"

Catherine opened her mouth, but no sound came out, and with another angry laugh, he was gone. Fear crawled up her spine. She listened intently, afraid he was still outside her door, but then she heard his retreating footsteps on the gallery. She remained at her desk, more shaken than she cared to admit. The Arceneaux house would burn like a torch. She should warn someone. But she would sound so—so melodramatic, telling people that a madman—a crazy Cajun?—was going to set fire to the Arceneaux house. She fought a hysterical giggle. How absurd. No one burned historical restorations. Did they?

When Gussie came in, Catherine was still sitting at her desk. "*Pour l'amour de Dieu,* Catherine," she exclaimed. "You look like you just saw a ghost! What's the matter with you?"

Catherine slowly shook her head. "I'm not really sure. Raymond Hebert came by here and threatened—sort of—to burn down the Arceneaux house."

"*What?*" Gussie's mouth fell open. "That's impossible!"

"It happened, I promise you."

Shock turned to indignation. "Why, that—that *salop*!" Gussie said loudly. Catherine didn't dare ask what the word meant. "He can't do that. We'll turn him in. We'll call Clarence, and the sheriff, and the state police, and—"

"It's all right, Gussie." Catherine broke in before Gussie could think of anyone else to notify—Blackie, for instance. "He just scared me. But I'm fine now, really I am." Automatically her hand came up to smooth her hair.

"Well, I'm not." Gussie shook a fist. "We've got to look into this. I don't trust him as far as I can throw him."

Catherine didn't, either, but she didn't want the incident blown out of proportion; in fact, now that it was over, she felt a little foolish. "I don't think he really meant it," she said. "People like that are mostly talk. If he threatens again, we'll tell someone. In the meantime, let's just try to forget it." She was determined to follow her own advice, but a queasy feeling remained in the pit of her stomach.

For a moment, Gussie looked as if she wanted to pursue the point. "All right, Catherine," she finally agreed reluctantly.

"Now...what did you find on the Arceneaux family?" Catherine asked, changing the subject.

Gussie handed her a manila folder, fat with photocopies.

"Ah," Catherine said, leafing through them. "These should keep me awake tonight. Do these tell us what we need to know?"

"I don't know. I didn't have time to go through everything. I'll probably finish copying tomorrow."

"Good. Hmm..." A group of old inventories had already piqued Catherine's attention. "Gussie, according to these records, the Arceneauxs owned a great deal more land than the Millards," she said in amazement. "They also owned nearly as many slaves."

"Well, sure," Gussie said. "Just because they didn't build a big fancy show-off house didn't mean they couldn't have if they had wanted to."

It's like everything else here, Catherine realized. *Nothing follows the rules.* She read on. "This land deed is dated 1767. Good heavens—by the time Joshua Millard bought his plantation in 1832, the Arceneaux family had already been here for over sixty years. I suppose they considered the Millards to be upstarts."

Gussie looked ever so slightly smug. "I told you the Arceneaux house was old. What did you decide about the site?"

"We need to stabilize the foundation. Clarence and Toni recommended Blackie Broussard. Why didn't you tell me he was an engineer?"

"You didn't ask me." Gussie's logic was indisputable, and so was the mischief in her eyes.

Catherine glared at her but refrained from comment. "Should I call him at his instrument repair number?" she asked.

"Sure. Or just call J. B. Broussard, Engineer, in Morgan City."

"J.B.?" Catherine said curiously. "Does the B stand for Blackie? I thought that was a nickname."

"It is. Blackie's full name is Jean Beausoleil Broussard. Mama told me his parents named him Jean because the pirate Jean Lafitte is supposed to be one of his ancestors. And another ancestor, named Joseph Broussard *dit* Beausoleil—that means he was *called*

Beausoleil—was a hero of the Cajun people way back when they were thrown out of l'Acadie.''

Jean Beausoleil Broussard. Such an imposing name—such a beautiful name. Saying it to herself brought vivid images to Catherine's mind: Blackie as he spoke of the Atchafalaya Swamp, as he hugged Uncle Bat…as he kissed her good-night. She was well acquainted with his lighthearted ''Blackie'' image, but she had only been given glimpses of Jean Beausoleil Broussard, the inner man—a man she felt an irresistible compulsion to know better.

''That's quite a name,'' she told Gussie. ''I suppose no one ever calls him that.''

''Just his mama. He's Blackie or Ti-neg to everyone else.''

The papers on Catherine's desk caught Gussie's attention. ''Did you see the bid on the acanthus molding?'' she pointed. ''What do you think?''

Catherine glanced at the bid again. ''If he's good, I think he's got the job. What's his name? Léger?''

''Yes, Dudley Léger. He's a cousin on Mama's side.''

Another cousin. Gussie's family tree would probably have to be drawn on a billboard, Catherine thought, feeling unaccountably envious. ''Tell me,'' she said casually, ''is Blackie your cousin, too?''

Gussie laughed. ''Why, sure. In fact, I think we're kissin' cousins.'' She shot Catherine a provocative look. ''See you later.'' She sauntered out the door.

Catherine looked fondly after Gussie's retreating form. How wonderful to be able to enjoy life the way Gussie did. Putting down the deed record, Catherine began to thumb through the rest of the pages, looking for names and dates. She found deeds, mortgages, marriage licenses, wills, the usual documents—enough to give her an idea of the life-style and possessions of the Arceneaux family.

Midway through the stack, a document caught her eye, and she stopped and began to read more carefully. It was from the Criminal District Court, an assault charge brought by one Michel Arceneaux against—she couldn't believe her eyes. One Joshua Millard. It alleged that Millard had, without provocation, attacked Arceneaux with a horsewhip on the main street of New Iberia. *How awful,* she thought. The ultimate insult. Millard hadn't even thought enough of Arceneaux to challenge him to a duel; no wonder the Acadian had filed charges.

Catherine sat, eyes narrowed in thought, fingernails tapping the desktop. She had to find out more. But where? Her only sources for information on the Arceneaux family, at least so far, were the courthouse and the library. No Arceneaux descendants had yet come forth with family papers, diaries or letters. The Millard records, however, might be a different story. Catherine went to a file cabinet in the corner of her office and pulled out a folder that read Millard Family Possessions. She studied it for a few minutes, closed it and walked to the door.

"Gussie?"

"I'm here, Catherine." Gussie poked her head out of the parlor door.

"Remember the little old lady who brought us that trunk full of Millard family correspondence? She told us she was the Millards' great-great-granddaughter."

Gussie nodded. "How could I forget? She almost talked my ear off. She stayed here at least three hours, wandering through the house and telling us everything she used to do when she lived here as a little girl."

Catherine smiled. "It's because you have such a sympathetic face. Anyway, I want that trunk, and according to the inventory, it's up in the attic..."

THIRTY MINUTES LATER, Catherine and Gussie came down from the attic, dusty but triumphant. Each held an end of a small, flat-topped trunk, its leather covering worn, and in places missing completely.

"This thing must be full. It's heavy!" Gussie said as they set it on the floor in Catherine's office.

"The Millards apparently liked to write. I just hope they discussed the Millard-Arceneaux assault case." Catherine fiddled with the rusty latch on the trunk. It was stuck. She hated to pry it open, but... She gave it another tug, and to her relief it opened with a reluctant creak. She opened the lid and stared into the trunk with mingled pleasure and dismay. As she had thought, it was full; the papers had been pressed down to make them fit.

"I won't be able to go through that in an afternoon," Catherine said. "I'll just leave the trunk here and read the letters as I have time." She stood and dusted her hands. "You'd better go, Gussie. Didn't you tell me yesterday you had a date tonight? With Alain?''

''That's the man.'' Gussie grinned. ''We're going to his parents' house for supper.''

''Supper at his parents' house?'' Catherine raised an eyebrow. ''Sounds serious.''

''You know, I think it is,'' Gussie responded in uncharacteristically quiet amazement. ''I've known Alain since we were in the first grade, but we were always just friends. He was so...so familiar, like one of my brothers. Then he went off to dental school, and I didn't see him much, and when he came back, he was different. Or maybe I was different. Anyway, the very first time we went out, we knew things had changed.''

''Seriouser and seriouser,'' Catherine teased. ''Fatal, in fact. But aren't you happy?''

''Ecstatic.'' Gussie said it as if she meant it. ''But I'm surprised, too. I thought I wouldn't marry till I got too old to have a good time, but now I don't have a good time unless I'm with Alain. I guess I got old without knowing it.''

Catherine laughed. ''The ruination of a perfectly good party girl. I think your time has truly come. Have fun, and I'll see you tomorrow.'' To her own surprise, Catherine felt a twinge of envy. Was it too late for her simply to learn to have a good time?

''Don't forget to call Blackie,'' Gussie called as she walked out the door. Catherine, unable to prevent her pulse quickening at the idea of hearing Blackie's voice, reached for the telephone. It was not until she heard the massive front door slam that she realized she had forgotten to ask Gussie about Blackie's problems with the Corps of Engineers.

THE FOLLOWING THURSDAY, Catherine watched Blackie walk across the field to where she waited near the Arceneaux house site. As he walked, he studied the ground, and she was able to stare at him unobserved. He was wearing his usual work shirt and jeans, which were snugly molded to his powerful body, and he carried himself like a prince surveying his domain. Although the day was warm, a breeze ruffled his dark hair, and Catherine could feel that same breeze lightly caress her neck.

Twenty-five feet from her, he looked up and saw her, and his grin split his handsome face. Catherine was unprepared for the surge of wanting that coursed through her body. All she could think of at that moment was walking right into his arms.

"Hello, Blackie," she said, clutching her clipboard against her more tightly than was necessary.

The grin didn't abate. Did he know his effect on her? "How you doin', *chère*? I haven't seen you lately." He walked toward her, his hand formally extended. Catherine hesitated, remembering how dangerous it was to touch him but unable to resist. Their hands had barely clasped when he pulled, gently but with enough force to tip her forward into his arms. Before she could speak, he had planted a quick, light kiss on her mouth. His lips tasted deliciously salty. It was over before she knew it, but the brief contact set her nerve ends tingling. "What was that?" she asked, trying to catch her breath. "A typical Cajun greeting?"

Blackie chuckled. "*Mais* sho'. That was your next lesson in the Cajun way of life. It's my particular favorite."

"I don't doubt it. At least it's short and sweet."

He looked at her speculatively. She felt his eyes on her, warm, intimate, as if he was touching her. "What makes you so sure I'm finished?" he asked, and laughed. "Come on, let's take a look at this ground and see what we can do."

For the next fifteen minutes Blackie inspected the area. He stepped off the distance the house would be placed from the bayou, dug into the ground at various points with a large pocketknife, stood at the water's edge gauging the slope. Catherine watched him as unobtrusively as possible, glorying in his expressions, in the graceful movements of his body, in the way his hair shone blue-black in the sun.

Finally he came back to where she stood in the shade of the hedge. "Whooee, but it's hot," he remarked, wiping his forehead on his sleeve.

"They're predicting an unusually hot summer," she said. "Do you think it's true?"

"Yes. It's only May, and it already feels like July or August. Uncle Bat says this much heat this early brings a hurricane, and he's usually right."

"Have many hurricanes hit the Teche area?" Catherine asked.

"Not really. We haven't had a big one here in years. But you never know." He knelt and wiped his knife clean on the grass, then closed it and put it in his pocket.

"I'll come back and do an official soil analysis for the record," he told her, "but unless this ground is different from all the rest along this part of the Teche, I can tell you right now what you should do about the Arceneaux house. This top layer is clay soil. It moves around, especially when it's close to water. On a slope like this, it needs to be stabilized." Catherine listened, fascinated.

"Will stabilizing it be difficult?" She had visions of the entire bank having to be dug away.

"Not really. The house will sit on piers. Everywhere a pier will be set, we dig a hole about six feet deep, then we fill it with concrete. In effect, we're extending the house foundation into the stable soil. I'd also recommend building a strong bulkhead along the bayou bank in front of the house to help support the whole area."

"That sounds fairly simple—and not too expensive," Catherine said, relieved.

"It isn't, especially if I do most of the work myself."

"Yourself?"

"Sure, why not? That's what engineers do best— work with their hands." Blackie made as if he were digging a hole.

"Blackie..."

"Yes, Catherine?" He cocked his head inquiringly.

"Why didn't you tell me you were an engineer? And don't say it was because I didn't ask you. We spent a whole afternoon talking about the Atchafalaya Swamp and its problems.''

He shrugged. ''To be honest, I don't really think of myself as an engineer, at least not much of the time, anyway.''

''So you don't do much engineering work?''

''Enough to suit me.'' He grinned at her. ''I wouldn't want to burn myself out on it. Playing the accordion's a lot more fun.''

''I'm sure it is. But is it as rewarding?''

''Some people might think so,'' he said lightly, but she sensed that he was pulling away from her. ''Everybody at the *fais-do-do* last week, for instance.''

''But you could do so much for those same people if you helped solve the problems with the Atchafalaya Basin,'' Catherine persisted. Why had she mentioned it, anyway? But all she could think of was how he was wasting himself. And if anyone ought to feel a moral obligation to help his people, it was Blackie.

''Those problems have been there since before I was born, *chère*. One person can't solve them all by himself.''

''You could try. I was told you once worked with the Corps of Engineers. You could at least serve as a liaison between them and your people. Think what a help that would be.''

''Sometimes a person thinks he's being helpful when he isn't. I'd rather do nothing than make things worse.''

Something akin to pain flashed across his face, then was gone, leaving his expression shut. She knew it was a warning, but she couldn't stop herself. "But, Blackie—you have ability, and you're wasting it."

He kept his voice even, but she knew she had gone too far. "Catherine, you have a habit of trying to direct people's lives the way you direct your restorations. I don't feel that I'm wasting anything. Maybe my music isn't universally important, but historical restoration won't change the world, either. Now, if you'll excuse me, I'm going back to *work*." He emphasized the word. "I have an accordion to repair and two gigs to practice for. I'll have your report for you by the first of next week."

Before she could reply, he was gone, striding across the field toward his truck. Catherine, feeling ineffably alone, wondered what in God's creation had possessed her to push him so hard for answers. And why those answers were so important to her.

CHAPTER SEVEN

CATHERINE WAITED in her office for Gussie and tried to calm the butterflies in her stomach. If she had forgotten anything, she would soon know it. Today, barely one month after the Preservation Society Board of Directors had approved the project, the Arceneaux house would arrive at its new location beside Bonne Journée. Laboring far into the evening the day before, the moving crew had jacked up the old house, placed long steel girders beneath it and slid it onto a waiting barge to ready it for the seven-mile trip. Now, if everything had gone according to plan, a tugboat was already pushing the barge up the Teche to New Iberia.

In spite of her nervousness, Catherine knew she alone wasn't responsible for the moving preparations—not by any means. Blackie, with a couple of his men, had done all the groundwork on the house site. He had worked on the house with Clarence and the moving crew the day before and was riding on the barge today to make sure everything went well.

Catherine realized that the expectation of seeing him today probably accounted for some of her nerves. The day he had agreed to engineer the Arceneaux house project, they hadn't parted on the best of terms. On the few occasions she had had to see him about the Arceneaux house, it had been strictly business between them. She hated to admit it, but she missed his Cajun lessons, his teasing, his engaging grin, his touch...

According to Gussie, he had been out of town, taking his band to play at various music festivals across the state and in other parts of the country. Gussie had proudly told her—as had Clarence and Toni—that he and his band were becoming nationally known as the foremost representatives of Louisiana Cajun music.

All well and good, but he was still wasting his other abilities. He had done a superb job on the Arceneaux house. And he could do even more as liaison between the local people and the Corps of Engineers. But her opinions had made him angry, and believing she was right didn't keep her from missing him.

Catherine glanced in her folder for the third time to make sure she had the checks for the moving crew—they would want their money at the end of the day—and came across Blackie's report on the preparation of the Arceneaux house site. Thumbing through it, she reflected that when he chose to work, he was more than competent. This report was as clear and concise as she could have wished.

She looked at the signature on the bottom. "J. B. Broussard," it read in bold, black strokes. Jean Beausoleil Broussard. Descended from Jean Lafitte, indeed. What a tale. But, remembering Blackie's rakish air and conning ways, she could almost believe it. Maybe he *was* descended from the pirate, after all.

"Bonjour." Gussie's voice came from behind her.

Catherine turned. "*Bonjour* yourself. My, you sound cheery this morning—and you look wonderful," she finished, catching sight of Gussie's face.

It was true. Gussie looked positively radiant. She broke into her brilliant smile and rushed across the room to give Catherine an energetic hug. "Look!" She thrust out her left hand. On the fourth finger winked a modest diamond solitaire. "Alain's asked me to marry him."

"Gussie, that's wonderful." In the midst of her delight for her friend, Catherine was suddenly horrified to find herself feeling a bit...not jealous. Forlorn. She had never seen anyone so deliriously happy, knew she'd never felt that way. Her mind conjured up molten black eyes, a devilish grin... She pushed the image aside; now was Gussie's moment. "When's the magic date?" she asked.

"Sometime in September. We both have so much family, it's going to take a while to arrange it so everyone can be here. Mama's already making such big plans, I'm afraid we're going to wish we'd eloped."

"You know you can't do that. You'd break her heart."

"Not to mention Alain's mother's heart. But it'll be fun." She hesitated uncharacteristically. "Catherine—my three sisters will probably be bridesmaids, and so will a couple of school friends. Will you be my sixth?"

It was a moment before Catherine could speak, and when she did, her voice caught. "Why, Gussie, I'd be delighted." In a gesture rare for her, she hugged the younger woman.

"That's great." Catherine wouldn't have thought it possible, but Gussie's smile became even brighter.

"Does this mean I'm going to lose my assistant?"

"Oh, no—give me a week for the honeymoon, and I'll be right back at work. I want to see both projects through."

"I'm glad to hear it, because I don't know what I'd do without you."

"Well, you'll find out someday, because I plan to be chasing kids as soon as possible. Alain and I want a houseful."

Catherine smiled at the picture. "By that time I'll probably be gone, so you can have as many as you like."

"Oh, Catherine, you can't leave." Gussie looked a little stricken, as if Catherine's eventual departure had never occurred to her. "You're a part of us now." Then her brow cleared. "Never mind—I'll find you someone here in Louisiana to marry."

Like Blackie Broussard? Catherine rapidly changed the subject. "Are you coming to see the Arceneaux house?" she asked. "It should be here shortly."

"I've got a few things to do here first, but I'll be over in a little while," Gussie said. "I wouldn't miss it for the world."

Catherine looked at her watch. "I'm going now. Come as soon as you can. And Gussie..." She smiled at the younger woman. "Thank you again for asking me. It means more to me than you can imagine."

"I couldn't get married without you." Gussie laughed. "You'd better get going."

Catherine hurried out the door, her heart full of joy for Gussie. But for herself, she felt a lingering melancholy.

As she walked toward the raw, new earth of the house site next door, she saw a tall, willowy form. Toni.

"Where's Clarence?" she asked. "I thought he was supposed to meet us here."

Toni laughed. "Clarence couldn't stand it," she answered. "He went down to catch a ride on the barge."

"Somehow, I'm not surprised." Catherine smiled. "All week, he's acted as if Christmas is coming." Even dignified Clarence had a little boy hiding inside him. Was that how it was with most men? *With Blackie?* Knowing Blackie, she felt sure it was true.

For an instant, she wished she had ridden on the barge, too. It would have been fun. Then she remembered she was in charge of this move. This was no joyride for her. Sternly, she dismissed the wayward idea.

A noise from the road intruded on her thoughts. Two big winch trucks swung onto the grass and chugged toward them, parking in the middle of the lot.

Catherine and Toni walked to the house site and inspected the concrete stabilizers, neat gray rectangles imbedded in the ground.

"Blackie's done a terrific job," Toni remarked.

"I know. Think of what he could do with his engineering if he really tried."

"Blackie's not had a very easy time of it in the past few years," Toni said gently.

"Oh?" Catherine's attention sharpened. Was Toni going to volunteer information?

"Blackie was working for the Corps of Engineers, when he lost his wife," Toni explained.

"How did she die?"

"She was a nurse. She went into the Atchafalaya Swamp to see about a sick child." Toni shook her head. "As she was coming back, the boat hit something in the water, a cypress knee, they thought, and she was thrown out. She hit her head and drowned."

"Dear God..." For an instant, the cheery songs of the small bayou denizens receded as shock reverberated through Catherine's consciousness. She'd assumed Blackie's wife had died of an illness. But the swamp had killed her—the swamp, where he had grown up, was responsible for the death of the woman he loved.

"I've never known all the facts," Toni continued, "but Blackie quit the corps right after Angéline died. Doug heard through the office grapevine that Blackie had some sort of run-in with his boss. Anyway, for all Blackie's carefree exterior, I suspect he's still grieving, and I think he's turned to his music for comfort. He's done some fine engineering work since he's been in private practice, but in general, he's lacked direction."

"I...see." And she had had the bad taste—no the sheer effrontery—to suggest that he go back to work for the corps. It seemed she owed him an apology. A big one.

"Angéline—what was she like?" Catherine hadn't realized she was into self-torture, but she had to know.

"Oh, she was a love," Toni said. "Warm, outgoing, caring—and beautiful, too. She had the blackest hair and eyes I've ever seen. She loved Blackie's music—in fact, he used to compose songs for her. They were the best dancers at the *fais-do-dos*. It was a pleasure to watch them."

"I'm sure it was," Catherine answered mechanically, remembering the tears Blackie had shed—for his wife, Gussie had told her—when she had heard him play. Angéline must have been perfect for him, and since her death, her memory remained, even larger than in life. No wonder he still wept for her. Deliberately, Catherine made herself turn to watch downstream for the first sight of the Arceneaux house.

THE TUGBOAT REVVED ITS ENGINES and slowly angled the big barge carrying the Arceneaux house toward the middle of the bayou. Blackie stripped off his shirt in the mounting heat and breathed a sigh of relief. The past few days had been full of hard work, but damn, it felt good. He made his way to the front of the barge, where a slight figure perched on a pile of huge wooden beams.

"Well, *Nonc*," he said. "What do you think, *hein*? Is this crazy? To float a house down the bayou?"

"*Oui,* Ti-neg. *Bien fou.* Dis I mus' see wit' ma own eyes, me."

"Ah, you just didn't want to miss all the fun." Blackie clapped him soundly on the shoulder, the gesture a caress.

Uncle Bat drew himself up with dignity. "I like to learn somet'ing new, me."

Blackie chuckled. "Yeah, me too."

"Ti-neg."

"Oui?"

"Da pretty *jeune fille*—Cat'rine. She know what to do wit' da house?"

"She says she does. We have to help her, though."

"I'm glad to help her, me. I'll tol' her anyt'ing she want ta know." He paused a moment. "Ti-neg—you been seein' dis girl, you?"

Blackie winced. He had expected this. *"Oui, Nonc,* I see her all the time, when I help her work on the house site," he hedged.

"Non, imbécile. I mean, *seein'* her."

"Sometimes," Blackie said lightly.

"She ver' smart girl, Ti-neg," Uncle Bat said thoughtfully. "But somet'ing make her *bien triste*— ver' sad inside. You make her happy, *oui?"* He looked hopeful.

"I don't think so. She's mad at me now. And to tell the truth, I'm mad at her, too."

"Ce n'est pas important." Uncle Bat made a dismissive gesture. "Dat don' matter. You make her happy, she make you happy."

"Nonc..." Blackie shrugged, giving up in the face of such awesome simplicity. He wandered over to the side of the barge and stared at the muddy brown waters of the Teche. Oh, yes, he was angry. What he did—or didn't do—was no business of hers. What kind of manners had she learned at her fancy finishing school, anyway?

And yet—there was the wanting. He couldn't rid his thoughts of the sight of her, the scent of her. Some-

times, when he was with her, it was all he could do to
keep his hands off her. He closed his eyes, felt his body
begin to respond even to the thought of her. At night
his dreams were haunted by a pair of sea-green eyes
and hair the color of moonlight. Then he'd awaken,
aching with the desire to join her slender body with his
in the fullest, most elemental way.

Propping his foot on a heavy wooden beam, Blackie
leaned an elbow on his knee and stared thoughtfully
at the passing scene. Modern houses sat next to ante-
bellum homes and the ruined smokestacks of sugarcane mills. Cleared land alternated with thickets of
tallow and palmetto. Cypress trees grew at the edge of
the water, spreading their brilliant, feathery foliage,
and the honeysuckle... He took a deep breath of the
fragrant air and felt his anger slowly evaporate.

This was his home, and he loved it. But he could
understand how foreign it might seem to anyone who
hadn't been born here, especially someone like Catherine, who had been reared in a different culture. It
was no wonder she didn't understand or approve of
how he lived.

He reminded himself that she was seeing his
world—and him—with an outsider's objectivity. What
if she was right? He didn't want to admit it, because
it would mean giving up his detachment, his self-
imposed isolation. Somehow, since Angéline's death,
it had been easier—and less painful—to stay unin-
volved. But look at him now, deep in this project.
Whether it was the project he was hooked on, or
Catherine, was another matter.

He straightened, wiped his hands on the seat of his jeans and headed toward the back of the barge; before they docked in New Iberia, he wanted to check the braces on the house.

But as he turned, he caught Uncle Bat's knowing eyes upon him.

A DEAFENING BLAST from a boat horn shattered the air. Catherine jumped.

"Here they come," Toni cried.

Sure enough, a few seconds later, the blunt, rusty nose of a big barge rounded a bend in the bayou, and then the peaked roof and weathered cypress siding of the Arceneaux house appeared, riding high on the center of the craft. Looking at the old house, Catherine realized it was much larger than she had remembered.

The tug, painted an eye-assaulting red and white, pushed the barge from the rear, chugging officiously and belching great clouds of black smoke from its stack. *I don't believe I'm seeing this,* Catherine thought. *A two-hundred-year-old house sailing up the bayou, being pushed by a tugboat.* A brief, graphic image of Gerrard Nolan's face witnessing this scene flashed into Catherine's mind and nearly upset her composure. She stifled a giggle.

Looking closer, she sorted out the separate figures on the deck of the barge. There was Clarence, in khakis and sport shirt, even from this distance looking as if he was enjoying himself enormously. And the shirtless, muscled figure next to him was Blackie. She couldn't prevent her eyes from dwelling on his powerful brown shoulders and muscular chest, bare in the June sunshine, couldn't stop her heart from beating faster.

A third figure on the barge captured Catherine's gaze. A slight, small figure, a little stooped. Definitely not a workman. Catherine looked closer, hardly able to believe her eyes. "That's Uncle Bat!"

Toni looked closer. "So it is." She laughed. "I'll bet he's having the time of his life." Slowly, laboriously, with much racing of engines and churning of the muddy bayou waters, the tug eased the barge over until it rested against the bank. Catherine could smell the hot, acrid diesel smoke drifting across the humid air.

The two winch trucks began to back down the steep embankment. Some men leaped from the barge onto the land, securing the barge firmly, and others began to unload the huge, oil-stained timbers that would form the ramp for the house to roll up the steep slope.

Blackie jumped off the barge and helped Uncle Bat climb down. They both headed in her direction. By the time they arrived, Catherine had already told herself a dozen times that she didn't care if Blackie refused to speak to her. In fact, he didn't look at her right away, but Uncle Bat kissed her hand with his soul in his black, sorrowful eyes.

"Uncle Bat, you've made my day." She took his hand in both of hers. "How on earth did you talk them into bringing you?"

"Cat'rine, *ma belle*. Ever' day you get prettier, you," he said in his laborious English. "I don' ask 'em nuttin', me—I jus' tol' 'em I'm comin'." He surveyed the old house, sitting in state on top of the barge, then the waiting site. "Cat'rine," he said, "you gon' make dis house look good. You ver' smart, *non*?"

Catherine smiled ruefully, made a helpless little movement with her hands. "Not really, Uncle Bat."

"*Mais* sho', you plenty smart, *mignonne*. Some other *bêtes* I know, dey not very smart." Uncle Bat threw a quick glance at Blackie and patted Catherine's hand comfortingly. He moved to speak to Toni, leaving Catherine to wonder if hers and Blackie's troubles were that obvious or if the old man was clairvoyant.

She braced herself to meet Blackie's eyes at last. They were shuttered, opaque.

"Catherine." He articulated her name carefully, nodding formally. He didn't attempt to touch her in any way, not even to take her hand.

Suddenly, nothing mattered to Catherine but that Blackie stop looking at her like that, stop treating her as if she was a distant and somewhat unwelcome acquaintance. Marveling at her own nerve and hoping Toni and Uncle Bat were too involved in their greetings to overhear, she held out both her hands in entreaty, and watched the look of surprise dawn in Blackie's eyes. Before she could say a word, he took them in his strong grasp.

She held on to his hands for dear life. "Blackie, I had no right to say what I did," she said quietly. "Please forgive me—I'm so sorry."

Blackie hesitated only a second before he smiled. This time it was not his usual grin but a quiet, loving smile that nearly undid her. "*Mais* sho', darlin'," he said gently. "So am I." She looked into his eyes and saw what she should have seen the first time she saw him—a shadow of the pain, always there. And then the warmth, that incredible warmth leaped to the fore of his gaze, turning his eyes molten. She felt it envelop her like a soothing, healing blanket. He kept one hand imprisoned in his, and she fought an irrational desire to kiss him. Blackie must have read her mind, because his eyes dropped to her lips.

Then his grin spread blindingly across his face. "We brought your house, Cat'rine," he said, his eyes alight with excitement. He looked like a little boy angling for praise. With a ridiculous surge of happiness, she understood that she was forgiven and that, as far as Blackie was concerned, the incident was forgotten.

"So I see." She tried to hide her gladness. "And you brought me a nice surprise, too." She nodded toward Uncle Bat, still in animated conversation with Toni.

"You like that surprise, *chère*? Well, I didn't have to talk him into coming, in fact, once he heard about the project, that was that. Nothing would've kept him away. You should have heard him on the way down— he was so excited, he was telling stories even *I've* never heard."

"Blackie..." Catherine hesitated; she'd put her foot in her mouth once before regarding Uncle Bat. "I'd like for Uncle Bat to be a consultant on this project. Do you think he'd mind?"

"*Mais jamais!* He'd be delighted. He's in love with you, anyway." But it was Blackie who kept his eyes on Catherine's face.

"Hmm . . . I might consider going after him myself," Catherine said pensively. "He's quite a catch."

"Don't build his ego too much. He's already hard to handle." With a last squeeze, Blackie let go of her hands. "I'd better go to work now, before they come to get me."

"Tell me," Catherine asked, wanting to keep him near just a moment longer, "are all your extra services today covered in your engineering fee? I don't believe I've ever known an engineer who rode down a bayou with his projects."

The grin widened. "*Chère*, I'm having so much fun with this project, there may not be an engineering bill."

Suddenly Catherine was acutely conscious of his shirtless state, of the way the muscles rippled under his tanned skin with his slightest movement and of how close they were standing. Almost as if she had spoken, he looked into her eyes, then his hand slipped up to cradle her cheek before he turned to go.

All afternoon the men worked, placing the beams, hooking the winch cables to the steel girders underneath the house, shouting, straining, sweating. At last, the winches began to pull, the cables sang with tautness, and the old house began to inch forward up the ramp on the last phase of its journey. Blackie was everywhere at once, directing operations, gesturing the winch trucks forward, helping the other men push when the slope became too steep.

The sun grew hotter, and the humid air grew steamier. Sweat poured off Blackie's face and ran in rivulets down his brawny shoulders and back. Tugging a red bandanna from his hip pocket, he rolled it and tied it around his forehead. Watching him, Catherine thought he looked more like a pirate than ever.

Uncle Bat presided over the activities like a visiting lord. As usual, his dolorous expression remained etched on his face, but Catherine could tell that he was enjoying himself enormously, because his currant-dark eyes darted here and there, never missing the smallest detail of what was going on. Catherine was glad he was there; his presence somehow bestowed a blessing on the entire project.

JUST AT DUSK, the work ceased. The winch trucks had gone, and the tug and barge departed with the workmen. Toni and Clarence had left, as had several other spectators, including Gussie, who had come down to watch the activity. Catherine stood with Blackie and Uncle Bat in front of the house. It sat squarely, if a little awkwardly, in the midst of its new surroundings, its great age painfully obvious. Its vacant windows and weathered cypress siding contrasted strangely with the newness of the turned earth and the temporary concrete piers.

Catherine stared at the old house. Here was her future, the job she must do. Time would tell if she could do it. She thought of the work ahead, the research she had to complete on the Arceneaux family, and silently renewed the vow she had made to Gussie to do her very best work on this restoration. She would tell the story of this family just as she was telling the story of the Millards. She would do this job right, for Clarence, for Gussie, for Uncle Bat . . . for this man standing beside her. And perhaps, most of all, for herself.

"There she is, Cat'rine," Blackie said, triumph in his voice. "The rest is up to you." He had put his shirt on and stood looking proudly at the house, but she could feel the fatigue that radiated from his body.

"I know," Catherine answered. In her mind's eye, she could see the house as it would look when it was restored: roof and siding repaired, front painted, furnishings in place . . . Suddenly she felt, *knew* the restoration would be a success. As the last rays of the sunset faded behind her and the fragrant air began to cool a little, she fancied she could hear long-ago voices, see shadowy figures moving from room to room in the house, going about their lives. Before her eyes, they became a real flesh-and-blood family. She had not expected the experience so soon, not with this house.

"It's going to be a good thing, Cat'rine, for all of us." Blackie dropped an arm across her shoulders. It was a casual gesture, but it moved Catherine more than if it had been done in passion.

Uncle Bat, who had gone inside the house to prowl around, came out onto the porch and climbed carefully down.

"Da house done fine," he announced. "She in good shape, her."

"I know, Uncle Bat." The move had not damaged the house at all. The massive cypress beams and the finely crafted woodwork were intact, as was the *bousillage*, the mud-and-moss mixture used to insulate between the wallboards. Structurally, the house was sound, and its craftsmanship was superb. This was no rustic cabin, she realized, but a house with a heritage as proud and pure as that of Bonne Journée. "It's going to be a real pleasure to work on," she said, truly meaning it.

"Cat'rine," the old man said. "In da yard you mus' put a *mamou* plant."

"What's that?"

"It has a ver' big root, *oui*? For make tea for ailments. And *citronnelle* for da bellyache, and sassafras, for make *filé* for da gumbo. In da ol' days, all people have dem in dere yards."

"We'll do that. Thanks very much. Can we still find all those plants?"

Blackie laughed. "No problem," he said, "the woods are full of 'em. I'll see to it."

Catherine turned to face him. They had had their moments, good and bad ... She thought of the dark, sweet pull of the attraction between them. But right now, Blackie was a person who had helped someone in need. And she was that someone. She had to tell him so.

"Blackie," she began, "if this restoration is a success, it'll be due in large part to your efforts. Somehow, I don't think that's part of the regular job description on a project like that. Thank you, more than I can say."

"It was just a little something extra." He shrugged. "We call that *lagniappe*, *chère*—and it's free. I do it for the good company." With a wink, he dismissed the subject. "*Nonc*, prowl around here for a minute more while I walk Catherine to Bonne Journée. I've got to protect her."

Uncle Bat snorted derisively.

"Protect me?" Catherine asked in bewilderment. "From what?"

"Why, the 'gators and moccasins sometimes crawl right up on the bank this time of day. You can't be too careful," he insisted. Catherine eyed him askance.

"*Mais jamais,*" Uncle Bat muttered behind them.

With a laugh, she gave up. "All right, Blackie. Protect me. Goodbye, Uncle Bat. I'm glad you came today."

Uncle Bat kissed her hand again. "Cat'rine," he said, "I already warn' you about dis guy. You remember what I say, you."

"I'm trying to." Just then, Blackie caught her hand and tugged. Together, they walked toward Bonne Journée.

"You must be dead on your feet," she said as they crossed the hedge and emerged onto the manicured lawn.

"Yeah, but it's a good kind of tired." Blackie stretched his muscular arms. "Of course, my shoulders *do* hurt, and it would really feel good if somebody rubbed them." As they reached the front doors of the mansion, he pointed to his shoulders and looked at her pleadingly.

Catherine laughed. "Poor fellow. All right, then— I suppose it's the least I can do. Turn around." But her breath came fast at the thought of touching him.

He obligingly presented his brawny back, and Catherine began to knead the muscles at the base of his neck, loving the feel of their corded strength and the healthy heat of his skin.

"Mmm..." He moved his head around. "You're pretty good at this. Just looking at your hands, I didn't think they'd be so strong."

"Engineers aren't the only ones who are good with their hands. I've done carpentry work for restorations. Besides, I used to do this for my father." For once, the thought of her dad didn't resurrect old resentment.

Blackie stood in wordless pleasure while Catherine's long, slender fingers traveled up his neck, probing, soothing, dissolving his aches and pains. She could feel his muscles begin to relax. His eyes closed, and he tilted his head until the ends of the jet-black curls brushed Catherine's fingers. She fought the urge to tangle her hands in them, touch their crispness, wind them around her fingers. She could feel the heat building between them in the fragrant semidarkness. She wanted to hold him—to love him.

"Blackie..."

"Mmm?" His voice was lazy, sleepy.

"I meant every word of my apology. It's none of my business how you live your life. It's just that—"

With the force of the rising sun, it suddenly dawned on Catherine that she had been about to say something she wasn't ready to say, something he almost surely wasn't yet ready to hear—if he ever would be. But it was the reason she'd meddled. "I suppose I care about what's good for you," she finished lamely.

Blackie turned around quickly, surprise and pleasure on his face. He caught her shoulders, and as his gaze met hers, his smile faded.

"Cat'rine—" His fingers tightened on her arms, and his voice sank to a husky whisper. "A man could drown in your eyes. Did you know?" He pulled her forward and took her mouth with his.

It was different this time. His lips, hot, moist, moved over hers with a fierce hunger that hinted at the banked heat within him. His mouth tasted like dark wine, and when his tongue invaded her mouth, she felt the breath go out of her body. She dug her fingers desperately into the muscles of his back, pressing herself into his hard body with an abandon she hadn't known she possessed. His hand slipped around to cup her breast, and his touch seared her through her thin cotton blouse. Need shot through her, frightening in its intensity. She felt her reserve being stripped away layer by aching layer.

Suddenly, she was afraid. "Blackie, no. I . . . we mustn't." She pushed against his chest, breaking the embrace.

Blackie let her go reluctantly, his eyes still clouded.

"You're probably right, *chère*." There was a sadness in his voice. When she heard it, her throat went tight. He looked at the front of his sweat-stained, grimy shirt and held it away from him between thumb and forefingers. When he looked up, he was grinning. "I probably could stand a shower."

"That's not what I mean, and you know it." Catherine smiled in spite of herself.

"Actually, you're not so clean yourself."

"What do you mean?"

"You've got dirt on your nose." He gave the tip of her nose a swipe with his thumb, then, before she could retaliate, kissed it quickly. "I'd better go find *Nonc* before he thinks I've seduced you." He brightened. "Not that that's such a bad idea..."

"No, Blackie." Laughing, Catherine held up her hands and backed away.

"Ah, me. Can't blame a fellow for trying. All right—let me walk you to your car."

"No, I think I'll work a little longer."

"You *are* a glutton for punishment. You worked all day, remember? Even workaholics have a limit. Where are you parked?"

Giving in, she pointed. He was right—she was exhausted. He propelled her to her car, helped her in. He leaned in, and she felt his lips, moth light, brush hers. He closed the door then, and as he walked away, she could hear him whistling.

As she put the car in gear, she remembered that touching Blackie was dangerous. She knew now that the danger was much greater than she had ever imagined.

CHAPTER EIGHT

CATHERINE STOOD in the dining room of Bonne Journée and held her breath as two workmen gently lowered the Waterford crystal chandelier into the waiting arms of Frank and another workman. The fixture, imported from Ireland by Joshua Millard in 1835, was one of the most valuable furnishings in the house.

"Where you want this, Cat'rine?" Frank asked.

"Take it to my office, Frank, and put it on my worktable so I can start cleaning it."

Shaking his head, Frank followed the two men through the door. "Hooee! Better you than me. What if you drop one of those little pieces of glass?"

"Don't ask. That's why I'm going to clean it myself. Then if I break a pendant I can't be angry at anyone else."

As the workmen laid the priceless fixture on her worktable, Catherine brought in a bowl of warm, soapy water and rummaged through her desk for her softest cloths. In spite of what she had told Frank, she was looking forward to this job. She loved to make old things shine. She picked up the first prism and began to rub.

The restoration was going so smoothly that Bonne Journée might be ready ahead of schedule. About the Arceneaux house she wasn't so sure, although moving it had sparked a lot of interest. Many people had come forward with offerings, not only of furnishings but also of family customs, stories and traditions. Overnight, she had gone from outsider to a sort of local celebrity—at least according to her professor in Acadian 101, Blackie Broussard.

It occurred to Catherine, not for the first time, that she thought about Blackie far too much. If she talked to an elderly Cajun about a piece of furniture for the Arceneaux house, she heard Blackie's musical accent. If she spotted a dark, curly-haired young boy on the streets of New Iberia, she saw Blackie as a child. If she heard the compelling, rhythmic Cajun music, she was instantly possessed by the vivid sights, sounds and smells of the night she had met him. He had become a part of her universe, and she didn't know how or when it had happened. She had to admit that she cared a great deal more for Blackie than she should. The question was what to do about it.

But no matter what, she always came around to the same answer. A relationship between them wouldn't work. And how did Blackie feel about her, anyway? He wanted her, she knew that; she could feel it when they were close, could see it in his eyes. But did he really care for her, the way she knew he had cared for Angéline?

As long as she was being honest with herself, Catherine had to admit that Blackie didn't fit into her master plan. She was just a wayfarer in Louisiana;

Atlanta was her home. She was still waiting for Gerrard to notify her that the job in Athens had come through. Given the chance, she told herself, she would go home. And Blackie would stay in Louisiana—his home.

She industriously polished a prism, then held it away to admire it. Its facets caught the morning sunshine, spangling the room with rainbow points of light. Musing, she watched them dance. Leaving Blackie would hurt, she knew; the time she could have walked away unaffected was past. But it would hurt even more later. She should break it off now.

But what would she say? She and Blackie had no declared relationship. No, she realized, she couldn't tell him anything. She was caught in limbo, too involved to break ties cleanly, not involved enough to have the right to voice her fears. She must prevent herself from becoming more emotionally involved with him than she already was. But could she do it? The memory of the dark, heady rapture of his mouth, hot and insistent on hers, filled her. She closed her eyes and her hands stilled. *Might as well try to keep the tide from coming in,* she admitted.

"Catherine?" The voice was Clarence's. She started.

"Come in, Clarence," she called, holding up a prism to the light. "You've caught me at one of my favorite jobs."

"Beautiful." Clarence, smiling, admired the crystal, but she could tell he was preoccupied. "Catherine—"

Arrested by his tone, she looked closer and saw the trouble in his eyes. "What is it, Clarence?"

"It's our funding, *chère*." He came right to the point. "It's a complicated business, but the bottom line is, our funding's been cut."

"Oh, no." Carefully, Catherine set the prism on the table. "What happened?"

"The bad economy. The state's cutting funds for museums and restorations. This type of project is nonessential because it doesn't put food in anyone's mouth." There was the slightest tinge of bitterness in Clarence's voice that, in all her dealings with him, she had never heard before. "We're only going to receive seventy percent of our grant money this year." He shook his head.

"Seventy percent! It'll wreck the budget for both projects."

He sighed. "It won't do them any good. And there's more, *chère*." His voice gentled, and Catherine knew she hadn't heard the worst. "Some of the society directors think the way you do things is too expensive. Toni and I have talked till we can't talk any more, trying to convince them that your methods are the best anywhere, that we can't afford to cut corners if we're going to get the kind of results we can be proud of. But they're just hung up on the figures."

"Are you saying my job is in jeopardy?" Catherine asked quietly.

"I hope not. Everyone likes you and has a great respect for your professional ability. No one wants to fire you."

"Let me think a minute," Catherine said. She began considering the possibilities, rethinking, mentally juggling figures, sequences.

"All right, Clarence," she finally said. "If they still want me, I think we can work things out. Give me a bottom line, and I'll start to work on the figures as soon as possible."

"Do you think we might work it out?" Clarence's face brightened. "It would kill me to lose you, and I know Toni feels the same way."

"I don't intend to be lost so easily. I should have something together to show the board within a week or so."

"I'll tell Toni." Fervently, he kissed her hand. "I can't thank you enough, *chère*."

After he left, Catherine sat still for a moment, shocked by the turn of events. In spite of the confidence she'd expressed to Clarence, she was far from sure she could finish her job with seventy percent of the budget, because she would not compromise her working methods. She would resign first. On the other hand, she could hardly stand the thought of leaving, of walking away from either of these restorations where she had invested so much of her expertise—and her heart.

She heard the front door open. "Gussie? I'm here, in the office," she called. Gussie was uncharacteristically late this morning.

She heard Gussie enter the room. "I'm washing the chandelier." She turned. "Wouldn't you just love to—" One look at Gussie's face sent Catherine instantly to her side. "Gussie, what's wrong?"

Gussie gripped Catherine's arm hard. Her face was white, still, lifeless—as if a flame had been quenched, Catherine thought. She looked closer and saw that Gussie's eyes were swollen.

"Alain—" Gussie began, and could go no further. Covering her face with her hands, she broke into a storm of weeping.

"Oh, God, he's not—"

Gussie shook her head between sobs.

Reassured that Alain was alive, at least, Catherine drew the younger woman to her and held her as the paroxysms of weeping shook her. Strangely, she gleaned comfort from the comfort she was giving Gussie—she, who normally found it difficult to touch another human being spontaneously.

Finally Gussie raised her head. "It's okay, Catherine—I'm better now." But her breath caught on another convulsive sob.

"Alain—"

"Alain's all right. It's—" Gussie closed her eyes a moment, took a deep breath and started over. "It's Alain's sister. She's been having some health problems…nerve problems. You know, numbness, tingling in her hands and feet, that kind of thing. Well, they took her to the doctor last week, and the test results came in yesterday afternoon. She's got Friedrich's Ataxia."

"What in heaven's name is that?" Catherine asked blankly.

"It's a hereditary nervous disorder that's carried in some Cajun families, because we've been isolated for so many centuries and we've intermarried a lot. Genes that are normally recessive become dominant when both husband and wife carry them.'' Gussie's voice sounded mechanical, dead, as if she was reciting the doctor's explanation by rote. "They've just recognized it in some of our families in the past few years."

"How bad is it?" Catherine dreaded the answer.

"It's bad. It's degenerative...and progressive. The victim loses mobility, gets weaker and weaker with the nerve damage. Sometimes it even affects the mind. And it's eventually fatal."

"Oh, Gussie." Catherine shivered. "Can anything be done for her?"

"Not really. Sometimes the disease goes into remission, maybe for five, ten years at the most, but no medicine has been developed yet. There's nothing to do for it but a lot of TLC."

And there's nobody better than these people for giving that, Catherine thought.

"But the worst part of it is that the disease is in my family, too," Gussie said dully. "A cousin and an aunt on my mama's side have it." Catherine flinched at the agony she saw in Gussie's eyes. "That makes Alain and me both possible carriers," she explained. "If we had children, they would probably develop it. Catherine—*we can't have children*." The words, stark, final, hung in the air.

Catherine took Gussie's hands, trying to telegraph strength to her. "I know how much you and Alain wanted a big family, but you can always adopt—" She stopped as Gussie sadly shook her head. "We can't do that. All our lives we've dreamed of having big families, and I've dreamed of having my very own babies.

I can't deprive Alain of having his own children, even if I was willing to give them up myself." Her mouth twisted. "If we both marry someone without the bad gene, we can have as many children as we want." She paused as if willing herself to go on. "So that's what we've decided to do."

Catherine gasped. "No, Gussie, that's no solution. Talk to somebody. Find a good geneticist."

"We've done a lot of talking to a lot of folks." She made a futile little gesture. "They've all said the same thing: no children. I can never hold Alain's and my baby in my arms."

The quiet hopelessness in her voice tore at Catherine's soul. "I'm so sorry," she whispered.

"My mama always said the sunshine follows the rain, but I sure can't see any light yet." She pulled a hand through her black curls, as if to try to restore her world to normal. "Well, I'm ready to go to work." She looked around blindly for a cleaning rag.

"Oh, no," Catherine said. "Not today. Go home. You need to be with your family. But if there's anything at all I can do..." The words seemed so inadequate that she let them trail away into nothing.

Gussie smiled sadly. "There's nothing you or anyone can do, unless you happen to have a magic wand. Life goes on, I know it does. But Catherine—" She took hold of Catherine's shoulders, and her black eyes shone with tears and love. "Thanks." A quick hug and she was gone.

Catherine stared unseeingly at the dismantled chandelier. Why did this have to happen to Gussie? Carefree, fun-loving Gussie, whose mere presence was a day brightener? She and Alain had been so happy. Feeling defeated, Catherine put her hand on the doorjamb and leaned her forehead on it.

Suddenly she was crying, weeping as she hadn't since she was a child. She knew life wasn't always fair, but at times like this it seemed almost too much to bear. She wept for Gussie, for Alain . . . for herself.

"Catherine?"

She raised her head and looked. Blackie stood there, in the hallway. Was he astonished? Shocked? It was hard for Catherine to read his expression through her tears. *Damn! Why did he have to drop by now?* But even as the words formed in her mind, she could feel her need for him gnawing at her.

"*P'tite*—what's the matter? What happened?" In an instant he was at her side. He spun her around, and just seeing the compassion in his eyes sent her into another fit of weeping.

"I—" She couldn't tell him for crying. She hardly ever wept; now she didn't know how to stop.

Blackie put an arm around her, guided her gently into her office and shut the door. He pulled her head to his shoulder and held her close to his hard, warm body.

"Go on and cry, *chère*," he said. "Those tears have needed to come out for a long time, *hein*? Then, when they're all out, you can tell old Blackie what's the matter." He spoke in a soft, musical whisper. His hand came up behind her head to cradle, to cherish, and he rocked her rhythmically as he spoke. Forgetting the resolve she'd made only an hour ago, she gave herself up completely to the unimaginable luxury of crying in his arms.

Tears finally exhausted, Catherine raised her head, and Blackie reached in his pocket and drew out a bandanna. He held her chin in one hand, as if she were a child, while he dried her wet cheeks. She drew a deep, steadying breath, inhaling the sunshine-and-fresh-air smell of the bandanna.

When he had finished, he paused a moment, his hand still imprisoning her chin while his eyes scanned her face. In spite of her grief, Catherine basked in the warmth of his gaze.

A smile, half wry, tugged at his lips. *"Ma belle,"* he said, very fast, almost to himself, "you're even beautiful when you cry." He put the bandanna in his pocket. "Now. Tell me what happened to make you cry so."

In a voice punctuated by an occasional sob, she told him. As she spoke, she could see the pain in his eyes. When she finished, he stood in silence.

"It's not fair, Blackie," she said.

"Nobody ever said it would be, *chère*," he answered, but his voice wasn't quite steady. He closed his eyes, pinched the bridge of his nose between thumb and forefinger. "But all the same, it's a damn shame, and there's nothing anyone can do about it, not yet. We just have to deal with it." He opened his eyes, and she saw that they were moist. *"La pauvre p'tite..."*

"There has to be another solution. They shouldn't have to give each other up—they've got something too good for that."

"I know, but you don't realize how we feel about our families, Cat'rine." He took her arms in an effort to make her understand, began stroking them rhythmically with his thumbs. "Next to God, our families—our parents, grandparents, especially our children—are the most important things in the world. To see in our children our own blood and that of our *bien aime*, human beings we've made together—that's true joy. If Gussie and Alain can't have that..." He spread his hands. As always, when he was moved, his voice fell more and more into the musical French cadences. "But they've got to work it out themselves." He gazed at her, the emotions playing across his mobile face, and reached out to cup her cheek with his hand. "So—you were crying for Gussie?"

"Yes," Catherine said. "I never had a sister..."

Blackie's fingertips had been caressing lingeringly along her jaw, but they stilled, and he grasped her chin, gently turned her to face him. There was an arrested expression in his dark eyes. "It takes somebody special to cry like this over someone else's trouble, Catherine," he said slowly, as if he was making a discovery. "Somebody loving—and good."

She couldn't speak, could only stare into his eyes, and the moment shimmered between them.

"Are you sure you're not Cajun?"

"I don't know," Catherine said. "I wish I was." *Now where had that come from?* she wondered. She didn't know any more.

"I told you before, *chère*," Blackie said gently. "We'll adopt you. Now I have to ask you something else. In fact, it's what I came by for. Did you hear more bad news this morning?''

"As a matter of fact, I did," Catherine said. "The society's funding's been cut.''

"Yeah, Clarence told me about it. What are you planning to do?''

"I haven't thought it out yet. But I've got some general ideas about how I can reduce costs without compromising my methods. I won't cut corners, Blackie. I can't. If it comes to that, I'll resign, if they don't fire me first.''

"They won't fire you," he said. "I've got some ideas of my own. The Arceneaux house project has generated a lot of interest around here. I think I can find some old-time craftsmen who can donate their labor to work on both restorations.'' He laughed. "In fact, I think I can find most of 'em in my own family. I know a few things about some of the old crafts myself, and so does *Nonc*. That should save a good bit of money.''

"If you can do that, we may be able to salvage the operation," Catherine said in wonder. "Are you sure you want to do this?''

"*Bien sûr*, I want to do it. After all, *chère*, it's my heritage," he reminded her gently, smoothing a strand of silver-gilt hair from her face. "And besides, we'll have a good time.'' He grinned. "I just had an idea. Do you have anything planned for next weekend?''

"No, I don't believe so," she said, trying to think. He was moving too fast for her, but Catherine couldn't bring herself to care. She felt dazed, drained, but somehow lighter, as if a burden had been eased.

"Then let me take you home," he said simply.

"Home?" she repeated. "But I've got my car. Besides, I can't leave the office."

He laughed. "No, no, I mean this weekend. Come home with me to St. Martinville." His strong brown hands were warm on her arms, and his voice was coaxing, pleading. "Let me share my family with you. You don't have a little sister—I've got two I can let you borrow, any time you want them. I have four brothers, too, in case you've ever wanted one. And my parents will love you. Come see them—they'll make you better, *chère*."

Suddenly, a yearning that was almost physical seized her—to know Blackie's family, to be a part of it, if only for a little while.

"All right, Blackie. I'd love to go." She spoke quietly, gratefully. Whatever else he was, this man was a healer.

"Wonderful." Blackie's face lit up like all the Christmas trees in the world. "We'll go down early Saturday morning." He squeezed her arms, cradled her face between his hands in a lingering goodbye kiss. "We'll have a good time, us." He left her then, and she could hear his voice, lifted in song, as he went out the door.

"Jolie blon'. . ."

Feeling strangely at peace, she rummaged in her purse for lipstick and mirror and began to repair her face for an eleven o'clock appointment.

AFTER WORK THAT EVENING, Catherine went to her apartment and fixed a quick supper. The day had been long and exhausting, and she intended to go to bed as soon as possible. But first she wanted to take a look at some things she had brought from the office.

The Millard papers. She hadn't yet had an opportunity to go through the contents of the little trunk, but thinking they might prove a welcome distraction, she had brought some home with her.

She settled herself on the sofa and began leafing through them, still looking for some mention of the assault case brought against Joshua Millard by Michel Arceneaux, whoever he might have been. Something she had seen buried about halfway down in the trunk had looked promising, a small packet of letters tied with a narrow ribbon, faded with age...

She untied the ribbon and picked up the first of the fragile, yellowed letters, felt herself transported to the vanished world of nineteenth-century Louisiana. The writing, carefully formed, almost childish, had faded over the years to a beautiful antique brown.

Dearest Mama,
I am sending you this quick note by Michel's cousin Ursin to let you know I am all right. Michel and I were married yesterday. I am sorry we had to leave like that, in the middle of the night, without telling anyone—I know you must have been frantic with worry. But we had to—Papa would not give in. When he tried to whip Michel in town the other day, I thought my life would end. I love Michel and don't ever want to be parted from him. I pray with all my heart that I will see you soon.

The letter was signed, "Your loving daughter, Laura Arceneaux." Catherine felt a tingle of excitement. Laura Millard was a daughter of Joshua and Eleanor who had disappeared from the records. So she had married an Arceneaux! But who was Michel? The son or grandson of the people who'd built the Arceneaux house? Catherine checked the date on the letter— 1837. According to Millard family records, Laura would have been nineteen. And if the Arceneaux house had been built in 1790, Michel was possibly the grandson of the original owner. She picked up another letter, dated a few months later in the same year.

Dearest Mama,
Apollonie brought me your letter today. I was so happy to receive it. I hope Papa does not find out you wrote me. We are now living with the Arceneaux in their house down the bayou from Bonne Journée. You might not know it, but the Arceneaux are wealthy. Papa Arceneaux and Michel's Grandpère Arceneaux have a big plantation with a lot of acres planted in sugarcane.

Down the bayou, Catherine thought. That's got to be our Arceneaux family—and our house. The excitement quickened her breath.

I am glad you are all well, even Papa, and that you, at least, have not disowned me. When I heard that Papa is telling people he does not have a daughter any more, I felt as if someone was tearing out my heart. Michel was very angry when

Papa tried to whip him—that is why he filed the suit against him. After he was not so angry any more he reconsidered and dropped it. Michel will be willing to forgive, if only Papa would, but, knowing Papa, I'm afraid. He hates the Cajun people so.

Catherine sighed. Bigotry flourished in the Louisiana of the nineteenth century, just as it did today. The fragments were starting to fit together. She picked up another letter, this one dated about a year later.

Dearest Mama,
I wished to let you know that Michel and I are well. Papa Arceneaux says that he will give us some land very soon, and Michel is planning to build a little house on it. We are going to farm. Mama, I want you to know I am very happy. I love Michel very much. Grandpère and Mama and Papa Arceneaux are very kind to me, and tell me they love me like their own daughter. And I have some wonderful news for you—Michel and I are expecting a child sometime in the early spring. Now I know that will make you happy! We will try to plan for you to see the baby. I miss you so much, dearest Mama.

Catherine read into the early hours of the morning, entranced by the story unfolding before her eyes. So Laura Millard, the mysterious daughter of Eleanor and Joshua, had eloped with Michel Arceneaux, the grandson of the original builder of the Arceneaux house. And rather than accept a Cajun son-in-law, Joshua Millard had disowned his daughter. From the tone of the letters, Catherine surmised that Laura Millard Arceneaux's happiness with Michel and his family was complete, except for the lingering regret that her father would not forgive her.

Catherine frowned thoughtfully. Joshua Millard had cut himself off from his only surviving daughter, a child he must have loved. And he had forced his wife to do the same, at least on the surface—apparently Eleanor had had enough backbone to keep in touch with Laura anyway. *Good for you, Eleanor,* Catherine thought. Remembering the face in the portrait at Bonne Journée, Catherine was not surprised. From the one-sided correspondence, Catherine gathered that Eleanor's relationship with her daughter had been very close.

She rose, restless, and moved to stare out the window. The lights of New Iberia winked at her through the heavy foliage of the massive oaks that surrounded the apartment house. It suddenly seemed that even the world of the past, the clearly defined universe she'd always thought was constant, had had its paradoxes, too. The Arceneaux, at first glance a simple provincial family, had been more prosperous than the Millards, Catherine's fellow aristocrats, who had lived in a white-columned mansion with imported furnishings. The strong family ties of the Arceneaux, who had loved an outcast woman as if she was their own, had put to shame the narrow emptiness of the Millards' existence, where a man who had everything had renounced the most important thing of all—his human values. The rules of that long-ago world didn't always apply, it seemed. Just at the edge of her consciousness, she saw Blackie's face.

Suddenly, the press of the long, long day fell squarely on her shoulders, and she felt the fatigue wash up from her toes in enervating waves. Tomorrow she would continue going through the papers, find out all there was to know about Laura Millard Arceneaux, but tonight she couldn't take any more news, bad or good.

Catherine fell asleep almost instantly, but she dreamed all night of a young woman searching through the swamps and bayous, crying for her father.

CHAPTER NINE

"HERE WE ARE." Blackie came around to Catherine's side of the car and opened her door. She took his proffered hand, as grateful for the moral support as for the physical assistance.

When she was with Blackie, she always felt somehow as if she was on her first date. And now she was going to meet his parents, his brothers and sisters. For the first time in her life, she was going to be a part, however temporarily, of a large, close-knit family. She wanted so much for them to like her, but she was well aware that sometimes, in unfamiliar situations, she came across as cold and aloof. On the other hand, Blackie had managed to breach her defenses in no time at all; his family should have no trouble doing the same.

She climbed out of the car and looked around. The Broussards' home, situated on the Teche a little way out of St. Martinville, was an ordinary frame house, set in a spacious yard a little way back from the bayou. A large porch spanned the front, and Catherine suspected that, as was often the case in this area, another porch crossed the back, on the bayou side. The house gleamed sparkling white in its setting of oaks, and multicolored flowers bloomed in carefully tended beds along the front. All in all, it presented an appearance of welcome, and Catherine relaxed a little.

"It's beautiful, Blackie," she said. "It looks so cared for. Your parents must work constantly to keep it that way."

Blackie laughed. "Mama and Papa said that once all of us left, it was easy. I guess we did keep them busy."

"This fronts on the bayou," Catherine observed. "Did your father inherit it?"

"Yes, this is the last piece of bayou land left from my ancestor's original grant. The rest was sold long ago. I can tell you, there were times when Papa thought he would have to sell, too, but he somehow managed to hang on to it."

As they walked toward the house, the door opened and a short, plump woman with salt-and-pepper hair came out, her pretty face wreathed in smiles.

"Jean, *bébé*," she called, "I thought you'd forgotten." She hurried down the steps, right into Blackie's arms. He hugged her tightly to him and gave her a resounding kiss.

"Now, how could I forget, Mama," he said, his face alight with tenderness, "when you're making gumbo? I want you to meet Catherine Nolan. Catherine, this is my mother, Azema Broussard."

Catherine took a breath, but before she could speak, Blackie's mother had transferred her embrace, hugging Catherine soundly. "*'Tite chou,*" she murmured, holding Catherine at arm's length, frank in her admiration. "You're so beautiful—I never saw such hair, me." She touched Catherine's hair, the gesture a caress. Her smile so resembled Blackie's that it took Catherine's breath away. "I'm so glad you're here."

"I'm delighted to meet you, Mrs. Broussard. Thank you for having me." Catherine felt overwhelmed, warmed and comforted all at the same time.

"*Non*—you have to call me Zema. And it's for us to thank you for coming. We love company, especially me. Then I have a good excuse to eat and dance." She looked a little regretful. "Except I don't dance much any more."

Blackie burst out laughing. "No, nor any less," he teased her fondly. "You can still dance the feet off all of us, and you know it."

"*Chia!*" She dismissed him. "By the time I raised you, I didn't have any strength left to dance. But I still like the parties." Although her French accent was more pronounced, her rapid speech and quick movements reminded Catherine of Gussie. And the heart-hugging warmth in her voice Catherine had heard before—from Zema's number-one son.

"We're going to dance here, tonight?" she asked, looking around. "Where?"

"Right here on the porch." Zema waved a hand. "For our family, and a few *cousins*. Just a *p'tit bal de maison*—a little dance. Cat'rine, do you like gumbo?"

"Very much, Mrs.—" Out of the corner of her eye she could see Blackie's look of unholy glee. "Zema," she finished with barely a pause. "And I'll help if you need me. In fact, I'd really like to learn how to make gumbo."

"*Oui*, I can always use more hands, and I'll be glad to teach you, me. I don't know what happened to

Elisa. She promised to help." She laughed, obviously unconcerned. "But you know how she is, Jean. Just like you. Her head's always in a book, or in the clouds, I'm not sure which."

"I wasn't that way, Mama," Blackie complained.

"Listen to him! He still is. Always fooling with his music. But what can I do?" She shrugged elaborately and turned to go inside. "If you see Elisa, send her in."

"Here comes Papa now—and Gil, and T'eo," Blackie said as a blue Chevrolet sedan pulled into the driveway behind his truck. "You'd better gather your strength for introductions," he told Catherine. "You're going to need it."

She looked at him quizzically but didn't have time to reply before two young men jumped out of the car and slammed the doors. As they heaved two large coolers from the trunk, an older man got out of the front seat and strolled toward Catherine and Blackie.

Amid much laughter, loud joking and slapping of backs, Blackie embraced them all. "Catherine," he said, "my brothers Gilbert and Theodore, and my father, Joseph Broussard. Papa, Gil, T'eo—meet Catherine Nolan." Joseph Broussard, a quiet, reserved man whose features greatly resembled Blackie's, bid her a quiet welcome. Gil and T'eo, dark, handsome young men with an obvious family resemblance, shook hands with her.

"Well, look at old Ti-neg," Gil said, in the same teasing tones Catherine had heard Blackie use all too often. "He finally got a respectable girl to go out with him."

"It's about time," a third man chimed in, walking up.

"This is my brother Alcide, Al for short," Blackie said. "They're all jealous because I've brought such a pretty one home. Careful, boys, I'll tell your wives, me."

"Tell us what?" A pretty woman demanded as she came up behind Catherine. Another young woman, possessed of a dark, quiet beauty, followed her, holding a child in her arms.

Blackie embraced them both. "Gil's wife, Yvonne Broussard," he said, indicating the first woman, "and my sister, Marie-Louise Theriot." His face lit up. "And my newest niece, Renee." He held out his arms to the little girl, who looked to be about eighteen months old. "Come see *Nonc* Blackie," he crooned.

The baby crowed with delight. *"Nonc,"* she said distinctly, and reached for him, nearly falling out of her mother's grasp.

Blackie caught her, laughing as he held the child high above his head, then brought her down quickly enough to make her squeal. Watching his face, Catherine's chest constricted. She turned to Gil. "Does Blackie always desert his guests like this when something better comes along?" she asked, surprised she felt so comfortable.

"You got to understand, Cat'rine," Gil said seriously, "he has to stick with the young ones. They're too little to run away from him." Everyone laughed.

Blackie looked hurt. "Cat'rine—how could you hand Gil a line like that?"

"Ti-neg, we've been worried about you," Al said. "You're too shy around the girls."

Another uproarious laugh.

"Leave Blackie alone, boys," Marie-Louise said quietly, with an affectionate smile. "He's my star baby-sitter."

Catherine was still watching Blackie with little Renee, but at that she turned, amazed. "You mean Blackie baby-sits for you?"

"Oh, he loves children." Her smile faded, and her voice dropped. "He spent a lot of time with us right after Angéline—his wife—died," she explained.

"I see."

"The kids are crazy about him," Marie-Louise said. "He sometimes keeps them overnight, and takes them fishing, crabbing, things like that."

"Lucky children." Catherine smiled.

"It's a shame he never had children of his own," Marie-Louise remarked. "Then, when he lost Angéline, he would at least have had them."

Blackie's children. The thought tumbled through Catherine's brain. *Lucky woman who could have Blackie's children.*

"Blackie!" A young boy, coltish in his adolescence, came galloping up, his mop of black curls flying. "You're here," he announced, looking at Blackie with patent hero-worship.

"*Mais* sho', I'm here. I told you I'd come, didn't I? Are you too grown up to hug your poor old brother?" Still holding baby Renee, Blackie held his free arm wide. The boy hesitated only a moment, then ran into

Blackie's embrace. For a moment, Blackie, the young boy and the child merged in a tight-knit, loving knot.

"The boys at school said I was too old for that," the youngster said when he emerged a moment later.

Blackie's eyes sobered as he shook the boy gently by the shoulder. "Don't ever let anyone tell you that," he said with quiet emphasis. "I still kiss Papa when I come home. And I always kissed him good-night when I lived here. Now, come make your manners. This is Catherine Nolan. Catherine, this is Marcel, my baby brother."

"How do you do, Marcel?" Catherine smiled and shook hands with him, thinking that Blackie must have looked like this at his age.

"Glad to meet you." Marcel's voice, newly changed, cracked a little. "Blackie, are we going crabbing this weekend?"

"Not this weekend, *chère*—I'm busy," Blackie said gently, flashing a grin at Catherine. "But soon." He handed Renee to her mother, then grabbed one end of a cooler. "Come on, let's get these shrimp and crawfish to the back porch. Mama needs them for the gumbo. Marcel, get the other end." Al and T'eo lugged the other cooler and they carried them to the back steps of the house, Catherine following.

T'eo set down his end of the heavy icebox. "Well, I guess I'd better go get Uncle Bat," he said.

"All the way to Lake Palourde?" Al asked.

"No, he's visiting one of his fishing buddies in Delcambre. I sure would like to stay and help peel 'em—" T'eo grinned and indicated both coolers "—but you'll probably be through by the time I get back. Too bad.'' With a jaunty wave, he headed toward his car. Everyone jeered.

"Just like T'eo to run out when the work starts," Al said in an aggrieved tone.

"*Mais* sho'," Blackie said. "I'm glad I'm not lazy." More jeers. "By the way, has anybody seen Elisa?" he asked. "Mama was looking for her."

"Last I saw her, she had sneaked down to the dock to read," Al answered.

They looked. Sure enough, on the large wooden dock, a black-haired girl was sitting on a chaise lounge, reading a book.

"Good. I want Catherine to meet her." Blackie looked sideways at Al and Marcel. "*I* sure would like to stay and help, but I can't."

"What about all these shrimp and crawfish?" Marcel asked indignantly. "We'll never finish."

"Sure wish *I* could stroll down to the dock with a *jolie blon'* on my arm, instead of having to do all this hard, hard work," Al said plaintively.

"*Tais-toi, pirate,*" Blackie said. "I'll help you in a little while." He took Catherine's arm and they headed to the water.

"Uncle Bat's coming, then?"

"Yeah. He wouldn't miss a *bal de maison*, or my mother's gumbo, either. Besides, it's been a while since he's seen *Gran'mère*," he explained. "A whole two weeks, in fact. They don't like to be apart too long."

A whole two weeks, Catherine thought. *I haven't seen my mother in almost six months, and I'm still not sure I miss her.* She felt a twinge of guilt.

"How many nieces and nephews do you have?" she asked, remembering Blackie's obvious joy in Renee.

"Let's see." He counted them off on his fingers. "Gil has three, Mar'Louise has four, T'eo has two—that's nine so far. But there'll be more. After all, Al just got married, and Marcel and Elisa are still single. And I don't have any—yet." His eyes glinted at her. *To have Blackie's baby...* She swallowed hard. This, then, was how Gussie felt about having children—hers and Alain's. Gussie, her carefree laugh gone, her buoyant spirits quenched. Suddenly, Catherine understood.

Elisa Broussard looked up when she heard their footsteps, and Catherine caught her breath. Here was the real beauty of the family. Elisa was a stunning girl, with eyes and hair as black as night. In her face, the strong Cajun features were softened and fine-honed, and her skin, instead of being olive-toned like Blackie's, bloomed magnolia-fair.

She rose, came forward with the same blinding smile that all the Broussards seemed to possess and walked into Blackie's embrace. It was obvious that Blackie loved all his family, but Catherine could tell by the way he held this sister that theirs was a special relationship.

When Blackie at last released her, Catherine extended her hand. "Elisa, I'm glad to meet you," she said.

Elisa's handshake was firm. "Hello, Catherine," she said. "I've heard so many wonderful things about you, I've been looking forward to meeting you." The musical French cadences were almost entirely absent from her speech.

Catherine glanced at Blackie. "She didn't hear anything from me," he said promptly.

"From Blackie, yes," Elisa said traitorously, "but also from Gussie LeBlanc."

"I love Gussie," Catherine said quietly. "I just wish I could do something for her."

"I know," Elisa said. "It's been especially hard for her, and for Alain, too. They're both miserable."

"It's a real shame." Blackie's eyes were heavy with sadness. He changed the subject. "How's your school coming, *chère*?"

"Fine. I've got a round of tests next week, so I'm going to try to study this weekend, if that's possible."

"Where do you go to school?" Catherine asked.

"LSU, in Baton Rouge," Elisa answered. "I'm getting a master's in economics. I'll finish this year, then I'm going to start interviewing."

"Around here?" Catherine asked.

"No." Elisa's answer was quick, definite.

Blackie chuckled, but Catherine received the distinct impression he wasn't too pleased. "Elisa's set on leaving us," he said, "the sooner the better. I've told her the big world outside's no different than Louisiana."

"Why shouldn't I leave?" Elisa asked. "You did. It's not my fault you came back." Catherine saw then in Elisa's face what she'd missed before—that the sensuous mouth proclaimed rebellion, and the night-black eyes held restlessness and discontent. "Look at

Catherine," she said. "She's had a taste of the outside world, of making her own way."

"I've had more than a taste, I'm afraid," Catherine said wryly. "Enough that I know the answers aren't as easy to find as I thought they would be." She caught Blackie's eyes on her face, and wondered if he was surprised she'd admit such a thing.

Elisa started to speak, but Blackie cut in. "Settle down, nobody's stopping you." He waved his hand. "Just remember, as Mama says, don't throw the baby out with the bathwater. I found what I was looking for here at home."

"Did you?" Dark eyes met dark eyes, and Catherine watched in amazement as Blackie's gaze dropped first.

"I don't know, *chère*," he said. "Sometimes I still wonder." He put one arm around Elisa's shoulders and the other around Catherine's. "Come on, Mama's looking for you—she needs help with the gumbo."

They walked to the house, Blackie's arms around both pairs of shoulders.

CATHERINE REALIZED LATER that Blackie's warning to marshal her strength hadn't been idle talk. In just a few hours, she felt as though she had been through the equivalent of several normal days. She had met the rest of Blackie's family, including the ancient *grandmère*, a tiny, wizened woman with Uncle Bat's sage, currant-dark eyes, who had called her a *jolie blon'* and had nodded approvingly; T'eo's wife, Mae, and Marie-Louise's husband, a dark, taciturn man named Robert Theriot; and the rest of the children. She had helped to cut mountains of green peppers, onions and celery, had watched in wonderment as Zema perspired over a huge black iron skillet, stirring the *roux*, a mixture of flour and oil the color of chocolate fudge; had watched Blackie and his brothers head the shrimp and crawfish; had sliced and buttered loaf after loaf of French bread; and had stared in amazement at the array of desserts, from tea cakes to custard, that lined one entire table. And over everything, she could hear the voice of Zema Broussard, directing, encouraging, occasionally scolding, but nearly always laughing. And not for one moment was Zema still.

Catherine had met Blackie's godparents, Onezime and Ursule Savoie, and the "few *cousins*" Zema had spoken of—uncles, aunts and cousins by the score, with names like Aspasie Guilbeaux, Felician Quebodeaux, Duplex Melancon. And she had joyfully greeted Uncle Bat, who announced that he would play a special song for her on his *beau violon*. She was complimented, made a fuss over and almost invariably embraced. She had never experienced anything like this day in her life, but found herself enjoying it immensely.

As the sun began to set, the meal was finally ready. With loaded plates, the family members headed for the front porch where, for lack of space inside, everyone was eating. Catherine took her food and sat down on the front steps, exhausted, but pleasantly so. She hungrily ate the hot, savory gumbo and listened to the lively conversation and incessant good-natured jibes that flew back and forth, particularly between Blackie and his brothers. Next to her, Blackie sat, eating—and talking—as heartily as all the others. His proximity, and her fatigue, combined to give her a feeling of contentment.

"Talk about good!" Blackie set down his dishes and, leaning back, gently rested his hand for a moment on Catherine's knee. It was with difficulty that she resisted the temptation to put her head on his shoulder.

"Just think," Zema said wistfully, "all the good food there is in the world, and I'll never have time to eat it all."

"Got' dog, I didn' realize I had ate so much," Onezime Savoie, Blackie's *parrain*, remarked, patting his ample belly. "Cat'rine," he asked, "I want to know somet'ing, me."

"Yes?"

"Did you ever see so many Broussards at one time?"

Catherine laughed. "I can honestly say I haven't."

"Say," another man, possibly one of Blackie's uncles, chimed in. "Did y'all know I ran across a *cousin* las' week who traced da Broussard line all da way back to Adam?"

"No kidding!" A couple of others bit.

"Yeah—and I tol' him dat if Adam was a Broussard, Eve mus' have been a LeBlanc." Everyone shouted with laughter.

"Hey, Blackie," Al called. "You fishin' with us next weekend?"

"I don't know," Blackie said, his forehead creased as if carefully considering. "When I go with you, we never catch anything. I think you're bad luck, you."

"Bad luck! What about that big bass I caught last time?"

"Big bass? What—oh, you mean that little thing? I thought that was your bait."

Amid the general laughter that followed, Blackie and Alcide exchanged good-natured punches.

"We gon' dance, or we gon' sit and talk all night?" Blackie's father asked finally.

"Oh, *bien sûr*, Joe, we're gon' dance," said Zema, walking over to give him a hug. Their children broke into applause.

"You two start the first dance, Mama," said Mar'Louise, who was holding little Renee, asleep on her shoulder. She beckoned Catherine to sit beside her.

"Crank it up, Ti-neg," someone called.

Blackie, Uncle Bat, Marcel and a cousin whose name Catherine had forgotten retrieved instruments from inside the house, moved to the corner of the porch and began to tune up. "Atta way, Blackie," people were shouting. *"Allons!"* and *"En avant*, Ursin—play da ting-a-ling!" The last provided positive identification not only of the cousin, but of his instrument, which Catherine could see was a triangle.

Within a few minutes the fragments of sound magically coalesced into a lively two-step, and the crowd whooped and clapped. Catherine felt the music tug, as it always did, at a place somewhere deep inside her.

Al played the guitar and Cousin Ursin played "da ting-a-ling." Uncle Bat sawed away at his violin with his usual dolorous enjoyment, and as usual, Blackie played accordion and sang the melody. He looked at her as he sang, and it seemed to Catherine that he was singing only to her. The music seized her, picked her up and rushed her along to a magical world, transporting her to the first night she had heard him play. But this time no unease marred her enjoyment. Entranced, she listened to Blackie sing and watched his expressive face to her heart's content.

"I think Blackie's music has saved his life," Mar'Louise commented, watching him.

Catherine thought of Angéline. He had played like this for her. "Yes, he seems happy when he's playing," she mused, a little sadly.

"He is, Catherine, but he seems happier now than I've seen him in years—since before Angéline died. And I think you're the reason."

"I'm ... I'm glad," Catherine managed to say. She found herself hoping Mar'Louise was right.

About that time, Joe and Zema walked out onto the middle of the porch. As they began to dance, Catherine could see what Blackie had meant. Zema moved lightly on her feet and in perfect time to the music, putting style into her steps. Even though Joe was more deliberate in his dancing, they made a fine-looking pair. Their movements, from years of practice, matched perfectly, and they obviously loved dancing with each other. Within a few moments, other couples joined them.

Suddenly Catherine ached to dance with Blackie, wanted to make up for the time she had missed before. As she looked up at him, longing to be in his arms, he glanced at her and lowered one eyelid in a slow wink. Once the gesture would have embarrassed her; now she smiled at him like a schoolgirl.

Just then, T'eo Broussard came up. "Now's my chance," he said. Although T'eo seemed to be the quietest of the brothers, the smile he gave her greatly resembled Blackie's. "I'm going to dance with the accordion player's girl." He took Catherine's hand, while she prayed that her years of ballroom training would be of some benefit in this particular situation.

She held her own, and was even able to enjoy it. When the dance was over, she thanked T'eo breathlessly, but before she could rest, one of Blackie's uncles claimed her for the next dance, fortunately a slow waltz. After the third dance, she was beginning to feel like the belle of the ball. Suddenly she thought of her father. He could make people feel at ease like this, she remembered. No wonder the women had loved him.

Her father would have felt right at home here, she reflected, and was surprised that the thought brought no bitterness. He had loved a good time. And he had loved her. She closed her eyes. Suddenly memories of her childhood flooded her, times her father had taken her places, spent hours with her, for the sheer pleasure of being with her. She had worshiped him. Irresponsible he might have been, but he had given her a spontaneous, unconditional affection that she had never received from her mother. The intervening years, when she had to bear the brunt of his poor management, his irresponsibility, his womanizing, had blocked out those fond memories, as had her mother's constant bitter remarks.

But tonight had made her realize just how wonderful her memories were and just how starved she was for that feeling of closeness. Her relationship with her mother seemed distant and cold compared to Blackie's with his family. Her eyes filled with tears so quickly that she had to look down to keep anyone from seeing them. She blinked rapidly to dispel them. Since she had met Blackie, she had carried her emotions right on the surface.

An hour and several songs later, the moon rode high in the night sky, bathing the yard in silvery light and casting long shadows from the huge oaks. The musicians took a break. Blackie laid down his accordion and came to sit by Catherine, holding a cold beer in his hand. "Hooee!" he said, drinking deeply from the beer and putting his free hand around her shoulders. "I need a rest. That's hard work."

"I thought you were having fun."

"Oh, I was *chère*. But the most fun comes during the breaks." He held her chin for a quick kiss, pulling away before she had time to protest. His lips were deliciously cool, and on them Catherine could taste the sharp tang of the beer.

"Watch it there, Blackie. Mama'll get you for disrespect," Al remarked.

Blackie pinched Catherine's cheek. "Oh, Mama'll understand about Cat'rine," he said fondly, leaving her to wonder what that was supposed to mean.

"I'll say," Al said admiringly. "She'd make good crab bait as far as I'm concerned."

"I beg your pardon?" Catherine wasn't sure she had heard right.

Blackie's rich baritone laughter rang out. "It's a compliment, Cat'rine," he said when he could stop laughing. "Just say thank you. If you could have seen the expression on your face..." The thought made him laugh again.

"Sorry, Catherine. I forgot you wouldn't know what it meant." Al grinned sheepishly.

"That's quite all right, Al. And thank you." What a crazy, crazy night, as the Cajuns would say. And she was loving every minute of it.

When it was time for the music to start again, T'eo picked up Blackie's accordion. "I'll sit in awhile, *mon vieux*," he told Blackie.

"Good. It's my turn to dance." He rose. *"Mamselle..."* He held out his hand to Catherine. Putting her hand in his and holding his eyes with her own, she rose. His arm circled her waist, and he swept her straight into the rhythm of a fast Cajun tune. T'eo sang the melody. If Catherine closed her eyes, she could almost hear Blackie singing, so alike were their voices. She only worried a moment about being able to follow him; he was so perfectly in control of his movements, and hers, that she had no trouble at all. She greedily absorbed the feeling of being held in his arms.

"Blackie," she said, "you're a wonderful dancer."

"So are you, darlin'." He sounded surprised—and pleased. He began to expand on the basic steps of the dance, moving faster and faster, turning her under his arm and pulling her to him, taking her on a giddying journey into a private world of sensuous pleasure. As the rhythm of the dance sank into her bones, Catherine felt a little bubble of pure happiness rise in her throat. *Dancing in Atlanta was never like this...* The words floated through her consciousness. Feeling amazingly free, she looked up and smiled into Blackie's eyes. His arms tightened and he drew in his breath sharply. "Ah, *p'tite*," he said huskily, "don't look at me like that. It's dangerous."

"Is it?" She felt reckless, giddy with the heady excitement of the evening. For the first time in her life, tomorrow didn't exist—or at least, if it did, she wouldn't think about it.

"*Oui—bien dangereux*," he said. And murmured something else in French she didn't understand.

Before she could ask him what he'd said, the tune came to an end. Everyone applauded, whistled, stomped boisterously, and Blackie held her for a lingering moment before he let her go. "*C'est bon*, T'eo," he called, holding his hands high to applaud.

"Thanks, Blackie." T'eo, looking pleased with himself, waved back.

"T'eo's good," Catherine remarked, feeling drunk without alcohol. Drunk on Blackie Broussard. "Does he play much?" she asked.

Blackie shook his head. "Just for *bals de maison*. He's gone a lot—works on a drilling rig out from Morgan City. We try to schedule our get-togethers so he can come." He grinned at her. "Otherwise, I'd never be able to dance. T'eo, *Nonc*," he called, "play 'La Valse de la Belle,' for Cat'rine."

"*Oui*, Ti-neg. For Cat'rine," Uncle Bat called back.

"What's that?" Catherine asked.

"It's one of my favorites," he said. "It's a wonderful song, about a beautiful girl—" his voice suddenly lowered, went intimate "—and I want to hold you while we dance, *mignonne*." She looked at him. The moonlight, canting onto the porch, played its eerie tricks, shadowing his eyes and throwing his strong features into sharp relief. *Jean Beausoleil Broussard.* Catherine stared into the fathomless depths of his eyes, seeing for the first time the full force of his personality. She saw a strong man's grief for himself and his people, respect for their long years of tradition and travail, pride in their heritage. *The laughter and the tears* . . . as she knew by now, they were both in him. Knowing what she knew, seeing him as she was seeing him now, how could she ever stop wanting him? At that moment, she knew she was in love with him.

The musicians swung into the haunting melody, and Blackie reached for her, slowly took her in his arms. The dark, rich tones of Uncle Bat's *beau violon* soared into the lead, and as if by tacit consent, the other dancers on the porch abandoned the floor to them. As they moved to the stately strains of the old waltz, Catherine felt at that moment that life could hold no greater happiness for her.

Suddenly, without breaking his rhythm, Blackie waltzed her through the wide-open front door into the living room, where there were other dancers, then through the rest of the house and finally onto the back porch. Their bodies molded together and they moved as one to the poignant melody. Catherine could feel the heat building between them. This was the way she had dreamed it would be. As the song ended, she tried to catch her breath. Her chest felt as if it was going to burst and every nerve end was alive and tingling.

"Well, look here. How did this happen?" Blackie feigned surprise.

"I have no idea," Catherine answered. "I wasn't driving. But it's cooler back here."

Blackie put his arm around her and they walked down to stand under an enormous tree near the bayou. The moon hung like a giant lantern in a cloudless sky, and a soft breeze whispered over the water to touch Catherine's hot cheeks. The scent of honeysuckle filled the air.

"Are you having a good time, *chère*?"

"A wonderful time, Blackie. One of the best I can remember."

"I'm glad. You've enchanted my family, you know."

"And I like them. Very much." She wanted to tell him how she felt inside, but didn't quite know how to say it. Long-buried feelings stirred inside her, fought to surface. "Your family's so close. I haven't had that since—for a long time," she finished lamely.

"Since what?" His voice was softly insistent.

"Since I was small and used to go places with my father."

"You didn't stay close to him after you got older?"

"No. My father loved me, and was wonderful to me, but he never learned to accept responsibility, I suppose you could say. There were not so nice things about him, too. As I grew older, I grew more resentful, and we sort of lost touch." Still she didn't feel the bitterness, the impotent anger that had been a part of her for so long; the magic spell of caring, from Blackie's family and from her memories, insulated her.

"Blackie, your family likes to have fun." She was groping for the truth, but it was still eluding her.

He smiled. "That they do."

"But they all work, don't they?"

He looked at her quizzically. "*Bien sûr.* They wouldn't eat so well if they didn't." He waved a hand. "Having a good time doesn't mean you're allergic to work, Cat'rine."

"What did your father do when you were growing up? To feed everyone, I mean?"

"He worked at everything he could find. When I was a kid, he hunted and trapped in the swamps, cut firewood and sold it, worked as a carpenter when he could get the jobs."

"College wasn't possible for him, was it?" she asked quietly.

"No. It wasn't even a consideration. When I was older, he got a job on an offshore drilling rig out in the gulf, but that meant he had to stay gone for several weeks at a time."

"That must have been hard for all of you."

Blackie kicked idly at a root. "It was hard. But he had to do it. He never made much money, not much more than what it took to feed and clothe us, but he always made sure we had everything we needed. It's only been lately that he and Mama have been able to afford some extras. He taught us to take care of our families first." He spread his hands. "That's what we believe, and that's what I'll do, if I ever have a family." He said it simply, as if it was so much a truth that no one would question it.

How could she ever have thought this man was frivolous or lazy? "I know you will, Blackie," she said softly at last, her voice unsteady.

His eyes rested a moment on her face. Very gently, he turned her toward him and took her lips with his. It was a long, lazy kiss, no less erotic for its gentleness, and Catherine could feel it tugging at her soul. Involuntarily, she leaned against him.

At last the kiss ended, but their bodies still touched, and neither made a move. "Cat'rine—" Blackie began.

"Yes?" She focused on what he was saying with difficulty.

"I care too much about you, *bébé*," he said huskily. He turned her so her back was against the oak. "And I don't know what to do about it." Like a thirsty man, he lowered his mouth to hers again. This time, beneath the lazy rhythm of the kiss, she could feel a deeper, more urgent power, and then, from deep inside her, the sweet ache of her great need, surging to meet it. Blackie pinned her between the unyielding trunk of the oak and his hard body, and still she wasn't close enough to him. She could feel his hand grip the back of her neck, then slide up to cup her head.

Hot, liquid desire came flooding, dissolving old barriers, evaporating her reserve. She wanted him, and the wanting was so strong it carried everything else away. She ran her hands over his wide shoulders, slowly down his arms and up again, feeling the strength in his rippling muscles. He moaned deep in his throat, and his hand crept up to cup her breast, while the last scrap of her rational mind screamed a warning before it was obliterated in an overwhelming rush of desire. "Cat'rine—I want you so bad—"

She shuddered, and the blood roared in her ears. His breath came in gasps hot on her cheek as his hand brushed her nipple, bringing it to throbbing, tingling life. She could feel his heart pounding, hard, against her own...

They heard laughter from the house. Slowly, reluctantly, they drew apart, each seeing their own feelings in the other's eyes what they were feeling.

"This is neither the time nor the place, *ma belle*," he said, his breathing still heavy. "But I promise you, there'll be another time..." He shook his head a little, as if to clear it. "Come on, let's go back to the house. It's about time for me to play again." He put an arm around her, gave her a quick kiss that was over before she felt anything but a single sharp rush of that treacherous warmth and gently propelled her to the party.

CHAPTER TEN

BLACKIE WOKE UP EARLY the next morning. He showered quickly and, without shaving, pulled on fresh jeans and a shirt and padded barefoot to the kitchen. It didn't surprise him to see that his mother was already up and making what looked to be an enormous breakfast.

"*Bonjour,* Mama." Leaning down, he kissed her good morning.

"*Bonjour, chèr.* Did you sleep well?"

"Mmm...more or less."

"Too many things to think about? Or maybe too many people?" She smiled, her eyes fixed tenderly on him. "Maybe one too many, *hein*?"

Blackie grinned wearily. "As you say, Mama."

"She's beautiful, Jean. And I like her very much, me."

"I do, too," he said wryly. "And I don't know whether that's good or bad." He gave her a quick hug and poured himself a cup of the black, savory coffee from the pot on the stove.

His mother said no more on the subject. "*Au lait?*" she asked, offering the pitcher of cream.

"*Noir.* I need all the energy I can get this morning."

"Your papa's already down at the dock. He wanted his coffee black this morning, too."

Cradling his cup of steaming coffee in his hands, Blackie headed toward the back door. It was still early—a little too early, he reflected, rubbing a hand over his unshaven face. It had been almost two in the morning by the time everyone had finished cleaning up. Even then, tired as he was, he hadn't fallen asleep immediately. His body wouldn't let him. He hadn't been able to banish the image of Catherine—the way her hair had shone in the moonlight, the way her skin had felt under his hands. Never had he seen skin so fair, so soft. And after only a few hours' sleep, he had awakened with her cool scent in his nostrils. He rubbed the back of his neck, trying to ease the stiff muscles. What was happening to him? He, a man who had never let grass grow under his feet, especially where women were concerned, suddenly felt as if events were moving much too fast.

And last night he had wanted things to go even faster. He had wanted Catherine badly, so badly he couldn't believe he had managed to stop. But he had, even though he knew she had been ready to be loved. Would there be another time for them? He ran a hand through his hair. If it happened, it would be no casual encounter, that much he knew.

He paused at the top of the back steps and took a first sip of the strong black coffee. That was the real problem, he admitted candidly to himself. He was very much afraid that things had gone too far.

He started slowly down, one step at a time. As far as he knew, Catherine still intended to leave when her work in Louisiana was done. And if he wasn't careful, she would hurt him badly when she left. While the wounds from Angéline's death might have healed, more or less, he wasn't ready to suffer new ones. He and Catherine had carefully avoided discussing the future, or anything else that implied making a commitment. But ignoring something didn't make it go away.

Joseph Broussard was sitting on the dock, drinking his coffee, peacefully watching the morning mists rising from the sluggish waters of the bayou. *"Bonjour, paresseux."* He indicated the chair next to him.

Blackie grinned and took the chair. "If I'm a lazybones, what does that make everybody else? I'll bet Marcel and Elisa won't be up before noon, at least."

"Young folks are lazy now. When I was a *jeune homme* I could dance all night and work the next day, me. Times have changed."

Blackie sighed. "Yeah, they have, Papa. And I'm caught right in the middle. Sometimes I don't know what to think."

"You got a lot of company, son," his father said, chuckling.

Blackie looked at him curiously. "Don't you miss the old ways?"

His father sipped his coffee in silence for a moment. *"Bien sûr*, I miss 'em—I miss the old folks, the old customs, the swamp the way it used to be." He leaned back, settled more comfortably in his chair. "But some things are better now. Before I went to work for the oil company, we had a hard time. You remember the year you wanted that gun?" He pointed a callused finger at his son. "You didn' get it until the next Christmas, because T'eo broke his leg and all the Christmas money went to pay the doctor." He smiled. "But I bet you didn' know all that, did you?"

"Well, no, I didn't," Blackie confessed. "I thought Santa just filled my order a year late."

They laughed together. Blackie leaned back and stared into the green canopy of leaves above them. It always did him good to talk to his father.

"You can't stop the change, *mon fils*," Joe said, "but you can't hide from it, either." He drained his cup and set it beside his chair. "You just got to try to make it work, use the bes' of the new and save the bes' of the old to pass on to your children. If you don' at least try, everybody loses in the end."

"Now, where have I heard that before?" Blackie said under his breath.

"Comment?"

"Nothing, Papa. I'm just thinking that maybe I should take another look at some of my ideas." He tossed off the last of his coffee, then set his cup down. "So, Elisa's still determined to go east, west, anywhere but stay here when she finishes school," he said, changing the subject.

"It looks that way," Joe Broussard said amiably.

"She's just like I was at that age—thinks she'll find what she's looking for somewhere else." Blackie laughed ruefully. "And everything she wants is right here. But she won't listen to me." He rose and walked to the edge of the porch, gazing out at the Teche.

"Ti-neg—" Joe shook his head. "Everybody's different. Maybe what Elisa wants isn't here. She's got to walk her own road."

"You don't want to see her leave, do you?"

"You know better than that, you. Your *maman* and I are happiest with all our kids around us. But it's better for Elisa to leave than stay here and be unhappy. And no one can decide but her."

"Maybe so, Papa." Blackie shrugged. After all, he could hardly call himself an authority on what people should do with their lives. Just then he thought he heard Catherine's voice, in murmured conversation with his mother, drifting across the yard from the direction of the kitchen. His pulse quickened. *Especially now,* he reminded himself.

"*BONJOUR,* CAT'RINE," ZEMA SAID.

"Good morning, Zema." Catherine savored the morning smells of coffee and frying bacon in the large, cheerful kitchen. "I don't know how I can possibly be hungry after all I ate last night, but I am."

Zema beamed. "Go to bed full, wake up hungry, my mama used to say. What she didn't tell us was that you can get fat doing that." Comfortably, she patted her ample hips. "How about some coffee?"

Catherine gratefully accepted a cup, reflecting that either this coffee was less potent than Uncle Bat's had been or she was becoming accustomed to Louisiana coffee.

"Jean—Blackie—is out on the dock with his father," Zema informed her. "I think they're both movin' a little slow this morning."

"Aren't we all?" Catherine laughed ruefully. "I haven't stayed up that late in years." She stopped and considered. "But then again, I haven't had that much fun in a lot longer than that." *Maybe ever.*

"Bon." Zema nodded vigorously. Her hands were never still. If they weren't busy flipping bacon, breaking eggs into a bowl, buttering bread or performing some other breakfast chore, they were helping her talk. "Having fun helps a person make it through the bad times," Zema remarked. "And the family parties, when all of us are here, are even better." She frowned. "I worry sometime, me, that my children won't stay close to each other after Joe and I are gone, that no one will remember to call everyone together. But I think Jean will. He loves his family, that one."

"Yes," Catherine agreed, remembering how happy he had seemed the night before. "Yes, he does."

Zema's pleasant face sobered. "You know about Angéline?" she asked hesitantly.

"Yes," Catherine answered. "It was hard for him, I know."

"When Angéline died, we were there when he needed us," Zema said simply. "He was never all alone." Her tone was matter-of-fact, but Catherine could see pain for her child in her eyes.

"I've never seen a group of people who have a better time together," Catherine said slowly, "or who care more about each other. I—" She hesitated. "I didn't grow up in that kind of family, so being here has been a wonderful experience for me."

"Oh, *chère*, I hope we didn' scare you to death," Zema said in alarm. "Sometimes we're a little loud," she confided as she poured a bowlful of beaten eggs, complete with chopped tomatos, onions, bell peppers and seasonings, into a large skillet.

"Not at all. I enjoyed every minute of it. I was a little nervous at first," Catherine admitted, thinking that she was becoming as candid as the Cajuns in expressing her feelings, "but no one could stay that way for long around all of you. Did you have *bals de maison* when your children were small?"

"Oh, my, yes, only back then we had them at *Gran'mère's* house. All Joe's brothers and sisters would come, and we would dance all night long. That's where Jean learned to love music." She smiled in reminiscence. "I mind one time for sure, when he was still a *p'tit*. His *Nonc* Amedée had told him not to touch his accordion, but when he came back, Jean was playing the chords to one of the old songs." Zema laughed, but her voice was proud. "Amedée didn't know whether to spank him or teach him more. The accordion was so heavy Jean couldn't hold it up by himself, and we almos' had to tie him to the porch post so it wouldn't pull him over. But he wouldn' quit, him. It was all he loved."

Catherine could see him, a small, dark boy with curly hair and snapping black eyes, almost overwhelmed by the heavy accordion. She laughed, but was touched by the image. "But he learned to play the violin, too, didn't he?"

"*Bien sûr*, he learned everything—accordion, fiddle, guitar, ting-a-ling, even washboard. And his papa didn' want him to play anything."

Catherine was shocked. "He didn't? But Joe loves the music. I could tell."

Zema nodded. "*Oui*, he does." She began forking the crisply fried bacon onto plates. "But he wanted Jean to go to college, so he wouldn't have to struggle like he did." She sighed. "Joe always had to work so hard. Anyway, he knew he couldn' stop Jean's music, so he tol' him that if he made good grades in school, he could play with the bands on weekends. And Jean always brought home straight As," she said proudly, "even in college."

"So he did what Joe wanted him to do." Catherine was beginning to understand Blackie's attitudes a little better.

"When he graduated, he gave his diploma to Joe, because he said his papa had worked the hardest for it," Zema continued, cutting off the fire under the eggs and hauling the toast out of the oven. "Joe was so proud he cried. Then, when Jean left Louisiana, he cried again. He wanted Jean to do well, but it hurt so much for him to leave. I cried, too. We were all glad when Jean got married and came back here to live." All at once, she seemed to remember she was talking to Catherine. "*Mais jamais*, how I talk-talk," she said hurriedly. "*S'il vous plaît*, go out and tell Jean and his papa that breakfast is ready. I'll go see who else is awake."

As Zema bustled off toward the other part of the house, Catherine opened the screen door and walked onto the porch. Blinking in the bright sunlight, she saw Blackie and his father seated side by side on the dock, apparently doing nothing more exciting than watching the bayou go by. She studied them for a moment. This family cared for each other; a bond existed among them that, quite simply, left her in awe. And even though it might only be because of Blackie that they had opened their ranks to admit her, she had never felt so loved, so cared for, as she did right now.

But it was only temporary, she remembered with a jolt. Atlanta was still her home, and she wasn't a Broussard. She and Blackie came from two different worlds, and nothing could change that. They had no future together. She had to remember to guard her emotions. All she could hope to keep from this idyllic visit were fond memories, and the realization tore at her heart.

Almost as if she'd called his name, Blackie turned and saw her. He beckoned to her, and she headed toward them across the dew-kissed grass.

"Bonjour," he said as she stepped onto the dock, his gaze drinking in her slim form from top to bottom. She had put on white linen shorts and a knit top of a soft mint green, bought when she had gotten her work jeans, and she could see the appreciation in his eyes. "You're the coolest thing I've seen around," he said, and Catherine felt her skin heat with pleasure.

"Thank you, sir. I'm finally learning to dress for the weather here." She basked in the warmth of his smile, all her admonitions to herself forgotten. He was even handsome when he hadn't shaved, she thought, looking at the stubble of heavy beard shadowing his jaw.

"It's a good thing—for you, and for the rest of us, I might add," he said, his eyes still on her shapely legs.

"Good morning, Joe," Catherine said, pointedly ignoring the remark. "I've been sent to tell you breakfast is ready."

"Good morning, *chère*. It's about time," Joe grumbled without conviction as he slowly got up. "I'm so hungry my stomach thinks my throat's been cut."

"I heard that, *mon homme*," came the retort from behind them. Zema was walking up. "Next time you're in such a hurry, you can cook it yourself, *hein*?"

"Uh-oh, Papa, you messed up," Blackie said gleefully.

"That's all right, son. I'll fix it up later." As Joe put his arm around Zema and guided her toward the house, he flashed Blackie a knowing grin that was all too familiar to Catherine.

"Now I see where you come by it," she said reprovingly. "You Broussards think you can solve anything with fast talk."

"Who says he's going to talk?" Blackie said, looking at Catherine with lazy, sensual eyes. "Oh, *chère*, I'm moving slow this morning," he said. "You'll have to help me up." He extended a hand, then, when Catherine took it, pulled her into his lap.

"I thought you said you weren't moving very fast this morning." But she didn't fight as he settled her comfortably against him. "I should know better than to believe that by now."

"*Mais* sho', you should." Unrepentant, he pulled her to him for a good-morning kiss. He smelled cleanly of soap, and when his lips moved on hers, his whiskers scratched her face. *God,* she thought, *it feels wonderful to be held like this*....

"Umm—you smell good," he said, inhaling deeply as he kissed a spot behind her ear, then worked his way down to her neck.

"Blackie, don't." She squirmed. "Someone will see."

"No, they won't, they're too busy getting ready to eat. We'll go in in a minute..." His mouth kept up its work.

"Blackie." She tried to sound stern.

"*Hein?*" Finally, he raised his head to look at her.

For several seconds she held his eyes, fascinated still by their black depths. Pirate's eyes. They were clouding now, and she felt an answering response welling up inside her. His arms tightened, and she felt his hand move caressingly on her leg.

Abruptly, she straightened. This was madness. "After we eat, I need to get back to New Iberia. I have to work on the budget."

"I know, *ma belle*, I know." Blackie sighed and reluctantly helped her out of his lap. Together, they headed toward the house.

THEY HAD TRAVELED only two miles down the road from Blackie's house, and already Catherine's stay there was beginning to seem like a dream. But she wasn't ready to wake up yet. All Blackie's family had gathered on the front porch to tell them goodbye, and once again she had been surrounded by love and a feeling of belonging. For now, at least, that feeling was still very much with her. She sighed.

"What's the matter, Cat'rine?"

"Nothing, really. I had such a good time that I hate for it all to end." *And I love the way you say my name.*

"We'll go back. I promise you."

Driving down the main street of St. Martinville, they passed a Catholic church. It was obviously very old, but it was immaculately kept, its plaster exterior neatly painted beige and trimmed in white. Its spire, topped by a large white cross, stood out against the sky and the dark green leaves of the trees in the church-yard.

"That's St. Martin de Tours church," Blackie said, pointing. "See the statue of Evangeline over there?"

Catherine caught a glimpse of the statue of a seated woman just behind the church. "So that's the famous Evangeline," she said.

"Longfellow's heroine. But in real life, her name was Emmeline Labiche. And her sweetheart didn't wait for her. He married someone else, and when she found out, she went insane."

"Not very romantic of her. Actually, pretty silly. I guess that's why Longfellow changed the plot."

Blackie laughed. "Poetic license." He looked toward the church. "My family should be here in a few minutes. Mass starts on the hour."

"That's where Uncle Bat said he was baptized," Catherine remembered.

"And everybody else in the family. I was baptized and confirmed there, myself."

Blackie's church. How many generations of Broussards had lived their whole lives in the bosom of this church, and when life was over, had been buried from it? Again Catherine felt a yearning, sharp as thirst, to belong to whatever was part of Blackie.

"Were you supposed to go to church?" she asked.

Blackie shook his head. "I can go this evening in Morgan City. That's where I usually go, anyway. I didn't know how you'd feel about going to church with all my family."

Catherine thought a minute. "I think with your family it would be wonderful," she said truthfully.

He smiled at her then, that smile that made the world fall into place. "Thank you, *chère*." He picked up her hand and kissed it lightly, looked at her as if he was deciding something. "You know all about my family now," he said. "At least, all anyone could stand at one time. But I don't know anything about yours, except what you told me that night in your apartment. Tell me about you, Catherine?"

"There's not much to tell." She shrugged. "My mother and I—aren't as close as you and your family are, but we keep in touch. As I told you, my father died several years ago."

"And?" he prodded.

"And what?"

"What sort of people are—were—they? I've seen pictures of both your parents, but all you've said about them is that your father used to take you places, and your mother is picky about her oyster dressing."

"Well, my family—both sides—has lived in the Atlanta area for several hundred years. Pedigrees, you know, the whole bit. I have a few cousins in Athens, but I really don't know them very well.''

''What are you doing in Louisiana? In fact, with a background like that, why are you working, period?''

''There's a small matter of money.''

''I see—a pedigree a mile long, but no cash, *hein*?''

''That's about it. Actually, there was even plenty of cash until my father got hold of it.'' She made a face. ''The Nolans were a very wealthy family, and my mother's side had plenty, too. But Dad only wanted to play, and Mother liked to live well, so they just spent. Pretty soon all the money was gone, and by the time Dad died, he was deeply in debt.''

''And then?''

''Debts have to be paid. By then I had my degree in restoration architecture, which isn't very useful in dealing with bankrupt estates. My mother—'' she hesitated, uncertain of how she should say it ''—was reared to be a lady. Period. She not only didn't know about money management, she didn't want to learn. Or even hear about it.''

''What about you?''

''Me?''

''Weren't you reared to be a lady, too?''

''Yes, but I suppose I couldn't afford the luxury.'' She smiled. ''Gerrard bailed us out. He took over most of the debts, but I salvaged what I could from the estate and eventually paid the rest of them. I started my first restoration job one day, the next, I met with my father's creditors.''

Blackie's jaw tightened, but he said nothing.

"We worked out a repayment schedule," she went on. "Even after Gerrard's contribution, it took most of my salary and all my ingenuity for the next four years to free us from debt and still leave Mother a little money to live on. Now, some of what I earn can go to supplement that. But I owe Gerrard, Blackie. I've got to pay him back. He doesn't expect it, and the Lord knows he doesn't need it—he's got scads of money. It's enough for him that, in his eyes, I'm going to vindicate the Nolan family name. But I must, for myself. I owe him for more than money."

"I see." Blackie was silent a moment, and she could tell he was displeased. But he said only, "What about you?"

"What about me? I have everything I need. I'm not deprived."

"You're not?" He was looking at her intently, and Catherine knew he wasn't referring to money. "Who loved you?" he asked tenderly. "Somebody used to. I can see you reaching for it again."

Catherine stared out the window. She thought back—to last night. For a moment, she couldn't speak for the lump that rose in throat. "My father," she said slowly. "He loved me." She drew a jerky breath. "I was so angry at him for not taking care of us... My mother was so bitter toward him that it must've rubbed off on me." The revelation stunned her. "He was an unfaithful husband and a terrible provider, but he was a loving father. When I was small, he took me everywhere with him. Mother never wanted to come when he took me to the zoo or to baseball games—

places she didn't like. She said he had a common streak in him.''

"But he knew how to have a good time with you."

"Yes, he did. And until last night, at the *bal de maison*, I had forgotten it." Unable to say more, she looked out the window and tried to blink away the tears.

"Our family party?"

"Yes." She recovered her voice. "Everyone was having fun, and no one was worried about appearances, or the guest list, or the oyster dressing. Everyone was drinking and dancing and genuinely glad to be with everyone else. My father would have loved it. It made me remember the good things about him," she finished.

"I'm glad, *chère*." For a moment, their eyes met and held. Blackie enveloped her hand in his. Then he turned back to the wheel, to drive them to New Iberia, and the real world.

CHAPTER ELEVEN

CATHERINE STOOD LOOKING, with considerable satisfaction, at the bulky report in her hands. Only a few
minutes before, she and Frank had been standing in
the yard of the Arceneaux house, discussing repairs to
the cypress-shingled roof, when Clarence had hurried
across the field from Bonne Journée, triumphantly
waving the report above his head.

"*C'est bon*—it's okay!" he had shouted when he
was no more than halfway to them. "We did it! They
approved the budget!" She almost believed he'd been
prouder of their success than she had been.

And considering all his hard work, maybe he should
have been. Strangely, that was one of the reasons she
felt so good about this project. In the time since she
had received the news of the budget cut, she, who had
always prided herself on her self-reliance, had shamelessly accepted help from anyone who would give it—
Clarence, Toni, Frank, Gussie, Blackie. They had
called on friends, relatives, anyone who could donate
labor, materials and anything else to cut restoration
costs.

Especially Blackie. He had done it all so casually, in
spite of all that was riding on the outcome. When
Catherine had told him that the board was to decide

on the budget that week, he had said, "Well, that's good, because I want to take you to the swamp for a picnic this weekend. To celebrate."

"What if the budget isn't approved?" she had asked him.

"Then you'll need consoling. Either way, we'll go," he had said with an easy grin.

She had agreed, with an eagerness that had startled her.

So, she thought as she leafed quickly through the report, it was to be a celebration. Blackie would pick her up early the next morning. Her stomach fluttered. She wasn't sure how much of her nervousness stemmed from the budget victory and how much came from the knowledge that they would soon be alone together—very alone.

It occurred to Catherine that this trip could be a big mistake. It was bound to worsen her already chaotic mental state. In the two weeks since they had been to his parents' house, she had found that she couldn't rid her thoughts of Blackie for more than a few minutes at a time. It was particularly frustrating to her, she who normally kept her mind in the kind of apple-pie order that some women kept their houses. Every day, every hour, a hundred renegade thoughts and feelings about Blackie cropped up like tiny forest fires, singeing her when she least expected it.

She kept warning herself that their relationship needed to cool a little. And to do Blackie justice, he had indeed seemed to be putting a little distance between them. It was what she thought she wanted, but perversely, it brought her no peace. Worse, it made no difference in her response to him. All he had to do was flash her a smile or look into her eyes for an unguarded moment and she was transported to a moonlit bayou night with Blackie calling her *hébé*.

"Catherine," a voice called from across the lot, and she looked up to see Gussie walking toward her.

Just looking at her broke Catherine's heart, but she made herself smile as if Gussie hadn't a care in the world. "Hi, Gussie."

"Hi." Gussie smiled, too, but the smile was lifeless. "I need to talk to you, if you have time."

"Of course. Let's head to my office. You'll be happy to know that Clarence just delivered the good news that our budget has been approved."

"That's wonderful," Gussie said, a tiny note of real enthusiasm in her voice. "I knew you could do it."

"I couldn't have if all you hadn't given me so much help. Tell me—is something wrong?" She could have kicked herself for that, but didn't amend the question. *Is something else wrong?* would have been worse.

"Catherine—" Gussie hesitated, looked down miserably. "I'm leaving."

"Leaving?" Catherine repeated stupidly. "But why?"

Gussie's eyes filled with tears. "I don't want to go," she said desperately. "Everything I care about is here. But that's the trouble. Alain's here, too, and it tears me up every time I run into him."

"I see," Catherine said with a sinking heart. It had never occurred to her what Gussie might leave, but she could understand. "Where are you going?"

"To New Orleans. Clarence helped me get a job as curator of a restored house in the Garden District." Suddenly Gussie's face crumpled. "I don't want to leave, Catherine. You know that. But . . ."

"I understand, Gussie. I really do. I'm so sorry." Catherine's own eyes filled with tears. "I also don't know what I'm going to do without you, and I'm not just saying that. Do you realize how much you've done on these restorations?"

"I loved doing it." Gussie wiped her eyes, made a gallant attempt to regain her composure. "Maybe I can come back someday, but I have to—get over Alain first."

"You'll come back. This town won't be the same until you do." To her chagrin, Catherine realized the tears were now rolling down her cheeks. "When are you leaving?" she asked, making an effort to control her voice.

"Tomorrow morning. I'm going to pack tonight. I want to start the new job as soon as I can."

"You'll be great, just as you were here. Gussie— take care." She embraced the younger woman, reluctant to let her go. "I love you. We all love you."

Gussie turned with a muffled sob, and without another word hurried toward Bonne Journée.

Wiping her eyes, Catherine followed at a slower pace. How would Gussie feel about the house in New Orleans? Would she care about it as she did for the projects here? Catherine remembered Blackie's words: *When anyone mentions the Arceneaux house, you look as though you dread it, but you're going to do it if it kills you.* How far she had come since then. Now she couldn't imagine working on a house that she didn't love—including the Arceneaux house.

No, Gussie probably wouldn't like her new job. She would probably hate the move as much as Catherine had hated to leave Atlanta. But maybe it would help her. Catherine hoped so. So much pain couldn't be for nothing.

Suddenly, she *needed* to see Blackie. As she walked onto the big front porch and headed for her office, she found herself counting the hours until the next morning.

"GIVE ME YOUR HAND and step down."

Catherine did as Blackie told her, then, struggling to keep her balance in the boat, sat down and took the picnic basket he handed her. He stepped in, flipped the rope off the piling and, balancing easily, seated himself next to her at the controls.

It was still early. That morning, Catherine had risen in the dark and, according to Blackie's instructions, had dressed in shorts and cool cotton blouse. "It'll be hot," he had said. They had left just after daylight and had driven a long way down winding Louisiana roads until she was completely lost. Finally, they had pulled off and parked by a narrow slough, where, next to a small wooden building, several boats were moored to a dock. Blackie had ushered her toward the largest one, explaining that it was his fishing boat.

Blackie started the engine, the motor roared into life, and he slowly began to reverse the boat out of its niche. When they had cleared the low dock, he straightened the wheel and pushed the throttle forward, and they were off.

He swung them out into the center of the stream and gunned the motor. The craft picked up speed, its bow lifting, its wake fanning out behind. Blackie raised his face to the breeze, his black hair blowing into wild curls. Catherine's own hair was escaping from its customary neat chignon in spite of her attempts to contain it. Blackie laughed at her. "Let it blow, *chère*."

She glanced around her. They were heading down a narrow, cattail-filled channel into what appeared to be a solid jungle. Catherine watched in wonder as the vegetation grew thicker and thicker, the sunlight grew dim and the outside world disappeared. Without warning Blackie turned the boat sharply, and Catherine gasped; for a moment she thought they were heading directly into the bank. But she was amazed to see that a channel existed there beneath a solid carpet of lavender-flowered green leaves that completely covered the water. Although the motor labored hard in the heavy stuff, the bow of the boat sliced through, and they entered an even narrower channel.

"Water hyacinth," Blackie explained over the roar of the engine. "It's pretty, but it's also a curse. It chokes all the channels and bayous around here and kills marine life."

They plunged deeper into the swamp, and in some places the thick growth blocked out the light completely. The smell of a primeval dampness, of life perpetuating itself, hung redolent in the air. Giant cypresses, draped with gray Spanish moss, stood majestically in the water on each side of the passage, surrounded by their myriad knees. In the spots of dappled sunlight, Catherine could see green, spiky sprays of palmetto leaves. Water stood everywhere, broken only by occasional ridges of land. It was hard to distinguish the channel from the shallower marsh around it.

The surface of the quieter waters was completely covered with what appeared to be a yellow-green scum. Repelled yet curious, Catherine dipped up a handful. Looking closer, she saw that it consisted of millions of tiny, separate bright green leaves. "Duckweed," Blackie answered her questioning look.

As she watched, the boat's wake washed up into the shallows and sent a small wave scurrying through the undergrowth, startling a huge heron wading at the channel's edges, its blue and violet plumage iridescent in the gloom. With a hoarse cry, it launched itself into the air, and Catherine caught her breath as it seemed to suspend itself just above their heads. An enchanted land, indeed.

On they went, winding through the perennial twilight of the swamp, until Catherine had no idea what direction they were going. But she could tell by Blackie's easy, confident navigation through the maze of narrow waterways and superabundant plant life that he was completely at home.

For the next two hours they explored. Blackie showed her secret places where unfamiliar plants grew and tiny, jeweled birds lived; huge cypress stumps, mute testimony to swamp giants felled by the lumberman's ax; alligator holes; and once even an alligator, who fixed them with a cold eye before silently sinking into the murky swamp waters. Through Blackie, she realized that, far from being a dismal place, the swamp teemed with myriad forms of life in a thousand vivid colors. Like most Cajuns, he was a born storyteller, and he regaled her with hunting, fishing and trapping tales from his childhood. And in those stories, Catherine could see the strong underpinning of familial love that had made him what he was.

Not all Blackie's stories were pleasant. He told of the dangers of the swamp—storms, floods, snakes, alligators—of how life and death coexisted equally in its depths.

Abruptly, he killed the boat's engine and aimed the craft toward a particularly large cypress tree, surrounded by its host of gnarled, stubby knees. They drifted in, and he pointed wordlessly. One of the knees, larger and flatter than the rest, had what appeared to be a shiny black growth on the top. To Catherine's horror, it uncoiled as they approached to reveal a stubby black snake, eyes fixed on the intruders in unwinking malevolence, tongue flickering in warning.

Catherine's skin prickled in horror, and in spite of herself, she shrank against Blackie. With an oar, he pushed the boat away from the tree, and the snake slithered soundlessly into the water. Blackie's face was grim. "Cottonmouth moccasin," he said. "But the cypress knees can be just as deadly."

Angéline. In spite of the warmth of the swamp air, Catherine suddenly felt chilled. Toni's words came back to her: *They thought her boat hit a cypress knee...*

Blackie started the motor, and they moved slowly away. She stole a sidelong glance at him. He was silent, but she could see the pain in his face. She sighed. If the memory of his wife still affected him like this, could he ever put it behind him?

At last they came upon a tiny cabin. It sat on cypress piers, its weathered sides blending with the muted colors of the swamp. "Our fishing cabin," Blackie explained as he shut down the motor and allowed the boat to drift in to the little dock. "Papa built it when my brothers and I were barely old enough to tote the boards."

The boat gently nudged the piling, and he jumped out and secured the rope, then helped Catherine out. Together they unloaded the gear, then mounted the steps to the minute front porch. He unlocked the door and ushered her inside. While he opened the windows to air out the interior, Catherine set the picnic basket down and looked around her.

It was undecorated and contained only a few pieces of furniture: a table, four chairs, a chest and four single beds covered by bright cotton spreads in a row by the windows. A small kitchen area occupied one corner, complete with potbellied wood stove, kitchen sink and cabinets.

"Why only four of everything?" Catherine asked. "What did Marcel do? Or your mother and sisters, for that matter, when they came?"

Blackie laughed. "We came in shifts, mostly. Mama didn't really like it out here. She said she had lived without modern conveniences too long when she was little." He opened the last of the windows and dusted his hands. "Elisa and Mar'Louise came some, but mostly it was just Papa and us boys. Marcel had to sleep on the floor in a sleeping bag, or with me. The few times we were all here, it got pretty crowded." He started toward the door. "Let's sit out here until the house cools off."

He opened an aluminum chair for her. Then he sat down in his own, propped his feet on the porch railing and stared out over the swamp. Catherine saw the brooding look on his face.

He looked her way then and caught her watching him. Their eyes held.

"Blackie . . ."

"Hein?"

"I know what you're thinking," she said gently. "It's been on your mind since you told me about the cypress knees." She reached for his hand. "That's what happened to Angéline, isn't it?"

He looked startled, and such a variety of emotions—guilt, pain, chagrin—chased each other across his mobile face that any other time she would have laughed. But then he let out his pent-up breath on a long sigh, and Catherine, unaware until then that she'd been holding her own, breathed with him.

"Yeah, *bébé*," he said. "That's what happened."

"Do you want to talk about it?"

"I think I do." She heard surprise and, incredibly, relief in his voice. He was silent a moment, staring unseeingly into the swamp. "I don't know whether you know it or not, but Angéline was a nurse. Raymond Hebert still had his family living back in the swamp—"

"Raymond Hebert?"

"Yeah. You know him, remember?"

"I certainly do," Catherine said dryly. So Raymond Hebert had been somehow connected with Angéline's accident. "Go on."

"Anyway, Raymond's little boy had a bad case of strep throat, and they didn't have the money for a doctor. Angéline took him some medicine that afternoon. She was later starting back than she'd intended to be, and it was getting dark. It's always darker in here than it is outside, anyway."

"I'd noticed."

"On the way out, her boat hit a cypress knee. When she was thrown out, she hit her head, probably on the side of the boat, and . . ."

"Don't talk if it—if it hurts too much."

"It's all right," he said, gripping her hand. "It makes me sad, it always will, but I need to talk about it. I had to work that night," he went on, "and I had told her not to go out there by herself, that I would take her when I got off later. I thought she'd wait, because the little boy wasn't that sick. But she didn't."

"It must have been especially hard for you, that her death was so unnecessary," Catherine said softly.

Blackie looked at her, and she saw the raw pain in his eyes. "You don't know all of it yet. Angéline knew that part of he swamp like the back of her hand. She had run boats in it since she was a little girl. But we—found her—a long way from the channel she should have been in. The swamp had changed, because the corps—*we*—were draining in that area, and she didn't realize it." He balled his free hand into a fist. "She was lost."

So that was the reason he was so against change. In fact, it explained a lot of things. "But Blackie, everyone says not to go into the swamp alone after dark, even people who know it."

Wordlessly, he nodded.

"Then why in heaven's name didn't she wait for you?"

He took a deep breath, then continued. "Everybody thought it was just because she was so dedicated. And she was. But this time—" He stopped again. "She was mad at me," he said finally.

"Just because you couldn't leave work?" Surely Angéline hadn't been that impulsive.

He shook his head. "I didn't get along with my corps supervisor. I asked him to let me off for two hours, so I could go with Angéline. Two hours," he repeated with suppressed rage. "But he turned me down. Said I had to finish my shift." His fingers clenched on Catherine's hand. "I knew he'd make trouble, and I still wanted to make my mark in the world, so I stayed.

"When I told Angéline, she got mad at me for not standing up to him and said she was going anyway. I thought she was just saying it. It would have been so easy for me just to have walked out."

"I was told that after the accident, you had a run-in with your boss," Catherine said softly.

He gave a short, bitter laugh. "Run-in is a little mild. I would've killed him if somebody hadn't stopped me. All I could think of was that if he had let me go, Angéline would still be alive. But it was my fault as much as his, and deep down inside I knew it. Anyway, I quit, and he got transferred not long after that, so it was over." He drew a deep, uneven breath. "All but the crying."

"And you still cry, Blackie." Catherine reached up to catch a tear that was making its slow path down Blackie's cheek.

Nodding, he carried her hand to his lips and lightly kissed the palm. "I do, sometimes. It's not Angéline—I've told her goodbye. Accepting death is a part of living. But I suppose I'll always feel responsible for what happened."

"Blackie, you're not Superman," Catherine said, her heart going out to him. "You did the best you could." Then the truth dawned on her. "All this time, you've never forgiven yourself, and nobody's known. But from everything I've heard about Angéline, she'd be the last person who'd want you to feel that way."

"You're right," he agreed. "She wouldn't have."

"And you've let it change the way you feel about everything, including your own people."

"I never thought about it that way," he said slowly. "Maybe I have." He looked at her. "You know, you've given me a lot to think about lately."

"Is that good?"

"I think it must be," he said after a moment. He tried to grin, but failed. "It hurts."

"Oh, Blackie," she said, horrified. "I would never deliberately hurt you."

"I know you wouldn't, *bébé*." He reached over, laid his finger on her lips.

They sat a while longer on the porch, hands clasped, talking at random, about the swamp, Blackie's family, the restorations, anything Catherine could think of. Gradually, she sensed that the heaviness was leaving him.

"Blackie?"

"Hein?"

"I'm hungry."

"Thank you, *chère*." He reached over to caress her cheek. "We all have to cry, but today's too beautiful for that—and so are you." He stood up and stretched. "Come on—let's eat. All of a sudden I feel like I could eat three 'gators, tails and all."

They went inside and began to unpack the lunch, taking out delectable-smelling fried chicken, potato chips and fruit. From the cooler, Blackie produced potato salad and ice-cold beer. Catherine had offered to bring the food, but Blackie had insisted. On the drive down, however, he had confessed that he had sweet-talked his mother into making the lunch.

Catherine's first bite of chicken affirmed what her nose had already told her. "Is there anything your mother doesn't cook well?"

He considered. "Nothing I can think of, but then, I'm not the one to ask. The rule at our house was, whoever criticized the cooking had to fix the next meal. So I was always crazy about everything she cooked."

Catherine laughed. "I like your mother's style. I'll have to remember that." *For what?* she asked herself, then pushed the thought aside. She looked at her empty plate. "What? No dessert?" she asked in mock disappointment.

"*Mais* sho'—can't have a picnic without dessert." Blackie rummaged through the basket, like a bear after honey, Catherine thought, smiling.

"Here they are," he said, waving a small package in triumph. "Mama never forgets them. They're her speciality." He unwrapped tiny, delicate, honey-golden rounds of candy, so translucent the chunks of pecans showed through clearly. "Pralines," Blackie announced reverently, popping a piece into her mouth. The sugared crispness of the candy melted quickly, flooding her tongue with its sweet flavor. She closed her eyes in sheer bliss.

When she opened them again, Blackie's eyes were on her face. "You looked like a little girl when you did that," he said gently, his eyes full of tender amusement. As he gazed at her, the amusement faded. Time was suspended as he leaned forward, caught her chin in his hands and put his lips to hers.

He tasted her sugared mouth, then deepened the kiss as his tongue explored, savored. Catherine made a little sound in the back of her throat as desire coursed through her in a hot wave. She felt the answering need in him. *There'll be another time,* he had said. She tried to summon up her earlier apprehension, but it wasn't there. A whole swamp lay between her and the outside world, and for now there were no consequences. She felt a sense of rightness, of coming home.

Blackie broke the kiss, and as he had when he had asked her to dance, stood and held out his hand to her. She rose and took it. Still holding her, he led her to one of the beds. They sat on the edge, and he pulled her toward him, kissed her again. This time the kiss was less gentle. Catherine felt as though she was on a roller coaster, poised at the crest of the first hill, awaiting the swift, inevitable descent. She began to tremble.

"Don't be afraid, Cat'rine," Blackie said huskily.

"I'm not."

He wrapped his strong arms around her, simply held her until, in her growing awareness of his body against her, her trembling began to subside. He put his fingers under her chin and lifted her face to his.

With the melding of lips and tongues, all barriers came down. Desire surged through Catherine's veins, thick, hot, honey-sweet. Behind Blackie's head her hands tangled themselves in the thick black hair. Her body molded itself to his, her softness to his growing hardness.

"P'tite," Blackie murmured hoarsely against her lips. He reached behind her head and one by one pulled out the pins that held her hair, his eyes never leaving her face. When the heavy mass at last tumbled free, Blackie buried both hands in it, looking as though he'd found the pot of gold at the end of the rainbow. *"Que c'est belle,"* he muttered. Then his hands moved to cradle her face, and his lips came to hers again. His kiss compelled, demanded. His hand drifted to cup her breasts, and his fingers found her nipples through the thin cotton of her blouse. She gasped. Through the haze of sensation, she could feel her heart pounding against his hand. A sweet fire began to ignite in her loins.

His hands moved to the buttons of her blouse, and slowly, slowly he undid them, his fingers against her skin nearly driving her mad. He slid the garment off her shoulders and tossed it to the floor. His hands came around her back, gentling her, and unclasped her lacy bra, freeing her breasts. "Ah..." The sound broke from him. His callused palms moved over her swollen nipples and she moaned, leaning into his hands. Then he gently laid her against the mattress and swung the lower half of his body onto the bed beside her, holding her against him. When their bodies came together, she felt as if the breath had been knocked from her. He lowered his head to one breast and gently took it into his mouth, sending another set of unfamiliar, electrifying sensations through her throbbing body. Dazed, she put her hands on either side of his head, feeling with her fingertips the rhythmic motion as he caressed her.

His hands roamed everywhere, touching her, warming her. Then he brought his mouth upward, his lips brushing the skin on her neck, the line of her jaw. The tip of his tongue touched the corner of her mouth as his fingers found her nipple, and the double contact sent a jolt straight to the core of her. As if she was drowning, she mindlessly clutched his sweat-damp shoulders, her fingers digging into his warm, muscled flesh.

He deepened his kisses to keep pace with their mutual hunger. "Ah, Cat'rine—*bien douce*—I've wanted this so long *chère*." Slowly, achingly, he retraced his route downward with lips and tongue, until Catherine's whole body shook with her need. He rained soft kisses down her quivering stomach, urged her legs gently apart so he could caress her through the fabric of her shorts. She opened herself to him, wanting to remove the last barriers between them.

Blackie raised his head to search her face, his eyes dark mirrors reflecting her own passion. *"Ma belle,"* he said hoarsely, "this time, I have to love you."

He put both arms around her, holding their bodies so tightly together that her shoulders came up off the bed and she could feel his heart pounding against her breasts. His hand slipped down to cup her buttocks, pressing her against his hardness, and she pushed her hips against him to intensify the contact. There was no future, no past; there were no differences between them. For now all her world was Blackie.

Reluctantly, he pulled away from her, sat up and unfastened the clasp of her shorts, then eased them gently over her hips. She thought then that she would drown in sensation. The humid air, blown in gently from the open windows, kissed her skin, leaving it deliciously cool. Blackie moved his gaze slowly over her body, and Catherine was awed by what she saw in his face. His hand came down gently to cup the dark blond triangle where her legs met. The sensation shot straight through her body, and she moaned softly. His eyes closed briefly, and when they opened again, their black depths glowed with such a wealth of mingled passion and tenderness that Catherine was lost in them, consumed by them. *"Dieu..."* His voice was thick, drugged. "You're so beautiful, sweetheart."

He stood, leaving her momentarily bereft. But in a matter of seconds he had removed his clothing.

Hungrily, she drank in the sight of his muscular shoulders, his smooth, tanned chest, his narrow waist and powerful thighs. She thought she had never seen anything so beautiful in her life. He saw her watching him and smiled crookedly. "You see what you do to me, *chère*," he said softly as he lowered himself to the small bed. "I want it to be good for you—but I don't think I can wait much longer."

"Don't wait," she said on a ragged whisper. "Teach me, Blackie . . . teach me how to love you." She heard him draw a sharp breath as he pulled her into his arms.

"Ah, Cat'rine," he murmured, "I need you, *bébé*." He opened her legs, and she felt his fingers touch her intimately, with a gentle urgency. He entered her fractionally then, hesitant at first. "I don't want to hurt you," he said softly. But Catherine, driven far beyond caring, raised her hips against him, and with a single smooth, hot motion, he slipped inside her. She flinched once, then moved against him again. With a hoarse sound from deep in his throat, he immersed himself completely in her, and they began to move together.

With each thrust, Catherine felt him enter deeper into her soul. Nothing could be more right, more natural than this. Nothing existed for her but Blackie and her own overwhelming need for him. She heard his breath coming in raw gasps, felt his weight on her and the convulsive pressure of his hands on her molding her more closely to him. Her hands moved up and down his back, over the curve of his hard buttocks, trying to touch him everywhere, caressing the places where their bodies joined, wondering at the compelling, unfamiliar sensations she was drowning in.

He surrounded her, filled her, completed her. Her body rose to meet him, but it wasn't enough. She wanted more. Their rhythm became faster, stronger, until she felt she could bear no more. Still she climbed. She was following Blackie. He pulled her along with him, set the pace for them both—teaching her. Just as the feeling became sweetly, painfully unbearable, it crested into a pulsing wave of joy so beautiful that, lost to herself, Catherine cried aloud.

Blackie watched her face, held her during her ecstasy, until his own overtook him.

HE DRIFTED SLOWLY BACK to the world, still joined with her. But it was several minutes before Blackie realized that she was weeping. Slowly, steadily, the tears welled from behind her closed lids, and one by one trailed warm and wet down the sides of her face. His muffled exclamation made her open her eyes. "*Mignonne*, did I hurt you?" he whispered. "I didn't mean to be rough." He caught her tears with his lips and kissed them away.

"Oh, no." Her voice was low, her tone wondering. "It was so beautiful. I didn't know…" She closed her eyes again, as if to hold back the tears, but still they flowed.

Blackie fought the tightness in his own throat. To be the first to give her that was a gift indeed. "I'm glad, darlin'," he said softly. He buried his face in her hair.

For long moments they lay together, and when Blackie moved from her at last, she made a small sound of protest. Leaning his weight on one elbow, he smiled at her. "Don't worry, *chère*, I'm not going anywhere." He caressed her face with his free hand. Tremulously, her face still dew-wet, she smiled back at him.

He studied her closely, memorizing each feature, wanting to preserve this moment in his own consciousness. He knew some women wept their first time—their first real time—of loving. He hoped it had been that good for her; God knew it had been for him. He had loved many women in his life, but he couldn't remember it being like this. His desire for this exquisite, complex woman was so tangled with the urge to protect, to cherish, just to hold, that he didn't know where one feeling stopped and the other started. He looked at her body, damp and fragrant from their loving. Even now, he wanted to bury himself in her again. To distract himself, he moved his eyes to her face.

She still had that look in her eyes, that look of a child, he thought, still vulnerable, but this time not so frightened. For the first time, he could see the trust. And something else? Blackie wasn't sure. He pulled her close, bent his head and blissfully willed the world to go away.

"BLACKIE?" CATHERINE WHISPERED.

He must have dozed. "I'm here, sweetheart," he answered drowsily. He moved his hand up to touch her shoulder, and his arm came to rest between her breasts. He looked at it, fascinated by its brownness against her fair skin. Suddenly she raised up on her elbow and her hair came cascading down behind her back, making her look like a child. She reached out a tentative hand, then touched him, her fingers as soft as a moth's wings. He held his breath. She so rarely touched him first. She traced his jaw, skimmed his mouth with the cushions of her fingers. He let his lips part under them, kissed one lightly, took another into his mouth. All the while, her eyes, those incredible green eyes, searched his own, boring into his very soul.

"Blackie—let it go." Her voice was soft, but carried a painful intensity.

In this tiny cabin they were so close, so at one with each other, that he could feel her emotions as if they were his own. He knew exactly what she meant. He suspended his thoughts for a moment, letting the feelings—the joy and the pain, the grief, the bitterness, the guilt—course through him. He closed his eyes, almost unable to bear it. When he opened them, they were wet. For the second time that day, Catherine lifted a hand to wipe away his tears.

With the aftermath, he felt as if a giant burden had been lifted from him. The memories were still there, the pain even, but they had all receded to a great distance. "I have," he whispered. Feeling his body begin to stir again, he slipped a hand into Catherine's hair and lowered her gently onto the bed.

CHAPTER TWELVE

CANE FIELDS BEGAN to give way to civilization as Catherine and Blackie drove to New Iberia late that evening. *Funny,* Catherine thought, looking out the window, *just because the world has changed for me, I suppose I think everything should look different.* She had not the slightest idea what the future held—her mind refused to dwell on that—but knew in her bones that, regardless of what happened, she had crossed a bridge, that she would never be the same Catherine Nolan who had come to Louisiana such a short time ago.

She stole a sidewise glance at Blackie, remembering the feel of his broad shoulders under her hands. Her eyes traced the strong line of his jaw, just as her fingers had done a few short hours ago. She looked at his brown, square hands, and at the memory of their touch, the honeyed heat once again coursed through her body.

Blackie turned to meet her look, and their eyes held. He reached over to take her hand in his.

"How you doin', *bébé*?" he asked, caressing her with his rich, warm voice.

"Fine." It was true, at least for the moment. She tried again to focus on the real world, to force her mind to face what was happening to her and, more importantly, to decide what she was going to do. But the thoughts simply wouldn't coalesce, so she gave in to the pure pleasure of being with Blackie.

Just then, she realized they were passing Bonne Journée and the Arceneaux house, and automatically she ran a critical eye over the grounds.

"Ready to go back to work?" Blackie asked, chuckling.

"Well, now that you mention it," she said, and laughed at his look of mock disgust. "I do need to check on things. Really. Would you mind stopping for a minute?"

Blackie shook his head. "I should have known better than to ask. You'd rise from the dead to see about your work, wouldn't you?"

"Probably. I know I'll sleep better tonight if I see they're still standing."

He shot her a look. "I can make you sleep better, *chère*," he volunteered.

Catherine's retort died on her lips. In the shadows at one corner of the Arceneaux house, she saw the fleeing figure of a man. "Blackie, stop!" She pointed. "Someone ran around the corner."

Before she could draw a breath, Blackie had swung the car onto the grass, braked quickly and jumped out. He disappeared around the corner of the house, and Catherine was left alone with her apprehensions. What if the man had a gun? She got out of the car, feeling helpless.

Not many seconds later, however, Blackie reappeared, barely winded in spite of the fact that he'd run so hard. Catherine, enormously relieved, hurried to him, putting her hands on his arms.

"Did you see him?"

"Just caught a glimpse. He ducked through the hedge and headed toward the back of Bonne Journée."

"Do you have any idea who it might have been?" Even as she asked, the words formed in her mind. *Raymond Hebert*.

"No. Maybe some kid, prowling around."

"Blackie?"

"Yeah?"

"Could it have been Raymond Hebert?"

He looked at her in disbelief. "What in the world makes you think it could be Raymond?"

"I didn't want to tell you, but a few weeks ago he threatened to set fire to the Arceneaux house."

"What?" Blackie's face was a study in thunderstruck amazement. "Why didn't you tell me?"

"I suppose I didn't want to worry you. I thought myself that it wouldn't amount to anything."

A scowl creased Blackie's forehead as her words soaked in. Catherine saw that he was struggling with his loyalties. After all, Raymond Hebert was a childhood friend. She wished she hadn't said anything.

"Well, that was wrong of him, but it doesn't mean he'll really do it," he said at last. "He's plenty mad at the world, but he's harmless."

"I don't think he's harmless, Blackie. He frightened me." Gussie would support her opinion of Raymond, but she was in New Orleans.

"Talk doesn't mean a thing—he's just had a hard time. He's got to have some outlet for his anger."

And I'm the lucky recipient, she thought. *Is that fair?* Catherine knew she should be angry, but right now all she wanted was to keep that shuttered look from Blackie's face. He was caught in the middle, torn between her and Raymond, and because of it she could feel him withdrawing from her. When it came to one of his own, she was still an outsider, she thought sadly. Afraid of being the loser, she didn't have the courage to force the issue.

"All right, Blackie. I'm sorry I said anything. I'll call the police when I get home."

"Sure, call the police," Blackie said stiffly. "Maybe they can catch whoever it was."

The incident was over, but it had served to remind Catherine just how precarious their relationship still was. Their unresolved differences hung like a tangible barrier between them, and all the old doubts resurfaced in Catherine's mind. What they had shared earlier didn't change the basic fact that their backgrounds, their cultures, were worlds apart. It had always been that way, would always be.

They didn't speak of it again. Catherine insisted on checking the interior of the house to make sure everything was intact. As far as she could tell, nothing had been touched. Blackie accompanied her willingly, and when he walked her to her door, she wondered if he would offer to stay with her, but he said nothing. The incident had altered the mood of intimacy subtly but significantly. But Blackie held her close for a long moment before he left, and Catherine took comfort from the strong, steady beat of his heart against hers. His goodbye kiss was tender, with just enough urgency in it to leave her trembling in the doorway.

Locking the door behind him, Catherine realized that she was as confused as ever. And she was now vulnerable, too. Blackie had breached her wall of reserve.

After she reported the incident to the police, she went into the kitchen to eat, but realized she wasn't hungry and decided to shower instead. She went into the bathroom and stripped quickly, running the water hot. She stared deliberately down at her body. Her skin was white and smooth, her breasts small and proud. This was her body, the same one she'd always had. *The body Blackie had loved*... Had it changed somehow? She fancied that her nipples glowed rosier, that there was an extra bloom on her skin. She hugged herself with both arms. Remembering how it had been, she couldn't bring herself to be sorry.

Late that night, restless and unable to sleep, she sat down again with the Millard letters. As she unfolded one, the scent of old roses brushed her nostrils. She began to read. The letter was dated April 7, 1843.

Dearest Mama,

I am writing to say that we are all well. I wish you could have been with us for little Armand's birthday. He is quite a little man and thinks he is a help to his papa. Of course his papa thinks so, too. Little Marguerite is so beautiful, and the baby is doing fine except for a touch of colic at night. Let me know when you can slip away to see us again.

Mama, I love Michel more with each passing day. He is so good to me and so loving with the children. My only sadness is that Papa will not forgive us. I thought if I could talk to him, to show him how happy I truly am, he must surely forgive us, but I was wrong. He would not even see me. I will never try again—the pain was too great. He has hardened his heart against me. But Mama—I still love him, as strange as it may seem. I send you my dearest love.

Catherine read on, tracing the years of Laura's happiness with Michel Arceneaux, their growing family—and Joshua Millard's continuing hatred and unforgiveness. She closed her eyes. Even from the distance of all these years, she resented Joshua Millard, what he had done to his family, because of his own bigoted beliefs.

The packet was growing smaller. She picked up another letter.

2 July 1843
Dearest Mama,
I wanted to reassure you that we are still alive. The fever so far has been merciful to us, although it has killed so many, but a few days ago one of our slaves came down with it. I of course have been seeing to his care, but I assure you I'm taking every precaution to avoid catching the disease. I haven't felt quite myself today, but I

feel sure it is simply that I'm tired. I'm going to try to rest tonight and I will no doubt feel better in the morning. May God preserve you all from this horrible plague, and keep you safe.

The fever. Meaning, in this part of the country, yellow fever, the ancient scourge of the hot, wet lowlands. Mosquitos carried it, of course, but back then, no one knew that; they thought it was from human contact. Catherine, reading the words, felt a dreadful sense of foreboding. She looked at the remaining letters—only two left. She picked up the next-to-last one. It was in a different handwriting—very primitive, with letters carefully formed, as if the writer had labored long over each one, but even so, the writing was somehow bold, assertive. The letter was very short.

Chère Madam Millard I grieve to tell you your beloved daughter Laura companion of my heart died early this morning of the cursed *fièvre jaune* we bury her tomorrow morning I will send someone for you her last words were her love for you and her forgiveness for her father may *le bon Dieu* pardon him I never shall

> With respect
> *votre beau-fils*
> Michel Arceneaux

So Laura Millard Arceneaux had died without her father's forgiveness. Across the chasm of the years, tears stung Catherine's eyes—for Michel Arceneaux's pain, for Eleanor Millard's. How must she have felt to

lose her daughter that way? The yellow fever couldn't
have been helped, but the estrangement could have
been.

The last letter was in yet another handwriting, elegant, feminine. The paper, though ivoried with age,
was obviously of good quality. *Charleston, South
Carolina,* it began, and was dated January 13, 1845,
approximately six months after Laura's death.

My dearest Eleanor, my heart grieves over the sad
news of Laura's death. Oh if only I could be with
you, impart some comfort to you on this dreadful occasion. If only the distance between us were
not so great. You must take care of yourself now,
for the dreaded fever strikes everywhere, and I
could not bear it if I were to lose you, too. You
must try to find it in your heart to forgive
Joshua—in spite of his unkindness about Laura,
he has within him the qualities of a good man. I
know he loves you dearly, and hating him will
only harm you in the end. I suspect he has en-
dured torture enough. We are all human beings in
the sight of God, and He will forgive us all.

The letter was signed, *Your loving sister, Caroline*.
Catherine put the letter down. Had Eleanor Millard forgiven Joshua? Catherine hoped so, for her
sake, even though he hadn't deserved it. The world of
the past was really no different from the present world,
she reflected—in both cases human beings tried to do
the best they could with whatever fate threw at them.
And then, as now, the human values were what mat-

tered. Because he couldn't bend, Joshua Millard had deeply hurt his daughter and, Catherine was sure, had ruined his own life, perhaps even that of his wife, in the process. And the people he had despised had opened their hearts to his daughter and given her the love he had denied her. Slowly, carefully, Catherine retied the letters with their faded ribbon, then put them away. So much for what she had always thought had been the safe, secure realm of the past. And so much for appearances.

In an attempt to salvage a little rest from the few remaining hours of the night, Catherine forced herself to go to bed. Tomorrow was her reentry into the everyday world, and she needed to make it as painless as possible.

"ANYBODY HOME?"

A soft knock sounded on the doorjamb to Catherine's office. She looked up to find Toni MacDonald standing there.

"Come in, come in," Catherine said, pleased as always to see Toni.

"I just dropped by for a progress report," Toni said. "What's going on?"

"A little of everything, I think," Catherine answered. "In fact, I was just reviewing both projects, and we're still on schedule. Our excavations at Bonne Journée have located the slave quarters. We'll mark them off so that as soon as the funds are available, we'll be able to reconstruct them."

Toni sighed happily. "We've been lucky twice. Once in hiring you, and again in being able to keep you."

Catherine looked at her quizzically. "I'm not sure how much luck had to do with keeping me. I heard how hard you pushed for me at the board meeting last week."

"I didn't say a thing I didn't mean one hundred percent. What about the Arceneaux house?"

"It's coming along beautifully," Catherine assured her. "We've been strengthening a couple of the floor joists, but the old-timers were right about that cypress. Most of it is still as strong as the day it was cut. It's such a wonderful house, Toni, even after all these years, and the move, it's still solid as a rock. The hardware is all handwrought iron, probably made on the place by the Arceneaux slaves. And it's cool inside, even in the heat we're having now, because the *bousillage* is a natural insulating material. The structural timbers are fastened together with wooden pegs..."

Toni smiled. "Catherine, look at your hands." Mystified, Catherine did. "You're even beginning to talk like a Cajun—with your hands. Is this the same person who so reluctantly agreed to work on this house three months ago?"

"I guess it is," Catherine said slowly. She looked up. Toni's brown eyes held amused understanding. "I've fallen in love with the house—and everything else here." *And with one Cajun in particular.* But Toni didn't know that; at least, Catherine hoped not.

"I knew you would."

"Is that what happened to you, Toni?" Catherine had always been curious about the cosmopolitan

Toni's background. "Did you come here and fall in love with it?"

"Beg pardon?" Toni looked blank.

"You're so enthusiastic about everything here, I've simply wondered when—and how—you learned to love it so."

"Catherine—" Pure amusement was beginning to show in Toni's elegant features. "I *am* from here. Born and bred in Franklin, right down the Teche from here." She spoke carefully, as if to a child. "I'm one hundred percent, pure-blooded Cajun. Didn't you know?"

"What?" Thunderstruck, Catherine groped for words. "I never dreamed," she gasped. "I thought you were from somewhere on the East Coast—" Realizing she was getting in deeper with every word she spoke, she floundered to a halt.

Toni burst out laughing. "Thank you—I think."

"I'd just assumed . . . never mind." Catherine had never felt so mortified in her life.

"I wasn't trying to keep anything from you," Toni said. "I guess it simply never occurred to me that you didn't know."

"But your name—"

"MacDonald's Doug's name, remember? My maiden name is Robichaux. Before I married Doug, I was Antoinette Robichaux."

"But why—"

"I'm like a lot of other people with strong cultural roots," Toni explained. "When I was growing up, I thought I had to deny them. So I went East for awhile. I spent several years in New York and thought I was

really something." She made a little self-mocking gri-
mace. "Then I got homesick in spite of myself and
moved to New Orleans. I figured that was a compromise. That's when I got into preservation work."
Her face lit up. "And that's how I met Doug. He was
working for the Corps of Engineers there. It's funny
how things happen." She smiled. "After we married,
he was transferred here, a few miles from where I was
reared. Back home for me."

"And now you love it."

"Of course. But do you know something, Catherine? It doesn't really matter where you live." She put
a hand on Catherine's arm. "If you're happy with
yourself, you'll be happy wherever you are."

"You're living proof of that."

"I've got to run—someone's coming by to discuss
a piece of furniture for the Arceneaux house. Keep
your fingers crossed that we can convince them to
donate it."

"I will. Bye, Toni." When she had gone, Catherine
stood in stunned silence. *Toni, a Cajun? That shows
me,* she thought. *Things are seldom what they seem...*
The old Gilbert and Sullivan line ran through her
mind. It seemed that she was being taught a few salu-
tary lessons, ones she was beginning to realize she
probably needed.

The phone rang.

"Ms Nolan?" A male voice came over the wire.

"Yes?"

"Lieutenant Vincent, with the New Iberia Police
Department. I wanted to let you know we've caught

the prowler you spotted at the restorations the other night.''

"Yes?" *Raymond Hebert*. Catherine held her breath and waited to hear the name.

"Yes, ma'am. It's a kid we've had an eye on a long time. He's not really bad, just on the verge of trouble. Someone saw him running away from the house, and we picked him up last night. He confessed, and his parents have promised to work with us to try to keep him out of worse trouble. I don't think he'll bother you again."

"Thank you, Officer." Catherine hung up the phone, deflated. Yet another lesson. Or was it? Maybe she had been wrong about Hebert, but instinct told her differently. Even so, she had fences to mend. She checked her watch, then picked up the phone and began to dial Blackie's number.

"That's okay, *chère*," Blackie said magnanimously, when she had apologized. "Everybody's wrong sometimes. I was once."

"I'm astounded to hear it." At least he felt like teasing her.

"Are you going to be in your office today?" he asked.

"I think so. Why?"

"Oh, I'll probably show up before the day's over," he said. Even as Catherine admonished herself not to get excited, her pulse jumped erratically at the thought of seeing him.

It was late in the afternoon before he appeared in her doorway. Their eyes met, and for a moment, she was transported to a world of dappled sunlight and shadows on still water—and Blackie's hands and lips working magic on her heated skin. Then a smaller figure appeared behind him.

"Uncle Bat!" She came around to meet him. "What brings you here?"

"I come to see how da Cajun house goin', me."

"Wonderful. We'll have a quick tour, if your chauffeur has the time."

"*Mais* sho', I've got time," Blackie said agreeably. "I want to see it myself."

"And I come to see you, too, *ma belle*," Uncle Bat added, a twinkle emerging from the depths of his unwinking black eyes.

"Watch it, *Nonc*," Blackie growled.

"I'm watching him," Catherine said. "I'm wise to his type."

"Hmph." Uncle Bat loftily ignored both of them. "Cat'rine—"

"Yes?"

"Somet'ing I mus' ask you, me."

"Name it."

"Careful," Blackie muttered.

"At da *bal de maison* you hear *mon beau violon*, and you do me *l'honneur* to dance to ma music. In t'ree, two weeks we gon' have a big *fais-do-do* in New Iberia. I invite you m'self, me. We give da money to you for fix' da Arceneaux house, us."

She was deeply touched. "I'm honored—and I'll be there," she promised, clasping his hands. She smiled questioningly at Blackie.

"It was his idea, Catherine," Blackie told her, looking at both of them fondly. "Come on," he said, jerking a thumb over his shoulder. At that moment, Catherine would have followed him anywhere. "Let's go look at the house. I've got to work on a fiddle this afternoon."

"Cat'rine, dis is sho' a *gran' maison*," Uncle Bat remarked, glancing around him as they walked down the lofty hallway of Bonne Journée. "Da Arceneaux house ain' near dis *gran'*."

"No, Uncle Bat, but it's just as important as Bonne Journée. Maybe even more so." A warm hand slipped into the crook of her arm, caressing the soft skin at her elbow. She looked up to meet Blackie's eyes, and had to look away quickly at what she saw there.

"Cat'rine, you foun' a *mamou* plant yet, for da yard?"

"Blackie's promised to bring me one," she answered, not yet daring to look up at him.

"*C'est bon,*" Uncle Bat pronounced. "I remin' him, me."

Laughing, they crossed the well-worn path from Bonne Journée to the Arceneaux house.

CHAPTER THIRTEEN

THE ANCIENT CYPRESS ARMOIRE stood in one of the back rooms of the Arceneaux house. Catherine ran knowledgeable hands over the old honey-colored wood. This was her first acquisition for the house, and it was a piece original to it.

A week ago, a tiny, elderly Cajun woman, brought to Catherine's office by her strapping son, had announced that she was the owner of a piece of furniture that had originally come from the house, and that she wished to donate it to the society.

"Are you descended from the Arceneaux?" Catherine had asked, wondering if she could have been lucky enough to find a direct descendant of Laura and Michel.

"Non, mamselle," the woman had replied. "Dis armoire come to ma *gran'mère* from da las' of da Arceneaux family. She was dere neighbor, her. Da Arceneaux who liv' in dis house are gone."

Disappointed but not really surprised, Catherine had begun verifying the story through available sources. Sure enough, she had found that, after Laura Arceneaux's death, Michel Arceneaux had never remarried. On his death, the house and part of the plantation land had gone to his and Laura's oldest son.

Somehow, the discovery that Michel had remained single after Laura's death had pleased Catherine; their love had indeed been real and, for them, forever. During the Civil War, the plantation, like so many, had fallen on hard times, and a couple of generations later, the property had been sold. It was a miracle, Catherine thought, that the house had been preserved at all.

At any rate, insofar as she could prove, this old armoire had indeed belonged to the Arceneaux—to Laura, in fact. It was superbly made. She opened its doors. Even after all these years, they moved easily and quietly on their handmade iron hinges. For a moment, she lingered, imagining. Laura Arceneaux had used this very piece of furniture, perhaps to store Michel's *cotonnade* work clothes, the children's baby things, even a fancy dress he had brought her from New Orleans. Perhaps she had stood, hand on the door, just as Catherine was standing now, for a moment of quiet thought in the middle of her busy day, thinking of Michel, her children, her parents....

"Need any help?" A female voice came from behind her. A very familiar voice.

Catherine whirled around. "Gussie!" She covered the distance between them in nothing flat, hugged her. She'd only been gone a month, but it seemed like a year. "What are you doing here? Just visiting?"

Gussie shook her head. "I've come home."

"For good?" Catherine hardly dared believe it.

"For good." For a moment, the pain was there, in her face. "The longer I stayed away from Alain, the more I realized that life without him doesn't mean much.''

"Oh, Gussie. I'd hoped you'd see things that way. What happened to change your mind?''

"He came to New Orleans to talk to me.'' Gussie chuckled. "But when he got to my apartment, I was all packed up to come home, to talk to him. Once we saw each other, it didn't take long for us to decide we needed each other more than anything.

"It's a funny thing,'' she mused. "Alain and I were so sure we were doing the right thing by not marrying each other. But after a while, nothing seemed as important to us as just being together. Sure, I'm still sorry we can't have our own *bébés*. But if we adopt, they'll be *our* kids, and Alain will be their father. That's all that counts. Whatever happens, Alain and I were meant to face it together.''

"No question about it,'' Catherine said, smiling. She studied Gussie's piquant little face. The *joie de vivre* was back in her expression, and now a look of fulfillment. But underlying the happiness was something else. Not a sadness, exactly—it was more of a new maturity. In life, the trick was to play the hand you were dealt. And Gussie was playing her hand well. Catherine wasn't surprised.

"Catherine—have you hired someone to replace me?''

"I—never got around to it.'' She smiled. "Maybe I knew you'd be back.''

"Thanks.'' Her face radiant, Gussie looked around, already noting, absorbing. "So,'' she said, "catch me up on everything that's been going on.''

Fifteen minutes later, Catherine had told Gussie everything she could think of about the two projects. "Now," Gussie said, "tell me what's really going on."

"I just did," Catherine said.

"No, I mean what's going on with you." She eyed Catherine shrewdly. "I've never seen you look so happy. You've got new roses in your cheeks. Did Blackie put them there?" she asked with her usual directness.

Did it show so much? Catherine wondered. "Well, I—" She hesitated, not knowing what to say.

"Never mind. I know he did." Gussie patted her hand. "Don't be embarrassed. You and Blackie are perfect for each other."

"How can you think so?" Catherine walked restlessly to the window and stared at the unfinished archaeological dig. "We couldn't possibly be more different. Oh, I'll admit I probably care too much for him." She'd never before spoken such a private thought, but it seemed her life was moving over uncharted ground these days.

"And Blackie?"

"Blackie and I have made no commitment to each other. I think he likes me well enough . . ."

"Oh, come on, Catherine."

"Well, then, he's attracted to me," Catherine amended, feeling her face grow warm.

"Watch those roses." Gussie chuckled.

"But I still worry about our differences," Catherine said.

"Listen to me," Gussie said, suddenly serious. "If you love somebody, it's worth more than anything else you'll ever have in your life. I know."

Catherine's throat tightened. Too bad things really weren't that simple. "Well, maybe things will work out," she said lamely, not believing her own words. Looking at the situation objectively, there seemed to be no solution at all. "In the meantime, welcome back. Things will be a lot more fun with you around to share them."

"Thanks. Do you want me to start work this afternoon?"

"I don't think so. It's almost time to quit, and anyway, I'm planning to leave a little early myself."

"Okay. Expect me Monday morning, then. And, Catherine," she said over her shoulder, "don't forget what I said."

"All right," Catherine promised. She thought a moment, then fished her grocery list out of her purse and checked it carefully. Some of these ingredients might be hard to find. Her insides fluttered a little in anticipation—tonight, after being out of town a week, Blackie was coming to her apartment for dinner, and she was going to feed him *haute cuisine*.

THE KNOCK, FIRM, ASSERTIVE, sounded on the door to Catherine's apartment. Her heart jumped. She automatically lifted a hand to her chignon, then remembered. Tonight she had arranged her hair to fall softly to her shoulders. Feeling wanton, she ran her fingers through it, tossed it back.

She had dressed with particular care, choosing a simple dress of jade-green silk that hugged her waist before falling in soft folds to the hemline. As she walked to the door, the fabric whispered against her, making her body come alive with remembered sensations.

She opened the door, a greeting on her lips, but stood transfixed instead. In place of the usual jeans and work shirt, Blackie wore tailored black slacks and a short-sleeved knit shirt of a vivid cherry red. Paired with his dark coloring, it made him look good enough to eat.

"Comment ça va, chère?" A lazy little grin played across his mouth.

"Blackie..." she floundered for a moment. "You look wonderful," she finally managed, sounding inane to her own ears. "I almost didn't know you."

"Didn't know me?" The grin turned wicked. "I thought we were better acquainted than that."

At the memory of their lovemaking, excitement shivered down her spine. "That's not what I..." she began, but before she could say more, Blackie stepped inside the doorway and pulled her to him for a quick, searing kiss.

"Now do you recognize me?" He chuckled as she stepped back, dazed, the little currents of pleasure now running unchecked through her body.

"I'm—not sure." She pretended to hesitate. "Again, please?"

"Anything to oblige, *chère*." This time he brought her into his arms, and the kiss was longer, deeper.

Catherine closed her eyes and gave herself up to the feel, the taste of him. A week was a long time.

She smiled hazily at him. "It's all coming back to me now."

"Speaking of looks—" He held her away from him, his eyes luminous with pleasure, then reached out and gently touched her hair. "You're easy to look at, you know. If you'd like to put off dinner a while..."

"Absolutely not. I've spent half the evening preparing this food, and we're going to eat it."

"Oh? Smells good." Like a little boy, he followed his nose into the kitchen, with Catherine, between amusement and exasperation, behind him.

She walked in just as he was lifting the lid from the pot on the stove. He inhaled appreciatively. "Mmm—coq au vin?"

"As a matter of fact, it is," Catherine answered in surprise.

He looked hurt. "Please, *p'tite*, give a man a little credit, will you? I've been out of the swamps a few times in my life, even as far as New Orleans. Besides, I know everything there is to know about eating."

Catherine laughed and shook her head. "Do you go to New Orleans often?" She measured out cognac from the bottle on the counter.

"Whenever I get a chance," he answered.

"What do you like to do?" she asked curiously, pouring the cognac over the chicken and preparing to ignite it.

He laughed. "Have fun. What else? That's what New Orleans is for." He took the matches from her hand, struck one and touched it to the liquid. "Eat, go hear a band. Pete Fountain, Preservation Hall. There're even some places that play pretty good Cajun music—not as good as mine, of course." He shot her a provocative look. "Sometimes I even go to the symphony or the opera."

Catherine stopped in the act of spooning in mushrooms and onions. Had she heard right? "Do you mean to tell me you like opera?"

"It's music, isn't it?" He shrugged, then grinned at her. "But don't tell anybody—it might ruin my image."

"Blackie, you're impossible." Catherine lifted the chicken onto a platter, then ladled the savory sauce over it.

"No, *bébé*, I just do what I like to do," he explained, dipping the tip of his finger in the sauce and licking it appreciatively. "If I want to play and sing Cajun music, I do it. If I want to hear opera, I go to New Orleans. If I want to eat Cajun food, I go home. If I want coq au vin, I go to a fancy restaurant—or con a good-looking woman into fixing it for me." He cocked a black brow at her. "What's so wrong with that?"

"Nothing, actually." His logic was unimpeachable. She carried the dish into the little dining alcove, where the table was elegantly and intimately set for two. She touched a match to two slender tapers in silver candlesticks and cut off the overhead lights. "Just as long as it's the right woman," she said, smiling at him as she retrieved the rest of the wine from the kitchen.

"Cat'rine," Blackie said as he took the bottle from her and deftly poured their wine, "I promise I'll never let anyone cook coq au vin for me but you."

"I'll remember that," Catherine said, and realized a little sadly that it was the nearest they had ever come to a commitment. Probably the nearest they *would* ever come. She pushed the thought from her mind. She would have him for tonight—for as long as she could.

She set the side dishes on the table. "Are you ready to eat?"

"Certainement, mamselle," Blackie replied, seating her with a flourish and taking his own chair.

By the time they had finished eating, Catherine knew a great deal more about Blackie's interests than she had. But the suspicion persisted that, as long as she knew him, he would continue to surprise her.

"Ma belle," he said, putting down his linen napkin and leaning back in satisfaction, "why aren't you a gourmet cook instead of a restoration architect?"

"I do enjoy cooking, when I have the time," she said, disproportionately pleased by the compliment. "I'm glad you enjoyed it."

"That's an understatement," he said, as he rose and took her hand. "Now, about dessert..." His voice was husky. He reached for her, his eyes on her face. "Ah, Cat'rine," he said, "I can't sleep for wanting you." His eyes were dark pools of longing. The pungent smell of the smoking candles mingled in her nostrils with the piquant aroma of his after-shave, making her head swim. His hands were warm on her arms. The undercurrent of desire that all evening had eddied between them suddenly caught them both, pulling them irresistibly into each other's arms.

He held her for a long moment, then broke away to bring his mouth down on hers. She could taste the wine on his lips, could feel the urgency within him, in the tightening of his muscles, the growing hardness of his body.

Blackie's mouth left hers and trailed to her neck, to her throat, where her pulse beat so frantically. Over the rushing in her ears, she heard herself whimper. His hand found her breast, and she felt the contact course through her body.

He raised his head, and she was lost in the darkness of his eyes. She saw his nostrils flare with the effort of breathing.

"I want to hold you," he said thickly.

She took him by the hand and led him down the hall to her pristine little bedroom. A dim light from a bed-side lamp threw half the room in shadow. This was the first time a man had ever entered this room, she thought irrelevantly.

"*Dieu*, I can't get enough of you," he whispered hoarsely. His fingers, not quite steady, found her zipper, and the dress floated in a shimmer of silk to the floor. He undressed her quickly, ran his fingers down her body, skimming her breasts, her thighs.

All at once she was starved for him. Reserve, caution, reason evaporated as though they had never been. She only knew that this man kindled in her a raging need that she was powerless to control. As he began to unbutton his shirt, she reached out a hand to stop him. "No," she said. "Let me."

He stood as she stripped off his shirt, and she could feel his muscles trembling. Unable to resist the sight of his chest, she touched it, reveling in the feel of the taut skin. In her haste, she fumbled with the catch on his slacks, and he helped her with it, his hands as unsteady as hers.

She turned down the covers and, taking his hand, drew him to her. They lay down together, their bodies entangling. Never in her life had she experienced such turbulent, violent need.

"Cat'rine—"

She hushed him with her mouth, frantically, desperately. Urging him onto his back, she took delight in the look of stunned surprise on his face. For now, for this moment, he was hers, and she was going to claim him. Every inch of him.

She felt her body begin to blossom again with the sweet, molten warmth as she trailed her mouth over his chest. She could hear his breath rasping softly in his throat. She wanted all of him, this man who had shown her what needing someone—and having someone—could mean. He had given her a priceless gift—a part of herself she hadn't known was missing. She wanted to give him back his own.

Her lips traveled across his stomach, rock-hard and quivering under them. She let her tongue linger, absorbing the salty-sweet taste of his damp, heated skin.

"Cat'rine—don't—" With a moan from deep within him, Blackie caught her with a brawny arm and rolled her to her back, covered her with his body. "I can't—*Dieu*—'' He thrust into her, filled her, set a desperate pace.

Catherine met him, glorying in his lack of control. She felt his muscles tense, his whole body move with an ever more urgent rhythm. With a cry, he went rigid. Catherine arched into him, then tumbled into a pulsing sea of sweet, sweet agony.

It subsided, leaving her as vulnerable as a newborn child. She heard his broken murmur—French endearments—but only caught the last phrase. She wasn't sure, but in the cocoon of silence that surrounded them, she thought he said *Je t'aime*. I love you.

THEY LAY TOGETHER, drained, as reality began to form itself around them. After a little while or an eternity, she didn't know, he propped himself up on one elbow to loom above her. His hand came to cherish her, and in his dark, dark eyes there was a world of tenderness. It still wasn't time for words, but she had a favor to ask him.

"Blackie." She reached up to cradle his face, to thread her fingers through his damp curls.

"Oui?" His dazed voice sounded as though he had never spoken English in his life.

"Tomorrow is Saturday. Will you . . ."

"Dis-moi," he prompted gently, his breath still coming uneven against her cheek.

"Stay with me tonight?" she whispered. "I want to fall asleep in your arms." Saying the words brought a fleeting wonder at herself.

He searched her face and seemed satisfied. Then, "I want it, too, darlin'—more than anything," he said quietly. He covered her, tucking the sheet and blanket around her as tenderly as if she had been a baby, then lay down beside her and drew her to him, settling her against his strong, warm body. In his arms, she felt a euphoric sense of well-being she had never experienced—except once before, in the same place. In a few seconds, she heard his breathing deepen, grow even, and she knew he slept. As she sank into the comfortable depths of her own fading consciousness, the endearment he had whispered in the afterglow of their lovemaking came back to sing in her mind like a lullaby.

Je t'aime. I love you.

CATHERINE AWOKE in the half-light of early dawn. Her body was curled comfortably against Blackie's, and she lay with her head on his shoulder. His arm lay across her, his hand cradling her breast.

He stirred in his sleep, and she eased her head around to look at his face. His hair lay across his forehead in tousled curls, and the one day's growth of beard showed blue-black on the lower half of his face. Black lashes, long as a woman's, swept his cheeks, belying the hard line of his jaw. He looked younger, more vulnerable, but the shadow of pain was gone.

Slowly, as if sensing her scrutiny, he opened his eyes. *"Bonjour,"* he whispered huskily, his eyes devouring her features, lingering in fascination at the mass of silver-gilt hair spread over the pillow. With his fingers, he traced the line of her jaw, her nose, her cheekbones, a look almost of awe on his face. Then he bent to her, and his lips, soft as the mists from the bayou, replaced his fingers, moving along her hair-line, behind the lobe of her ear, to the corner of her mouth.

She saw desire mist his eyes, and his fingers tightened on her arms. She felt his body, so close against hers, begin to change, and felt the answering current begin to stir her own body, to awaken it to throbbing life again. When his mouth came down on hers, she was ready for him.

CATHERINE AWOKE AGAIN, from a heavy sleep. The sun was shining through the gaps in the draperies. The space next to her was empty, and she could hear the television in the next room. She glanced at her clock radio. Nine o'clock. As she fought to clear her head, Blackie appeared in the doorway, dressed, with two cups of steaming coffee in his hands.

"Bonjour, paresseuse," he said, grinning. "I finally had to fix my own coffee." He set her cup on the bedside table, then sat on the edge of the bed. Before she could stop herself, Catherine made a small, instinctive movement to pull the sheet up over her breasts. Blackie laughed out loud. "It's a little late for that, *chère*."

"I was just—" Catherine stopped and smiled. "I suppose it is a little silly." Still, she didn't drop the sheet.

"Catherine..." She heard the laughter fade from his voice. He tipped up her chin to meet his eyes. "You're beautiful." For an instant his eyes darkened, and his fingers tightened on her chin. "There's no need to be ashamed of anything. Anything,'' he repeated with emphasis.

''Would you believe I'm not?'' she said softly, in wonder.

''Good,'' Blackie said gently. He touched his lips to hers in a fleeting, tender kiss. ''Drink your coffee before it gets cold. It tastes bad enough hot.''

''Good heavens,'' Catherine said after one sip. ''How much instant did you put in here?''

''Oh, enough to make it respectable,'' he answered.

''Respectable is not the word I'd use,'' Catherine said, grimacing.

''It's not the word I first had in mind,'' Blackie said. ''But I don't think you'd like that one, either. Unless I said it in French.''

''Very funny. Why do you have the TV on?''

''There's another hurricane building up in the gulf, the sixth this year. Uncle Bat was right. This has really been a season for storms.''

''They've all missed us so far.'' On such a sunshiny morning, when her personal world was so at peace, it was hard for Catherine to imagine catastrophe.

''I hope this one does, too. But I want to keep an eye on it just the same. We may be pushing our luck.''

Catherine stretched. ''I suppose I'd better get moving,'' she said reluctantly. ''Do you—ah—want to wait in the living room?''

''No, I think I'll wait right here.'' Blackie sipped his coffee.

''How about handing me my robe, then?''

"Nope." Blackie shook his head. "I might miss a lovely view."

"*S'il vous plaît?*" Catherine cocked her head in a perfect imitation of him.

Blackie shouted with laughter. "Well, if you put it that way..." Rising, he gave her a quick, hard kiss and headed for her closet.

They were lingering at the dining room table, drinking coffee and eating croissants and using any excuse to touch each other, when the phone rang. Catherine frowned, unwilling for anything to break the spell. "Oops! Be right back." She rose to answer. "Hello?"

"Good morning, Catherine." As though from another planet, the measured, even tones of Gerrard Nolan came over the wire. Catherine's eyes flew guiltily to Blackie.

"Gerrard! Good morning," she blurted. Blackie raised a brow.

"Did I wake you?" Gerrard asked.

"No, not—not at all," she stammered.

"Good. I won't keep you long. Are you well? I haven't heard from you lately."

"Oh, very well, thanks. I've just been busy." She glanced again at Blackie, who examined the ceiling.

"I've received some nice reports on your work at Bonne Journée."

"Thank you, Gerrard," Catherine returned politely. *How like him to check on me,* she thought. For the first time in her life, she felt resentment toward him.

"I've called to tell you that I've worked everything out for the Athens project," he explained. "One of the conditions of my accepting the job was that they budget money for an assistant, and I'm offering you the position. I think you're ready for it." *In other words,* Catherine thought, *this is a genteel way of telling me what I'm going to do.*

"I see," she said. She didn't look at Blackie, but she could feel his eyes fixed watchfully on her. "What's the time frame on the job?"

"We'll begin in January. By then, I think Bonne Journée will be near enough finished to turn over to an assistant."

"But I've got to finish the other project. Remember? The Arceneaux house."

"Oh, yes." Catherine could imagine him waving a hand in casual dismissal. "I'd forgotten about that. See if someone local can take over."

"I . . . don't know if that's possible," she said, her eyes flicking to Blackie.

"Of course it is." Gerrard's even tones never varied by the slightest inflection. "This new job is an important career move for you." He paused, but Catherine said nothing. "You need to come to Atlanta next week," he went on.

"Next week?" She saw Blackie tense.

"Yes. Then we'll have time to talk before your interview with the Athens board. Although, since I've agreed to hire you, that should just be a formality."

"All right, Gerrard." She wanted to say no, but couldn't quite do it.

"Good, it's settled. I'll see you next week." With a click, the line went dead.

She hung up, leaned her head against the door-jamb. Before she had to tell Blackie, she wanted to keep what they had shared, hug it to her for just a little longer. But it was no use. This was the moment they had been heading for from the beginning. She walked slowly to the table.

"What was that all about?" He was carefully keeping his voice neutral, but she knew he was concerned.

"Gerrard has offered me a job as his assistant in Athens, Georgia, starting in January." She spoke in a rush, thinking she might somehow take the hurt from the words.

"In January? You won't be finished with the projects by then." He shoved his coffee cup away.

"Bonne Journée will be complete, all but a few details. The Arceneaux house won't." She had said it. They were both going to be hurt. She had known it. He should have known it.

Blackie's eyes narrowed. "You told him you had to finish the Arceneaux house. What did he say to that?"

"He said—" She couldn't bring herself to quote Gerrard. "He thinks this job is too important for me to pass up."

"Important for you or for him?" Blackie stood, and she saw the anger smoldering deep in his eyes. She didn't want to look at him, but forced herself to meet his eyes. "He's asking you to drop everything, run to help him and damn the consequences. That hardly sounds as if it's in your best interests."

For a moment, she didn't answer. No matter what, Catherine knew she had to go back. In Atlanta lay security, everything she had worked for. She couldn't give it up for something unknown—the risk was too great. "I'm just going for the interview," she said finally. "It doesn't mean I have to take the job."

"But he expects you to, so you will." It was a flat statement. She hadn't fooled him a bit. Angrily, he jammed his hands into his pockets, but she saw the hurt flicker in his eyes.

"I owe him, Blackie, both gratitude and money. You know that."

"But you don't owe him your life," he said tautly. "You can't live in his shadow forever."

"I've got to try to repay my debts."

"You pay your debts, but you don't bother to fulfill your obligations. What about the Arceneaux house?" The question hung in the air between them.

She looked down. He had her there. She knew she was running out on it. "The society can hire someone to take my place, and Gussie can help. Maybe they can find someone local." Even to her own ears, her words sounded lame.

He turned away from her and paced to the window. "How long will you be gone?"

"I'll leave this Tuesday, and I should be back the following Tuesday or Wednesday. Gussie can handle everything until then."

"Everything?" He turned around, his eyes flashing black fire. Involuntarily, she stepped back. "What about Uncle Bat's *fais-do-do* next Saturday? The one he's doing for you?" he added bitingly.

"Oh, no." She closed her eyes. Everything was crashing around her. "I...I forgot about that, Blackie. I'll talk to him. I'll just have to hope he understands."

"Don't bother." He made an abrupt, dismissive motion. "I forgot something, too. I forgot you've got your own fish to fry, and you're not going to be frying them here, no matter who it hurts." He jerked a hand through his hair. "I thought you had learned to care for this job—for all of us."

"I do care for all of you," she said desperately. "A great deal. But I've got to work for a living, remember? I can't pass up an opportunity like this one, because it'll lead to more jobs. After I finish the Arceneaux house, there'll be nothing for me here."

The moment she said it, she could have bitten out her tongue. Blackie looked as if she had struck him.

"If that's the way you feel, then you'd better go," he said, white lipped. He headed for the door, but stopped with his hand on the knob. When he turned, she saw that the anger had drained out of his eyes, leaving only the pain. "What about us, Catherine? Can you walk away from what we've had?"

The question hurt her more than his anger. Her eyes filled. "What we've had together—you and I—means more to me than you'll ever know," she said past the lump in her throat. "I've wanted so badly to be a part of your world. But from the beginning, I've known I couldn't."

"Catherine—" He held out his hand, and she wanted nothing more than to go to him. But she knew she couldn't. Blindly, she shook her head, and his arms dropped. "You're afraid," he said simply. "*Pauvre p'tite.* You're afraid of yourself." His voice was ineffably weary. "For a while there, I thought we might make it. *Au 'voir,* Cat'rine." Then he was gone.

CHAPTER FOURTEEN

"GOOD MORNING, DEAREST." Elizabeth Nolan rose gracefully from the breakfast table.

Mother always looked as though she was about to confer knighthood on someone, Catherine thought, amusement momentarily overriding the ever-present ache in her heart. "Good morning, Mother." She kissed Elizabeth's cheek and sat opposite her.

"Did you sleep well?" Elizabeth asked.

"Not very. The drive probably tired me out too much," Catherine hedged. She wasn't about to go into the sleepless nights, the gray days, the general feeling that nothing was going to be right, ever again.

"You're looking awfully thin," her mother commented in the same perfectly modulated voice. "You must not be eating properly."

The trouble isn't my diet, Mother. But Catherine, remembering her mother's singular ability to block out explanations that didn't suit her, said nothing.

Covertly, she studied Elizabeth. Although she had always been told she looked like her father, she knew that in some ways—carriage, mannerisms—she resembled her mother. Now she looked at the permanent lines of discontent worn into Elizabeth's features and hoped that was where the resemblance stopped.

"Come and have your coffee," Elizabeth said. "These croissants are from that little bakery, remember? You used to love their things."

"I do remember, and these look delicious." But they didn't. Nothing had lately.

Elizabeth poured her coffee from the silver pot. "It's wonderful to have you home again. I don't see why Gerrard couldn't have worked this out a long time ago. You've lived on the edge of civilization long enough."

"Louisiana's not the edge of civilization, Mother." Catherine knew how her mother felt about Louisiana. But now, for some reason, she could feel her hackles rising. "You do understand that I have to go back, at least temporarily, don't you?"

Elizabeth came as close to looking displeased as she ever did. "No, I don't suppose I realized that. Gerrard indicated that after you went to collect your things and to take care of a few loose ends, you would be home for good."

Catherine shook her head. "I'll still have to finish Bonne Journée. Besides, I haven't definitely committed myself to the job in Athens," some imp of perversity made her add.

"But Gerrard has it all worked out. If he thinks it best, I'm sure you'll take the job." She sipped her coffee, complacent in her own artificial little world.

With an effort, Catherine squelched her exasperation. She had almost forgotten what life with Mother was like. Or was it the reference to Gerrard's controlling her life that irked her? "We'll see," she said,

shamelessly deflecting Elizabeth's insistence. "I'm
sure everything will work out for the best."

"Of course it will." Elizabeth passed the butter and
marmalade, her equanimity restored.

Catherine took a deep breath. Suddenly her
mother's elegant little Haversham Street apartment,
perfectly scaled and furnished with family heirlooms
in the very best taste, seemed awfully small. No, it
wasn't the size, it was the atmosphere. It was cold,
impersonal, stifling. Catherine remembered Zema's
kitchen the morning after the *bal de maison*, warm,
busy, full of good smells...

"Now that you're home," Elizabeth continued,
"we can have a small gathering here, sometime in the
next few days. It might be nice, don't you think? So
many of your old friends are still here."

"I'm not really going to be here very long," Catherine reminded her patiently. "I'm driving to Athens
Friday morning to take a look at the building. Then,
the early part of next week, I'll be going back to
Louisiana."

"That shouldn't be a problem." Elizabeth inclined
her perfectly coiffed head. "I'm not talking about
anything complicated, maybe tea next Monday afternoon, just for a few friends." She poured more coffee for herself, then filled Catherine's cup. "Oh, I
nearly forgot. Todd and Emily Woodward are di-
vorcing. Such a shame." She looked anything but displeased.

Here we go, Catherine thought. Todd Woodward,
her high-school sweetheart who, she had heard, had
already crawled into his bourbon bottle. Trust her

mother to resurrect someone like him. "No, you didn't. But from what I've heard, Todd has a drinking problem, and I don't want to start something I've no intention of pursuing," she said bluntly.

"Oh, I don't think Todd has a real drinking problem," Elizabeth protested mildly. "Perhaps he does take a bit too much now and again, on special occasions, but nothing serious."

A talent for self-delusion like her mother's occurred only once an age, Catherine reflected. Her father's early death had been a direct result of alcoholism. In his quest to avoid all responsibility, John Nolan had found increasingly numerous "special occasions" to blot out unpleasant realities, until life had become one continuous special occasion. But she was just now coming to realize how much her mother had contributed to his problem.

"Maybe not, but he's a complication I don't need right now." Realizing the futility of discussion, Catherine stood. "I'd better get dressed. I'm supposed to meet Gerrard at the Driving Club, and I don't want to be late."

"Dear Gerrard," her mother said. "He took me there for lunch last week. It was so good to be back. Hurry on, then. You know he doesn't like to be kept waiting."

Grateful for the dismissal, Catherine fled upstairs to dress, leaving her mother to preside over the remaining croissants.

She looked hurriedly through the things she had brought, searching for something suitable to wear to lunch at the most exclusive private club in Atlanta.

Dull, dull, dull, she thought. Everything she owned was dull.

Her hand touched the ivory linen dress that she had worn to that first *fais-do-do*, the night she had met Blackie. At the thought of him, pain pierced her again, this time so sharply that it stole her breath. She couldn't keep thoughts of him at bay—not for long. All throughout the sweltering drive to Atlanta yesterday, she'd had plenty of time to think, plenty of time to rehash the events just prior to her departure.

She had gone to Toni first, then to Clarence, had been entirely frank with them both. They had been understanding—in fact, their sympathy had made it even harder for her to leave.

"Of course you must go, *chère*," Clarence had told her. "I'll just pray you don't take the job. We want you here. If things don't work out, come back. We'll always find something."

Toni had been more direct. "I don't want to influence you, Catherine, but between us, Clarence and I probably have enough connections to help you find work around here, if you decide to come back to us. And I hope you do," she added impulsively. Catherine had been deeply touched at their caring.

When she had asked Gussie to take charge of the two restorations in her absence, the younger woman had waved away her apologies, and her knowing eyes had taken in the misery she saw in Catherine's face. "Come back to us, Catherine," she had whispered. "Blackie may not know it right now, but he needs you."

Lucky Gussie, to be so secure in her love and to have it so surely reciprocated. Catherine couldn't reply because she had no answer. But she had asked a favor of Gussie. On the day before her departure, she and Gussie had left work a little early and had driven past Morgan City to Uncle Bat's house, because Catherine had not been sure she could find the way.

With Gussie's help, she had painstakingly explained the situation to the old man, and although he seemed disappointed she wouldn't be at the *fais-do-do*, he had understood.

"Cat'rine, *ma belle*, why you worry so about work, you?" he had asked. "Why you not let ma wort'less Ti-neg take care for you, *hein*?"

"He doesn't want to do that, Uncle Bat. I—I don't think he likes me any more." And to her horror, her eyes had filled with tears. They seemed so close to the surface these days.

"Sacré misère!" The old man launched into a rapid stream of French that had Gussie laughing and covering her ears. Recollecting himself, he took Catherine's hand and patted it gently. *"Ça me fait de la peine,"* he said sadly. "It hurt me here." He placed a gnarled hand on his chest. *"Mignonne*, I unnerstan' you have to go. Ever't'ing fine. Excep' ma *imbécile*…"* He muttered ominously in French. "Come see ol' *Nonc* when you come back," he told her. "I straighten out dis mess, me."

"I will, Uncle Bat," she said, not having the heart to tell him she would probably never be back to stay. "I'll always keep in touch. And thank you." This old man had become infinitely dear to her. Whatever else happened in her life, wherever she spent her days, she would carry his image in her heart.

She had left before she shed more tears. It was a shame that Uncle Bat blamed Blackie, but their relationship would survive it, she knew. Early the next morning she had left for Atlanta. And here she was. She was going to have to make the best of whatever happened.

Catherine finally chose a suit of dove-gray raw silk and a tailored white blouse and tied a red and gray paisley scarf at her neck. Once she would have found no fault with her appearance; now, she knew she looked fatigued, lifeless. Dull. The Louisiana influence had rubbed off on her, she thought, amusement warring with sadness. About one Jean Beausoleil Broussard, *dit* Blackie, she tried not to think at all. But she couldn't stop the ache from the gaping void in her heart, sometimes dull, sometimes acute, but always there, hovering just at the edge of her consciousness, ready to overtake her when she least expected it.

CATHERINE STEPPED INSIDE the door of the Piedmont Driving Club, noting that it hadn't changed since she had left. But that was hardly surprising, since it hadn't changed within her memory. That was part of its aristocratic tradition. The large, high-ceilinged reception area had the same comfortably used yet exquisite antique tables and chairs; the same fine oils hung on the walls. Even the scent was still the same. How many times had she come with her parents to this place? And how many times in the past few years had she met Gerrard here? For every stage of her life, she could recall a memory of the Driving Club.

A tall, gray-haired man in a perfectly tailored charcoal suit rose from a nearby seating area and came leisurely toward her.

"Gerrard." He was in his sixties by now, but he never seemed to change. She held out her hands to him in genuine pleasure.

"Catherine." He took her hands, bestowed a formal kiss on her cheek. His pale green eyes, which Catherine knew from experience never missed a single thing, rested on her a moment. "I'm delighted to see you," he said. "You're looking a little thin."

"So Mother tells me." How like them both to notice, Catherine thought. And to comment.

"Come in—our table's ready." He indicated the dining room, and instantly the maître d', a dapper-looking man just past middle age, materialized beside them, ready to lead them into the inner sanctum.

"Good day, Mr. Nolan," he said with courteous dignity. "How are you and Miss Nolan today?"

"Albert." Gerrard nodded absently.

Catherine, who had never quite gotten over her awe at Albert's memory for names, smiled. "Fine, Albert," she responded. "How are you?"

"Fine, miss." He gave her a perfect little bow. "It's good to see you. If you'll step this way, please."

"I'll acquaint you with the details of the job as we eat." Gerrard took her arm as they moved toward the dining room. Although always impeccably correct, he never wasted more time on the amenities than was necessary. The rare times Catherine had ever seen him animated had been when he was discussing his work.

An hour and a half and a marvelous lunch later, Catherine knew all she needed to know about the proposed job. When Gerrard had described it as an important career move, he had understated the case. It was much more than that. It was Catherine's dream, her chance to accomplish the goals she'd set for herself. Afterward, Gerrard would take her into partnership as his assistant. He'd implied as much during lunch.

The real problem, of course, was the Arceneaux house. She hadn't mentioned it today, and neither had Gerrard. She was sure he had forgotten about it.

"Gerrard..." She hesitated. "I told you I had one problem with the time frame on this job."

Gerrard's brows rose a fraction. "The little Acadian house? I thought you had settled that."

Catherine winced as she recognized her own words—and former attitude—being unwittingly thrown in her face. "Not quite. I had no idea you'd have anything for me this soon, so I agreed to handle the restoration. I—I gave my word."

"That's unfortunate." He frowned. "You'll miss the opportunity of a lifetime. Why don't you just resign?"

Catherine took a deep breath. "I don't think I could reconcile it with my conscience."

"People do it all the time," he said evenly. He glanced at his watch. "I have to run. I have a two o'clock appointment." He brushed an invisible speck of dust from his sleeve. "You have a meeting in

Athens Friday morning at ten o'clock with the directors of the project."

"I'll be there. Thanks for lunch, Gerrard. And I'll think about the proposal."

"I can't see that there's anything to think about," he said mildly. "I'll drop by your mother's for cocktails around six."

"I'll see you then." Catherine hurried out of the exclusive club, feeling as if the familiar walls were suddenly closing in on her.

LATE FRIDAY AFTERNOON, Catherine stood in her room, staring blindly out the window, trying to sort out her tangled thoughts and feelings. As Gerrard had dictated, she had met with the directors of the Athens project and had toured the proposed restoration, a beautiful Greek Revival mansion very like Bonne Journée. It was a measure of Gerrard's prestige that they had been willing to hire her before the interview. The job would be her ticket to a prestigious career, not to mention financial stability. She had only to make the final commitment and the job was hers. Instead, she had told them she would consider it.

Why hadn't she accepted the job outright? If she neglected this opportunity, she might never have another like it. Actually, another competent restoration architect could finish the Arceneaux house, and she already knew that no one there would hold anything against her if she left. And as far as her personal life was concerned, there was nothing to hold her in Louisiana—not any longer.

On the other hand, she had given her word that she would restore the Arceneaux house. She gazed through the tall pines at the city that had always been her home. Even if the little house wouldn't establish her reputation nationally as a restoration architect, it was very important to her, and to the people whose heritage it represented—the people she had grown to love.

Suddenly, memories came flooding back: the Arceneaux house, battered and forlorn, riding up the Teche on a modern-day barge; her vow, in the warm twilight that evening, to make a good job of it, for her friends and for herself; the mystical kinship she had felt, first with Eleanor Millard, the chatelaine of Bonne Journée, then with Eleanor's daughter Laura Millard Arceneaux, who had followed her own heart to happiness. The bright fragments of memory shimmered, faded, sharpened again. Gussie teasing her; Clarence waving the funding report over his head in jubilation; Gussie again, her young face ravaged with grief; Toni, gently confirming her Cajun heritage when Catherine should have seen it all along. Uncle Bat. And Blackie...

Blackie. His image suddenly sprang full-blown into her mind, so vivid she felt as though she might reach out and touch him. And with it, the pain, knife-sharp. In flesh or in spirit, he had the power to pierce her to her soul. He had accused her of being afraid, and she had been—of many things, but mostly of herself. She had lost him, as she had somehow known she would. But he had changed her forever.

She turned from the window and wandered to the dresser, picked up a framed photograph, an old snapshot of herself and her father. It had sat on her dresser since it had been taken, but she hadn't really looked at it in years. It showed a handsome young man and a little girl, both blonde, both slender, both obviously excited about their outing together. Looking at it, she saw in her father's face, so like her own, the *joie de vivre* she had loved in him but had come to despise. And his love for her. Her eyes misted over.

In that moment, she knew what she would do—had to do.

CATHERINE RANG THE DOORBELL of Gerrard's palatial Peachtree Road residence. Gerrard answered the door; it was getting on toward six o'clock and his servants had gone for the day. Like his ancestors, he had retained servants all his life, and he could well afford them; unlike her father, he had hung on to his inherited wealth, then had augmented it with the fruits of his formidable career.

"Thanks for letting me come by, Gerrard," she said. "I know it's late."

"No, indeed," he said imperturbably. "Come in, Catherine. We'll have a drink in the study, and you can tell me about the meeting this morning."

"It went very well," she told him as he ushered her through the spacious rooms of the mansion. "The restoration is everything you said it was. White wine, please," she replied to his questioning glance.

He indicated a Queen Anne wing chair by his desk, and she sat down while he prepared their drinks from a well-equipped bar. How many times had she sat in this very study, in this very chair, in fact, while Gerrard talked to her, first about her dream of a career in restoration architecture, then finally of the reality? Too many to count.

Gerrard handed her the wine and took an identical wing chair opposite her. He settled himself comfortably with his George Dickel and water, his customary drink for as long as Catherine could remember.

She took a firm hold on her courage. It was impossible to predict how Gerrard was going to react, because, quite simply, she'd never gone against his wishes before. But this time she knew she had to do it.

She took a large swallow of wine. "Gerrard, I'm not going to take the job on the Athens project," she said bluntly.

"Oh?" His expression never changed. But she had never known him to betray surprise, or any other emotion, for that matter. "That's too bad," he said finally. "I was looking forward to working with you."

"Aren't you surprised at all?" she asked.

"Not really." Gerrard took a leisurely sip of bourbon. "When you mentioned something about having given your word the other day, I suspected this was going to be the result." He smoothed his thin moustache. "I tried my best to shame you, but I see it didn't work."

"I gave my word to my friends—people I care about."

Gerrard sighed. "Conscience can be such a nuisance. I saw your father give in to it so many times. 'I've got to do it, Gerrard,' he would say. 'I've given my word.' To tell you the truth, I'm really grateful I haven't had the problem.'' He smiled, and the smile was genuine. ''You know, Catherine, I hadn't realized you were so much like your father.''

A rush of gladness coursed through her. ''That makes me very happy,'' she said. ''I've just lately come to appreciate him.''

''Your father was a good man, in spite of what you may have heard to the contrary,'' he said.

So he had been aware all along of how it had been with her mother.

''Thanks so much for understanding,'' Catherine said. ''If you hadn't, I think it would have killed me.''

''Don't get me wrong, Catherine,'' Gerrard said. ''I do believe it's the wrong career move for you, and I'll admit to being disappointed in your decision. But you're a good restoration architect, in case I haven't remembered to tell you lately, and you'll do well wherever you are. And of course they're doing some interesting things in Louisiana, even if they are a little backward.'' He sipped his bourbon. ''I'll certainly put in a good word for you on anything that develops there. And someday, maybe we can still collaborate on something here.''

And that, coming from Gerrard, was as good as a promise. The joy, the relief washed over her. It seemed she hadn't closed any doors, after all.

She rose to go, and Gerrard saw her to the door. She turned to him. ''Gerrard, I'm well aware of what you spent to retire Dad's debts, and I intend to pay you back, every penny. I realize I could have done it if I'd taken this job, but I'll manage it someday, one way or another.''

"As I've told you before, I don't want your money. The wolves aren't exactly howling at my door, you know."

"Maybe not, but I *am* going to pay you back."

Gerrard sighed. "You're behaving like your father again. I'm sure you'll do whatever pleases that troublesome conscience of yours, but there's no need."

"There's something else, which I'll never be able to pay you for." Her throat tightened. "And now that I think of it, I'm not sure I've ever told you. I owe you everything. In a lot of ways, you've been the father to me that Dad wasn't able to be."

"Nonsense." He never changed expressions, but Catherine could have sworn that a faint color swept his aristocratic cheekbones. "Catherine—" He hesitated, something she'd never seen him do. "John and I were cousins, but we were also close friends." He cleared his throat. "He always took the lead. He loved life, loved people. He was—everything I was not. When I was with him, I didn't feel scholarly, studious, unattractive. I never understood why, but he actually liked me." Catherine listened in astonishment. She couldn't believe Gerrard was talking about himself, much less confiding in her.

"Even when we were young men, I could see his unfortunate tendencies, and I knew how it would end. But I still loved him. When his money was gone, I helped him. Just as I've done for you. I never had children, but . . ."

Catherine put her arms around his neck, held him close for a long moment. "Gerrard?" she whispered. "I love you." It was the first time she'd ever told him so. And she was gratified to feel his arms tighten briefly around her.

She drove to her mother's apartment, still warmed by his words. The biggest hurdle was over; now there was only her mother to contend with. Catherine knew the upcoming scene with her would be far more unpleasant.

She was right. Elizabeth Nolan was by turns incredulous, genteelly furious, then determined to change her daughter's mind by any of the considerable means at her disposal.

"I simply can't believe it, Catherine," she said for the fifth time. "I'd so looked forward to having you near me again. How can you do this to me? And think of all Gerrard's done for us—for you. How can you repay his generosity like this?"

"I'm fully aware of everything Gerrard's done, Mother. It's just that I've promised to finish this project."

"Why? From all I can understand, it's nothing but a simple country cabin. You'll be squandering your talent and your training for nothing."

Catherine grimaced. "Not for nothing, Mother. For my friends. I have wonderful friends in Louisiana. They're depending on me."

"Friends?" Elizabeth came perilously close to raising her voice. "What's happened to you, Catherine? Your real friends are here."

"Oh, no, Mother," she shot back. "My friends in Louisiana are real. They care about me, and I care about them. I can't—won't—let them down."

"You're beginning to sound like your father," Elizabeth said bitterly.

"That's exactly what Gerrard said, Mother," Catherine said gently, laughing a little in spite of herself. "In case you didn't know, I loved my father. As for Gerrard, he doesn't necessarily approve of my going back, but he understands why I'm doing it."

Deprived of her chief crutch by Gerrard's defection, Elizabeth fell back on her old weapon of her own helplessness. She appealed to Catherine's filial loyalties, her sense of guilt, anything else she could bring handily to mind. She reminded Catherine of how unwell she'd been the past few years, of the fact that she was getting older. She declared it was Catherine's moral duty to care for her.

As her mother came to the end of her beautifully restrained tirade, Catherine decided it was time to end the discussion. "Mother," she said gently but firmly, "you know I love you, and I'll always take care of you. But I'm not going to allow you to blackmail me into doing something I know is wrong. It used to work on Dad. I can remember. But it's not going to work on me."

"How can you say that, when you know how much I suffered all those years from your father's neglect?" Elizabeth said, and pouted. Catherine had always thought it was one of her most masterful expressions. "You suffered, too, if you'll remember."

"Yes, I did. But not only from what Dad did—or didn't do. You actually had me convinced I didn't love him." In spite of her best intentions, Catherine's voice hardened. "Maybe if you'd been more supportive of him, he wouldn't have been so neglectful—of either of us. But you drove him away."

There was a moment of total silence. Then Elizabeth drew herself up to her full height. "Catherine, I will not allow you to talk to me like that," she said in tones that would have frozen any ordinary mortal.

"Then I won't, if it distresses you," Catherine said calmly. "I'm going back to Louisiana in the morning. I'll say goodbye now, because I know you hate being wakened early. I'll probably be gone by the time you get up."

"You're going in the morning?" her mother repeated, stunned. "You can't leave tomorrow. I've already invited several of my friends, your friends, too, to come by Monday afternoon for tea."

"You'll have to uninvite them," Catherine said firmly. "I won't be here."

"But what will I say?" In the face of this social crisis, Catherine's ungrateful behavior faded, in Elizabeth's mind, into insignificance.

"I'm sure you'll think of something," Catherine said. "You do that kind of thing so well." She kissed her mother gently, lovingly on the cheek. "Goodbye, Mother. I'll call you next week." Leaving her mother staring after her, she headed toward the stairs.

As she went, she glanced at her watch. She had time to catch the ten-o'clock news. On the drive from Athens, she had caught a newscast announcing that

Hurricane Florence had slammed into the upper Texas coast early that morning. It had caused extensive damage, then, with the capriciousness common to Gulf Coast hurricanes, had changed direction and spun due east into South Louisiana. Immersed in her problems, she hadn't paid much attention to the progress of the storm, but if it hit Louisiana, she might run into some bad weather tomorrow. Maybe she'd better leave a little earlier in the morning than she'd planned; then she could allow for delay. She wanted to be sure to make Uncle Bat's *fais-do-do* tomorrow night.

And this time, she must remember to pack that snapshot of herself and her father. Her mother would never miss it.

CHAPTER FIFTEEN

"...MAY NOT BE A HURRICANE any longer, but it's not finished yet."

Catherine turned up the radio so she could hear it above the monotonous clack of the windshield wipers. She had been driving since seven o'clock that morning. At first, the clouds hadn't looked all that threatening, but as she approached the Louisiana state line, she ran into waves of increasingly heavy rain showers. The wind blew fitfully, then lulled, then blew harder. Now, although she'd turned the wipers up to their maximum capacity, she'd had to slow her speed almost to a crawl, and she had to strain to see the road. It was doubtful she'd arrive in time for the *fais-do-do*, but if the weather grew any worse, it wouldn't be held anyway. At any rate, the dance was rapidly becoming the least of her worries.

"So far," the commentator continued, "dying Hurricane Florence has dumped over fifteen inches of rain in the south and central Louisiana area and is now stationary over the northern part of the state, where she could drop another ten inches before she rains herself out. Morgan City's having a rough time of it. Our live weather eye is there now. Come in, Glen."

A sharp blast of static crackled from the radio, making Catherine jump. Then another voice came over the air. "Glen LeDoux here, Bob. I'm in Morgan City, at one of the concrete flood walls that protects the town from the Atchafalaya River. People have been working here since last night, sandbagging the tops of the walls to keep the water from flooding the town."

Blackie would be there, Catherine knew, sandbagging as he had during the last flood, expending his considerable strength to save his neighbors' homes and his. She wondered how dangerous the work was and sent up a silent prayer.

"The watchword here, Bob, is cooperation," the announcer continued. "Civil Defense workers, the Corps of Engineers, local citizens, people from the surrounding area, everyone's working nonstop. Most of them have been here for at least twenty-four hours, and it looks as though they'll be at it at least another twenty-four."

"Thank you, Glen." The first announcer came back on. "Well, folks, that was Glen LeDoux on location at Morgan City. The Atchafalaya River won't crest for at least another twelve hours, so those people have a long vigil ahead. They need volunteers to help with the sandbags. By the way, any of you folks in the Morgan City area who are flooded out can go to the refugee center in the Municipal Auditorium building; they'll give you food and a dry place to sleep.

"That about wraps it up for the weather. Stay tuned for the next bulletin on former Hurricane Florence as we receive more information. For KCAJ in Lafayette, Louisiana, this is Bob Charles.''

The expiring storm, billed as the storm of the century by the media, seemed to be wreaking its personal vengeance on Louisiana. Catherine turned down the volume and frowned at the rain-slick highway stretching before her. Something was tugging at her memory, something Blackie had said... *The Atchafalaya River.* The rain would pour into the bayous, creeks and rivers that fed into the already engorged Atchafalaya River, then the water would head in a raging torrent toward Morgan City. *It's a very dangerous situation,* Blackie had told her that long-ago day on the bridge. *Morgan City is at the bottom of the sock—it gets all the water.*

Dear God, keep Blackie safe.

She took a deep breath and stretched her cramped muscles. By now the sharp pain that flared inside her every time she thought of Blackie was familiar to her. She almost welcomed it, in fact, after those first days in Atlanta of feeling that there was nothing left for her. Anything was better than the numbness, the emptiness of that time. The minute she had started on her way this morning, she had begun to feel better. She no longer felt torn in half, as though she had betrayed someone. Louisiana was where she belonged, even though she wasn't coming back to Blackie. She had to remind herself of that from time to time, because in spite of everything, her heart kept forgetting that there wasn't any hope for them. Compressing her lips together, she drove on through the rain.

Suddenly, she snapped to attention. "I've just received another bulletin," the radio announcer was saying, "that the Lake Palourde area, just north east of Morgan City, may be in trouble from the floodwaters. There are several weak spots in the dirt levees out there that authorities are watching carefully for washout. They're evacuating the area now, just in case."

Lake Palourde. *Uncle Bat.* The tiny, weathered cabin perched on stilts suddenly seemed so frail, so all alone on its little bayou. Would the levees hold? The area was being evacuated, but if the water in the lake was too high from all the rain, if it was moving too swiftly—but Blackie would get Uncle Bat out, of course.

She was breathing easier when the second thought struck her. *Blackie would be working on the levees. What if he couldn't leave? What if he didn't hear about the problem at Lake Palourde until too late?* She had to know Uncle Bat was all right. She wouldn't go home, she would go straight to his house. A few minutes later she hit Interstate 10 near the small Louisiana town of Slidell, but instead of taking the easier interstate route to Lafayette, then to New Iberia, she turned south toward New Orleans, then to Morgan City, praying she could get through.

BLACKIE STRAIGHTENED from the row of sandbags he was working on and massaged his tired, aching muscles. He surveyed the result of his labors. He had gone all night without sleep, and for the past five hours without even a break. At this point, the sandbags were probably stacked high enough to keep the waves from washing over the wall. He hoped so; the Civil Defense had called for the loads of sand as soon as the storm had turned eastward, but they were already running short.

If it would only stop raining. Not that it would help the flooding, because as long as it rained to the north of them, the real danger lay in the water coming down the Atchafalaya River toward Morgan City. But if it stopped, he thought ruefully, then at least the rain wouldn't pour down the back of his neck. He unfastened the top clasp on his slicker; the upper part of his body had long since become soaked.

He looked at the town below him. It was safe, for now. The levees and flood walls were holding, and the sandbags were blocking the overflow. But still it looked terribly vulnerable, and the danger wouldn't be over for a while, not until the river crested. When he thought about it, it was downright crazy for anyone to live in a town that was only one foot above sea level. Particularly when it was right next to a river like the Atchafalaya.

Only a few feet away, only inches below the wall where he stood, churned that treacherous river. Blackie looked at the angry, rushing waters that strained against the concrete. The walls seemed too small to hold back so much water. But so far they had. And so far the sandbags had stopped the wave action from driving the water over the top. With a little luck, and not too much more rising water before the river crested, everything would be all right.

The levees at Lake Palourde, though, were another matter. They were lower than those around Morgan City, and overflow was very possible there. Besides, some of the levees in that area were weak.

Anyway, he was glad he had gotten Uncle Bat out safely, just in case. Despite his exhaustion, he smiled as he remembered the old man's protests, then his final grumbling acquiescence. Uncle Bat hadn't wanted to leave his house, was afraid it would be gone when he got back. When Blackie had pointed out that that was all the more reason for him to leave, Uncle Bat had only snorted indignantly. He had finally packed his things, however, stowing most of them under a tarpaulin in the bed of Blackie's truck. But he had carried the old violin tenderly in his arms as he rode beside Blackie on their way to Morgan City.

The thought of the violin made Blackie think of Catherine. His insides twisted. She would have been glad to know the violin was safe, even if she hadn't cared about anything else.

Damn Catherine. He wanted to hate her, but all he could do was ache from wanting her. She had helped him to let go the last of his anguish for Angéline, then had left him with a new agony that was all-consuming. In an effort to rid himself of it, he had looked around for work, wanting to lose himself in it, to exhaust himself beyond thinking about her. When the flood came, he had almost welcomed it. But so far, no amount of backbreaking labor had rid his soul of its pain.

Why had she done it? Dropped everything and gone to Atlanta? He believed the reasons she had given him, but the fact that she would even consider going back after all that had happened between them proved to him that she had only considered their relationship a temporary diversion.

No, he chastised himself, realizing he was feeding his own anger. It was easier to do that than to hurt, but he knew better. Even that night, after his anger had passed, he had known better. Her involvement with him had been genuine. He could remember, much more clearly than he liked, how she had responded to him, body and soul, when they had made love. But still he couldn't quite believe his own memories—was afraid to believe them. And in the end, her fear had proved too strong for them both.

He wiped a wet hand across his dripping brow, then grimaced as he realized he was smearing himself with mud. He was filthy, tired and hungry. What he wouldn't give for a real meal, a hot bath and a soft bed—with Catherine in it. He would have sworn he was too tired to feel anything, but the longing that surged through him at the thought of her lying in his bed, reaching for him, whispering his name, staggered him.

A wave of fatigue washed through him like a flood tide. But he forced himself to pick another sandbag. In a few minutes he would have food and drink, and possibly by tomorrow he would have a hot bath. Eventually, he would even be able to go home to his nice, soft bed. But it would be empty.

CATHERINE SLOWED THE CAR and turned onto Highway 70, the two-lane road leading north between the

Atchafalaya River Basin levees and Lake Palourde. If she had kept on going straight, she could have been in Morgan City in a matter of minutes, but she had to see about Uncle Bat, had to make sure he was all right. She leaned over the steering wheel, squinting to see through the rain-splattered windshield. The turnoff was only a few miles down the road, and she didn't want to overlook it.

The rain continued to fall steadily, heavily. She gripped the wheel a little tighter. Thank heaven she had gone to Uncle Bat's house with Gussie; otherwise she wouldn't have been sure of the way.

The road was clear of traffic—deserted, actually. Come to think of it, Catherine hadn't seen anyone since she had turned onto this highway. Surely someone was around. She looked, but it was desolate. A prickle of fear touched her backbone at the thought of going through the wooded path to Uncle Bat's house alone. But after all, he would be alone—that was why she was going.

From time to time she glanced at the huge dirt levees that made up the east bank of the Atchafalaya Basin, the only thing preventing millions of gallons of muddy water from inundating the entire area. She tried to ascertain if they were holding firm or about to give way, but realized ruefully that she wouldn't know the difference, unless a wall of water actually came roaring down on top of her. It was funny, she thought. On this side of the levees all was quiet except the steady patter of the rain, while on the other, an enormous volume of water roared, pounding steadily at them with incredible force. Such a small levee to keep all that in, when she thought about it. She looked up, wondering how near the top the water on the other side had risen. She shivered.

Only a mile or so now, she calculated, until she reached the turn to Uncle Bat's place. For that she was glad; the sooner she found him, the sooner they could get to the relative safety of Morgan City. Then she laughed at the idea. Morgan City, that tiny settlement tucked into the shadow of a great, gray concrete wall, buffeted by a great, angry river. Morgan City wasn't safe at all.

She rounded a curve in the road, then slammed on her brakes when she saw barricades stretching across her path. As she drew closer, a uniformed figure moved into the road and flagged her down. Her heart sinking, she braked to a stop. She was so close to Uncle Bat's turnoff...

The man was dressed in the uniform of a Louisiana highway patrolman. She rolled down her window as he walked to her car.

"Ma'am, I'm sorry," he said politely, "but the road is closed."

"Why? What's happened?" Her heart lurched with sudden fear.

"Nothing yet, but there's a spot in the levee up ahead that we're watching. It's low, and the water washing against it has weakened it, so we're sandbagging the top of it."

"It hasn't gone yet?" Relief rushed through her.

"No, and we hope it won't. But we've closed the road just in case. You'll have to go back." He indicated the road behind her.

"But I can't, officer. Someone I know lives here, on one of the bayous. An old man. He lives alone. I've got to see if he's all right." The fear was returning, this time approaching panic.

"We evacuated the entire area this morning," he said soothingly. "I'm sure we got him out."

"But he doesn't have a radio or telephone, or any transportation except his boat." Catherine spoke very deliberately in her effort to make him understand. "He might not know anything about it. Can't you let me through, just for a little while?"

The man shook his head. "I'm sorry. No one's allowed in there until the flood danger's passed. Are you part of his family?"

"No—no, I'm not," Catherine answered. "Just a friend."

"Does he have any family? Wouldn't they have gotten him out?"

"Yes, he has a nephew in Morgan City. But he may be working on the levees there, and wouldn't have heard they were evacuating."

"I'm sure he's been taken into town. Check the refugee center, he'll be there." The man was sympathetic, reassuring, but Catherine could tell he was eager for her to go.

Defeated, she turned her car to head to Morgan City. Uncle Bat was in town, she told herself. He had to be. Remembering Blackie's protectiveness of him, she was almost sure of it. But she wouldn't be easy until she saw his wonderful old face. She didn't think she could yet face Blackie with any degree of calmness, but she knew if she didn't find Uncle Bat right away she would hunt Blackie down.

As she approached town, Catherine noticed there weren't many people on the streets; most who weren't working on the levees were inside, out of the rain and wind. Those who were out seemed to be wearing olive-drab slickers and big boots, as though the outfit were a sort of town uniform, Catherine thought.

Finally, she spotted someone crossing the street ahead of her and asked directions to the Municipal Auditorium building. Within a few minutes, she was there. She parked and hurried across the lot toward the brick building. *Just a few more steps and I'll know Uncle Bat is safe.* She could feel her nerves jangling. If he wasn't—but he would be. She wouldn't think about anything else, not yet.

She pushed back the hood of her raincoat and opened the front door. For a moment she simply stood in the doorway, overwhelmed by the number of people she saw. The building was packed; people were clustered in groups of various sizes over all the available floor space. In the foyer, the Civil Defense authorities had set up tables, which were laden with coffeepots and boxes of food. Blankets were stacked on the floor beside the tables.

Catherine began scanning faces, looking for Uncle Bat. *Please let him be here...* She saw ancient, wizened *grandmères*, frightened young couples, men who reminded her of Blackie, tiny babies in arms, children darting in and out. In a secluded corner, she saw a young mother nursing her baby, the father standing protectively nearby.

She searched everywhere, peered frantically into every cluster of wet, bedraggled people. She had just decided with a sinking heart that Uncle Bat wasn't there. Then she glanced down a side corridor. There, at the end of the hall, perched on a chair, a stack of belongings beside him and on his face an expression of cosmic indignation, sat Uncle Bat.

CHAPTER SIXTEEN

CATHERINE WENT LIMP with relief.

"Uncle Bat," she called out, hurrying toward him. He rose to meet her, and she thankfully enveloped him in her arms. "You're safe!" She stepped back to look at him more carefully. He seemed the same as always. She glanced at his small pile of possessions, recognizing the box that held his violin and the chair on which he had been sitting—the chair his people had brought from Acadia so long ago.

"A course I'm safe," he said scornfully. "I tol' Ti-neg I need ta stay in ma house. I been t'rough a lotta storms, me. But Ti-neg he say da swamp, da river diff'ren' now. He say dey change dem so much, da water flood my house. He make me come wit' him, so I bring ma t'ings and come, oh, six, five hours ago. *C'est ridicule.*" Uncle Bat folded his arms, obviously unhappy with everyone from the Corps of Engineers to his erring nephew.

"But he might be right," Catherine pointed out. "This is the worst flooding they've had in years. There's no way of knowing what will happen."

"Hmph," he said. Suddenly the fact of her presence dawned on him. "What you doin' here, *hein*?"

he asked her in surprise. "You suppose' ta be in Atlanta."

"I didn't take the job—I told them I was coming back to Louisiana to finish the Arceneaux house." She kneaded an aching muscle in her neck, moved her hand gingerly to stretch it. The long hours of driving in the rain were beginning to take their toll. "I was so frightened when I saw they'd closed the road to your house. They wouldn't let me pass, and I was afraid you hadn't gotten out..."

"You come ta fin' me, Cat'rine?" he asked wonderingly.

"Yes, of course I did."

"*Mais jamais.* I never forget dis, me." He put a hand to his heart.

"I care about you, Uncle Bat," she said simply. "I care about all of you. That's why I came back." *All of you,* she reaffirmed silently. She didn't want to ask, but she had to know. "Where is...ah...Blackie?" She tried to make her voice casual.

"He tol' me he he'p put da bag on da levee," Uncle Bat answered solemnly, but his eyes shone with knowing amusement.

Sandbagging the levees, Catherine thought. *I knew he'd be there.*

"Don' worry, *chère*," Uncle Bat reassured her, seeing the concern in her face. "He plenty safe. Dat *pirate* take care hisself, heem. I done tol' heem I want ta he'p, but he tol' me stay here." Again the grievance surfaced in his voice.

"He just wants to be sure you're all right." She patted his arm, still thankful he was safe. "Why don't

I go up front and see if I can find out what's happening?''

Near the entrance to the building, she cornered a harassed but courteous young Civil Defense official who was shepherding new arrivals. ''We don't yet know how high the waters will go, ma'am,'' he told her. ''There is still flooding in the north part of the basin, and we probably won't have any definite idea about when the river will crest until after midnight, maybe later.'' Wearily, he rubbed his face. ''Right now, we're worrying about overflow and leakage along the floodwalls downtown, so we're sandbagging them like crazy.''

Catherine thanked the man. *Was Blackie safe?* With a sigh, she made her way to Uncle Bat. It was going to be a very long night.

In spite of the old man's confident words, Catherine could tell he was worried about Blackie, too. In the ensuing hour, he mentioned his nephew several times and finally suggested, very casually, that he might walk down to the floodwall just to see what was going on.

''Oh, no, Uncle Bat,'' she protested halfheartedly. ''Let's wait here. Surely we'll hear something before long.''

But half an hour later, when they still had heard no news, the old man declared in no uncertain terms that he was going to find Blackie.

''All right, I'll drive you,'' Catherine told him, giving in to her own need to assure herself of Blackie's safety.

Uncle Bat left his things in charge of relatives he had discovered down the hall, but leave his *beau violon* he would not. Catherine couldn't really blame him. They walked out into the remnants of the storm, Uncle Bat clutching the battered box tightly in his arms.

The rain had diminished, but the wind still blew too hard for comfort. In the gathering darkness, they drove the short distance to the river and parked on a side street. Then they walked to the concrete flood-wall, new—and four feet higher—since the last terrible flood, towering twenty-seven feet above the organized chaos taking place at its base. Trucks were dumping huge loads of sand, which crews of workmen in slickers were shoveling into bags. The filled bags were stacked on front-end loaders, which lumbered to the wall to deposit their burdens. Then the bags were used to fortify the wall.

"Excuse me." She stopped a burly man swinging a sandbag onto a carrier. He looked around impatiently. "This man is looking for his nephew," she explained, indicating Uncle Bat. "Have you seen—"

"Nonc," the man exclaimed before she could finish. "What are you doing out here?"

I should have known, Catherine thought, smiling in spite of her worry.

"I come ta find Ti-neg, me," Uncle Bat declared. "You saw heem aroun' here, Sosthene?"

"Mais sho'." Sosthene pointed. "There he is, up there." Catherine's eyes followed the direction of his finger. At the very top of a tall ladder, she could see a muscular figure, slicker-clad but bareheaded, just starting down. Blackie. The breath rushed out of her

lungs in a sigh of relief. She watched him climb down, starved for the sight of him, incredulous still that one man had such power over her mind, her senses, her whole being. But even at this distance, she could tell by the way he moved that he was exhausted.

He reached the ground and headed in their direction, still oblivious to them.

"Ti-neg," Uncle Bat called.

Blackie's eyes found his uncle first. *"Qu-est-ce que c'est, Nonc?"* he asked, amused annoyance on his face. "Couldn't stand it, *hein*? Couldn't stay out of the. . ." He saw Catherine, and the words died on his lips.

For a second they both froze, eyes locked, and she saw the startled gladness, the hunger on his face. Through the rush of emotions that filled her, she saw, too, that his exhaustion went bone-deep, that even his phenomenal energy was nearly depleted. Under its tan, his face was a grayish color, and dark circles shadowed his eyes. His hair curled wildly in the humid air. Catherine thought she had never seen such a beautiful sight in her life. She had to forcibly restrain herself from going into his arms.

But as she watched, his face shuttered. "I thought you were in Atlanta," he said warily, his voice flat.

"I—" She hesitated. Now wasn't the time for explanations. "—didn't take the job," she finished. "I was coming back for the *fais-do-do* but heard about the storm and decided to come here first."

"She come ta get me, Ti-neg," Uncle Bat told him solemnly.

"She what?" Blackie looked at her blankly.

"I came in on Highway 70," Catherine explained, a little embarrassed. "But they'd already blocked off the road. I finally found Uncle Bat in the storm shelter."

"Yeah, I brought him in this morning," Blackie said slowly, his eyes still on her.

A tall, rangy figure in the proverbial olive-drab slicker materialized beside them. "Hello, Catherine, Uncle Bat. How's it going, Blackie?" Douglas MacDonald was genial as always, but his craggy features mirrored the tension in the air.

"Doug." Blackie turned and shook hands, and the moment between him and Catherine was gone. "Okay, I guess," he answered. "Right now we're still ahead of the water."

"The next few hours will tell the tale," Doug said. "We're not out of the woods by a long shot. The latest word is that the storm's stalled over the north part of the basin, and it hasn't quit raining up there yet."

"Hooee." Blackie grimaced. "This is worse than the flood of '73. Well, all we can do is watch and keep sandbagging. I'd better get back to—"

"Ti-neg!" The voice, harsh, penetrating, cut Blackie off in midsentence. In the darkness, Catherine could see him, a slight, familiar figure—clothes soaked and filthy, black hair stringing wetly down his face. He emitted pure rage. Raymond Hebert. Her stomach knotted in fear.

"Raymond!" Blackie's head snapped around in surprise. *"Qu'est qu'il y a..."*

"I been lookin' for you, Ti-neg. I come to tell you something." Hebert stepped closer. "I thought you quit the corps, after what they did to Angéline," he taunted. His eyes looked glassy, unfocused, and Catherine could see a sheen of sweat across his upper lip. "An' here you are, workin' for 'em again."

"That's crazy, Ray." It occurred to Catherine that Blackie didn't mean the words literally; he still didn't fully realize—or didn't want to realize—how crazy Hebert truly was. Beside her, she sensed Uncle Bat and Doug waiting in tense, watchful silence.

"This isn't just for the corps." Blackie spread his hands, pleading. "Everybody's got to pitch in this time, or a lot of people are going to die."

"Let a few of 'em die—maybe there'll be some engineers in the bunch." Hebert's voice held a peculiar disembodied quality, as if it didn't belong to its owner. "That'll pay 'em back for everything they done to us."

Alarm—and at last comprehension—dawned on Blackie's face. "Ray, you can't mean that." He grabbed Hebert's arm.

Hebert shook off Blackie's hand. "Nah, Ti-neg," he snarled. "Don't touch me. You're just like the rest of 'em. *Défecteur* . . ." He hissed the word.

"I'm no traitor, Ray," Blackie protested, and the anguish Catherine saw on his face tore at her heart.

"I come to tell you, Ti-neg." Hebert jerked a thumb behind him. "I put some things on the levee that'll fix everything up, me. Then Morgan City won't have no more to worry about."

"What are you talking about?" Blackie's voice was taut.

Hebert laughed. "It's a surprise, Ti-neg. For you and your friends. And I knew just where to plant 'em so the whole town'll go away." He began edging side-wise. "That'll fix 'em."

Explosives, Catherine thought numbly. *He's going to blow up the levee.*

Suddenly Hebert turned and ran. Blackie lunged for him, but he was too late. Hebert melted into the rainy darkness and disappeared, Blackie close behind him. Doug MacDonald followed them.

"Bien fou," Uncle Bat commented, touching his temple. *"Bien dangereux.* But I know him when he was a *bébé,* use' to play wit' Ti-neg . . ." His eyes grew sad.

In a very few minutes, Blackie came back alone, breathing hard. "He got away," he said between gasps. "I didn't know he could move that fast." He met Catherine's gaze for the first time, and she could see in his eyes the knowledge that he had been wrong about Hebert and Catherine had been right. "I'm sorry, Cat'rine," he said simply.

Catherine thought in that moment that it was worth a dozen rainy, nightmare trips to hear him say her name like that again.

Doug hurried up. "I've called the law, Blackie. What do you think?"

"We've got to stop him before he blows everything away," Blackie said urgently. "I think I know where he's talking about. There's a low spot in the levee a little way north of town."

"Will you help us find him?" Doug asked. "You know that area better than anyone."

"*Bien sûr*. In fact, I want to be the one to find him," Blackie said grimly. "I've got some things to settle with him."

"Blackie, no!" Catherine astonished everyone with her outburst, but no one more than herself. "You can't do that. He's dangerous—he's got explosives. He may even have a gun."

"I've got to." Blackie's eyes were bleak pools of agony. "This is my fault, in a way. I should've seen this coming."

"Don't be silly," she begged. "You couldn't have known. You mustn't do it. Leave it to the police." She put a hand on his arm, willed him to stay.

"I've got to go," he repeated stubbornly. "I may be the only one who can find him in time." He turned to Doug. "We'd better get started. What did you tell the police?"

"I gave them a description of Hebert," Douglas said, "and the general direction he was heading when we lost him. They're putting out an APB on him now, and they're sending a couple of officers to meet me. They should be here shortly."

"Fine. As soon as they get here, we'll go."

Catherine could have screamed in frustration. He wasn't listening to her, seemed not to see her. "Uncle Bat," she said in a low voice, "you've got to try to stop him. He could be killed."

"I can' stop heem, Cat'rine." Uncle Bat shook his head worriedly. "He got da *tête plus dure*—da mos' hard head," he explained, "dat I ever know, me. Us got ta let him go."

"Blackie..." She turned to him in one last desperate appeal.

"Hush, Cat'rine." Blackie held his finger gently but firmly over her lips, looked at her as if he was committing every one of her features to memory. "Take Uncle Bat to the shelter," he said. "I'll find you there." Then he was gone.

THE HOURS CRAWLED BY. Catherine marked the passing of every minute. She made desultory conversation with Uncle Bat's numerous friends and relatives who had made their way to the shelter, peered over his shoulder as they played a spirited game of *bourrée* and finally took a turn dispensing coffee and blankets to tired, hungry refugees. Even through her worry and fatigue, she was conscious of a feeling of homecoming, of being where she belonged.

But always at the forefront of her consciousness lay the nagging fear for Blackie's safety. And although Uncle Bat never said so, she could tell by his frequent glances toward the front of the building that he was worried, too.

As the night wore on, he forsook the *bourrée* game and became silent, thoughtful, sitting on his ancient little chair in grave contemplation. When she took a break from her work she came to sit by him. After a little while, he spoke.

"Cat'rine?"

She turned to him. "Yes, Uncle Bat?"

"I been t'inkin', me. Dis storm, she a bad t'ing."

"That's true."

"A course, she don' scare me."

"Of course not."

"But ma t'ings . . ." He paused.

"Yes?"

"I don' want nuttin' to happen to ma t'ings," he said, gesturing to where they lay. "I decide somet'in', me. I want ma chair go ta da Arceneaux house. An' when I die, den *mon beau violon* go, too. Den it belong ta all da Cajun people."

When she could see him again through the tears that filmed her eyes, Catherine embraced him. "Uncle Bat . . . are you sure that's what you want to do?"

"*Mais* sho'," he said with simple conviction.

"Thank you," Catherine said simply. She knew she had finally gained the full measure of his trust.

After that, the old man seemed relieved, and with renewed energy he plunged again into the continuous *bourrée* game. Catherine's fatigue, on the other hand, increased with every passing second.

Finally, around two in the morning, Doug MacDonald appeared. In her relief at seeing him, Catherine threw her arms around his neck. "Oh, Doug, you're all right. Where's Blackie?"

"Take it easy, Catherine." He patted her shoulder. "Blackie's safe."

"Thank God," she breathed, not even caring that he knew her concern was for Blackie.

"He's safe, all right," Doug said, then, incredibly, broke into a broad grin. "Actually, as it turned out, Blackie was safer from Hebert than Hebert was from him."

"What do you mean?" Catherine stared at him.

"Well," he explained, "we found Hebert about where Blackie thought he'd be, just north of town, where the levee makes a sharp westerly bend." He sobered. "He was setting up his explosives. There were four of us—Blackie, me and a couple of policeman. We surprised Hebert. We were going to take him by force right away, but Blackie wanted to talk to him, to reason with him." Doug's face softened with sympathy.

"I don't think Blackie wanted to believe Raymond was crazy," Catherine said quietly.

Doug nodded. "He would have felt disloyal to him. I suspect he was also fighting his own feelings, about Angéline's death and a lot of other things." He shrugged. "Anyway, it didn't work. Hebert got crazier and crazier, and Blackie got madder and madder. Finally, Hebert insulted you. I won't repeat what he said, but Blackie couldn't stand it any more. He cold-cocked him."

"He *what?*" Through her stupefaction, she dimly heard Uncle Bat's quiet chuckle. It was the first time she'd ever heard him laugh aloud.

"Coldcocked him. Knocked him out with one punch. The damnedest thing I've ever seen. The policemen didn't even have to draw their guns." Douglas shook his head in wonder. "They'll be telling that one around the *bourrée* tables for a long time."

"I can't believe it." Catherine stared at Douglas in horror.

"I don't think I would've if I hadn't been there. Anyway, the police have taken Hebert into custody, so he shouldn't be giving anyone any more trouble." He pulled out a cigarette and lit it. "It's lucky we found him, though—he had laid out enough explosives to make mud pies out of that levee. Blackie saved a lot of property tonight, and probably a lot of lives, too."

"Ti-neg?" It was Uncle Bat who spoke. Catherine couldn't seem to find her voice.

"He went to the police station. He should be along in a little while." He began unfastening his slicker. "By the way, I just heard that it's stopped raining in the North Basin, and it looks as though we're going to be able to contain the floodwaters." He took a drag on his cigarette, then exhaled a long stream of smoke. "I think we've got it made."

After he left, Catherine fell prey to so many conflicting emotions that she couldn't begin to sort them out. At last her exhausted mind fastened on one aspect of their ordeal: Blackie's behavior. In the first place, he could easily have been killed. What did he mean by playing the hero and frightening them all like that? Especially after all those months of disbelieving her warnings about Raymond. How typical of him, to go to the other extreme, to plunge inconsiderately into the swamp after a madman.

She had begged him not to go, had put her feelings on the line for him, with plenty of witnesses—and he had ignored her. Then, adding insult to injury, he had insisted on subduing Hebert single-handedly, even though he had with him two perfectly good armed policemen who could have taken him. That Blackie had been needed, and that he was a genuine hero, her overtaxed emotions rejected. That she was being irrational, she refused to acknowledge. Her anger began to simmer, and as she waited it escalated to a slow boil.

Toward four in the morning, muscles aching and eyes gritty with fatigue, she was huddled on a bench, watching the seemingly indestructible Uncle Bat playing *bourrée* with *cousin* Celestin and several other cronies. Uncle Bat, with his usual aplomb, had won the last four pots, most of which were Celestin's.

"Uncle Bat, how come you so lucky?" Celestin reached into his pocket for another penny.

"Lucky? I ben playin' *bourrée* all ma life. Dat's not luck, it's skill," Uncle Bat said haughtily.

"But you takin' all ma money," Celestine groused.

"*Mais jamais.* If you gon' *bourrée* ever' hand, you gon' lose all you money. An' I tell you, I'm happy to take it, me." Catherine smiled at the pennies and nickels stacked on the table in front of Uncle Bat. Celestin was lucky the game was only penny ante.

"*Comment ça va?*" The voice came from behind her shoulder.

She jumped as though she'd been struck. *Blackie.* She whirled around, and for one glad moment, all she could see was Blackie's face, streaked with mud, eyes hooded with exhaustion, grin in place as though absolutely nothing had happened. The grin did it. Suddenly, everything was obscured by the red mist rising before her eyes.

She fixed Blackie with a frosty glare. "What do you mean, *Comment ça va?*" She jabbed a finger at him. "How do you think we are, anyway? You're out in the storm somewhere, knocking people out and doing heaven knows what else, while we have to wait here, not able to do a thing but worry ourselves sick about you. What does that tell you?''

Blackie's mouth fell open in amazement.

"You could have told the police where to go. You could have stayed here. You could have had the common courtesy to call from the police station to tell us where you were, but no—we had to hear from Doug that you were all right.''

"But Cat'rine—" Blackie protested feebly.

He never finished the sentence. As the corridor suddenly grew very quiet indeed, Catherine proceeded to give Blackie the dressing-down of his life, in a voice as loud as it was condemnatory. Then, out of words, she faltered to a stop and stared at him. He stared back, speechless, as stunned by her outburst as she was.

Of them all, only Uncle Bat retained his vocal powers. *"Mon fils,"* he said into the tomblike silence, "I t'ink she loves you."

"Of course I do, but that's no excuse..." Catherine's voice faded away. Suddenly, it was all too much: the quarrel with Blackie, the cutting of her home ties, the storm, the worry, the fear. In a reaction that any Cajun would have understood perfectly, Catherine buried her face in her hands and burst helplessly into tears.

Through the tumult of her emotions, she heard Blackie's quiet chuckle. His big, warm hands grasped her shoulders, pulled her against his muscular chest. For several minutes he rocked her gently in his arms, still shaking with silent laughter. Finally spent, she lifted her head and he kissed her. To a man, the assembled friends and relatives cheered loudly.

"Chère," Uncle Bat announced, his eyes twinkling like Christmas lights, "you done tol' heem, you. *Bien magnifique.*"

What else could happen? Catherine wondered. The crowd was tactfully slipping away, melting into the recesses of the corridor. Her fatigue was almost palpable, driving away every coherent thought. She looked cautiously at Blackie, not knowing what to expect.

"Cat'rine?"

"Yes?" Her voice sounded far away. In the distance, she could dimly hear people laughing, joking, preparing to go home now that the flood danger was lessening. But between her and Blackie there lay a profound stillness.

"I hit him, Cat'rine." He looked disbelievingly at the knuckles of his right hand. They were swollen, turning blue. Painfully, he flexed his fingers. "He's one of my oldest friends, and I hit him." A shudder went through his powerful frame at the memory.

"Blackie, he's ill," she said gently. "He needs help. This way, he'll get it. It had to happen." Now it was her turn to comfort. "Don't blame yourself."

"But I didn't have to hurt him. It was just that he said something—" he stopped quickly.

"I know. Douglas told me."

Blackie looked at her sharply. "He told you what Ray said?"

She smiled. "No. He only told me that Hebert insulted me, and that's when you hit him."

"I was so wrong about him," he repeated dazedly. "Maybe I've been wrong about a lot of other things, too." In an indescribably weary gesture, he closed his eycs and rubbed them. Then, with a visible effort, he focused them on her. "Cat'rine?"

"Yes?"

"Why did you come back?" he asked, carefully enunciating each word.

"I told you. I didn't take the job."

"Why?" The single word hung in the charged air between them.

"I have to finish the Arceneaux house, remember?"

"Is that the only reason?" She could hear him trying to keep his voice level. Suddenly, her numbness evaporated, and her heart began to pound against her chest.

"No, that's not all."

"What else, then?"

"I kept remembering," she faltered. "Gussie, Clarence, Toni, Uncle Bat—" Her voice quivered, broke.

"Oui?" He stood very still.

"And you..." She heard him exhale.

"Cat'rine, when you were chewing me out a little while ago, you said you loved me. Is that true?"

"I'm afraid so." Catherine was beyond deception, beyond defense. She couldn't offer him anything but the simple truth. He knew, anyway. If her love wasn't enough for him, if he didn't return it, then so be it. She bowed her head. The tears were coming again, but she was powerless to stop them. Irrelevantly, it occurred to her that she had never cried so much in her life as she had since she had come to Cajun country.

She felt rather than saw him move closer to her. His finger lifted her chin, and what she saw in his eyes answered all her questions.

"Cat'rine," he said huskily, "*Je t'aime*. I love you, *bébé*, more than I can ever say. When I thought I'd lost you..." He took her face between his hands, cradled her head. "*Dis-moi*," he whispered, "will you share your life with me? Have my children?"

At her wordless nod, he pulled her to him, and for a few moments they simply held each other. Through a haze of happiness, Catherine could feel his heart beating strongly against her cheek, his big hands holding her tightly to him, could hear his deep voice murmuring softly in French.

At last he raised his head, and the kiss he gently placed on her lips was like a benediction.

"Come on, sweetheart. The news is that the levees are going to hold, and they don't need me right now. I've got to get some rest before I fall on my face." His arm went around her, and he drew her close. "Let's go home."

THE SUN WAS COMING UP when they finally reached Blackie's house. Uncle Bat, with innate delicacy, had gone home with *cousin* Celestin. Catherine heated soup while Blackie took a hot shower, and when he emerged, clad in a terry robe, they ate together at his kitchen table.

Blackie sighed in satisfaction. "That shower almost made a new man out of me, and the soup's going to finish the job. I've never been so tired in my life."

Watching him, Catherine believed it. "Go to bed," she admonished him as she picked up their empty soup bowls and headed toward the sink. The understanding between them was still new enough, fragile enough, that she was afraid to speak of it. "I'll finish cleaning up. When I'm through, I'm going to borrow your shower."

At the mention of the shower, Blackie's eyes lit with an unmistakable light. "That's not a bad idea, *chère*," he drawled. "In fact I'll volunteer to scrub your back for you. I'm plenty good at that..."

"I thought you were tired," Catherine protested, too late. The idea seemed to rejuvenate him, and all her protests were in vain. Scrub her back he did, and bathed the rest of her, too, finally joining her in the shower in his zeal for the job, and by the time he finished both were fairly consumed with their need for each other. Carefully, he dried her off with a big towel, then led her to bed.

He began to stroke her, and in spite of her fatigue, she could feel her desire threatening to overwhelm her. But then his hand stilled, grew heavy on her body.

"Blackie?" she whispered. His deep, even breathing gave her her answer. His exhaustion had finally conquered even his desire to love. Reflecting that this must surely be a first for him, maybe for any Cajun, she settled contentedly against him. After all, she thought as the world slipped away, they had a lifetime left to love.

EPILOGUE

SPRING IN THE BAYOU COUNTRY was wonderful, Catherine reflected as she inhaled the familiar fragrance of the honeysuckle blooming on the banks of the Teche. It was hard to believe she had come here only a little over a year ago, even harder to believe she hadn't fully appreciated such lovely surroundings at the time.

She and Blackie sat on the wide front porch of the newly completed Arceneaux house with assorted dignitaries, among them the mayor of New Iberia, the president of the Council for the Development of French in Louisiana and the governor of the state, a Cajun. Before them in the yard, a crowd sat on folding chairs, waiting expectantly.

"Thank you, ladies and gentlemen, for joining us on this beautiful May morning." Clarence held out his arms in welcome. "This is a very special occasion. We're celebrating not only the opening of the Arceneaux house, but a milestone in the preservation of the Cajun culture. All the residents of this area, Cajun and non-Cajun alike, can take pride in this restoration."

As Clarence spoke, Catherine's gaze moved to the adjacent lot, where the chimneys of Bonne Journée rose tall and stately in the sunshine. The mansion had been open for a while now, drawing visitors regularly. It was a superb restoration, if she did say so herself.

And already she was receiving recognition for her work. The Arceneaux house was right next door, showing another facet, equally important, of Louisiana culture. In fact, in a way, it was even more important, she reflected; the plantation way of life had died with the Civil War, while the Cajun culture, warm, vital, alive, still existed all around her, as Clarence had told her so long ago. *Human values.* Wasn't that what Blackie had taught her? Wasn't that what she had learned in working on both houses? Wasn't that the secret the old Millard letters had imparted to her?

She smiled, thinking it appropriate that, in the final chapter of the Millard-Arceneaux saga, the two houses stood next to each other. Somehow, she thought their respective mistresses, Eleanor Millard and her daughter Laura Millard Arceneaux, would be pleased. And Catherine was pleased that she had helped bring it about, had perhaps laid two lovely ghosts to rest.

And after all, though Bonne Journée represented her heritage, the Arceneaux house represented her children's heritage—hers and Blackie's. She laid a hand on her swelling abdomen. Only last night, Blackie had felt the baby move for the first time. He had been beside himself with joy. She had never seen him so happy, unless it had been at their wedding.

At the thought of their wedding, her throat tightened. They had been married one crystal-clear morning the previous October in a small ceremony at St. Martin de Tours, the ancient little church in St. Martinville where generations of Broussards had been baptized, married and buried. Clarence had given her away, and Gussie, newly married to Alain, had been her only attendant. Blackie's father had stood with him. Only his immediate family, Uncle Bat and Toni and Douglas MacDonald had been present. Catherine had worn a simple ivory silk dress, edged with antique lace, and white roses, Blackie's gift, in her hair. Blackie couldn't seem to take his eyes off her.

For Catherine, the only thing marring the otherwise perfect marriage ceremony was the fact that neither Gerrard nor her mother had been there. Gerrard had been tied up with the restoration in Athens, but he had sent his love, along with the very handsome sterling tea service that was his wedding gift. Her mother had been so angry when Catherine had called with the news that she hadn't spoken to her for a month, but once she had accepted the finality of the marriage, she had come around. In fact, when she had found out about the baby, she had even condescended to pay them a visit. As Catherine had discovered long ago, Elizabeth Nolan could adapt remarkably quickly to any situation over which she no longer retained control.

Even though the ceremony had been private, Zema Broussard was not to be cheated out of the festivities. She invited the entire Broussard clan to a *bal de noce* at their house. There was much eating, drinking and celebrating in general, and Catherine and Blackie led a wedding march to the cheers and clapping of dozens of her new relatives. Uncle Bat had played the old songs for them on his *beau violon*, and Blackie had looked so handsome in his gray morning suit that she had fallen in love with him all over again.

Just before she and Blackie had finally left his parents' home late that evening, Elisa Broussard had come to her and embraced her tenderly. "Take care of him, Catherine," she had said, tears in her eyes. "He's a good man. And you've already made him so happy..."

"I'll take care of him, Elisa," Catherine had answered. "And I'll wish for you to find your own happiness—wherever it's waiting for you."

Blackie had promised Catherine a wedding trip to New Orleans, but instead of going north from St. Martinville toward the interstate, he had headed in the opposite direction, passing through New Iberia, resisting all Catherine's pleas that he tell her where they were going. When at last they rounded a familiar curve and the car's headlights hit the brick pillars and gabled roof of Petit Coeur, Catherine was too surprised and touched to speak.

"It's for you, darlin'," he told her gently, pulling up to the porch and stopping the car. "For us. I bought it before you ever said you'd marry me, hoping for the best. And then when I thought I'd lost you, I figured I'd at least have the house we both loved." He laughed softly. "I don't know what I would've done if it hadn't worked out between us—roamed the halls with the other ghosts, I guess. But I'll enjoy it a lot more with you in it, that's for sure." He turned serious, caught her hand. "This will always be your home, *chère*," he whispered. "Always. I told you once that my family came first, that I would always take care of them. And I will."

He had more than kept his word. Since their marriage, he had involved himself in various construction and development projects in the Teche area. Best of all, he had lately begun to show an increasing awareness of problems between local residents and the Corps of Engineers. He still refused to be pushed, but he had talked several times with Doug MacDonald, and Catherine could see that he was gradually becoming an unofficial liaison. No one could do that sort of thing like Blackie. Thinking of it, Catherine quietly exulted. It seemed that he had exorcised a few ghosts of his own.

And his music... Blackie would always have his music. It was as much a part of him as his breathing. He couldn't give it up, and she wouldn't let him. After all, she had begun falling in love with him the very first night she had heard him play. As Clarence had said, anyone could be an engineer, but it took a special talent to make people happy with music the way Blackie did. And he had written a beautiful love song for her...

With a little start, Catherine focused on the present. "...our beautiful restoration architect," Clarence was saying, "and now one of our very own: Catherine Nolan Broussard." She rose easily, her condition not yet so advanced that she had difficulty moving. But beside her, Blackie rose with her, his hand at her elbow, ready to steady her if she needed it. He had been so careful, so cherishing of her since the onset of her pregnancy.

She stepped to the mike. "Ladies and gentlemen," she began in her cool, firm voice, "I'm delighted to be here with you today as we celebrate the opening of this wonderful house. When I first came to Louisiana fifteen months ago, I knew it would be a new experience for me, but I can truly say that I had no idea just how new it would be." She threw the briefest of glances at Blackie, who flashed her his blinding grin. The audience laughed appreciatively.

"Of course, I didn't know it when I accepted the job, but I also feel that I've helped to preserve my own children's heritage." She smiled. More laughter.

"At any rate," she continued, growing serious, "I do want to tell you what a rare and precious experience restoring this house has been to me. And for this, I have many people to thank—not only all of you who shared your knowledge and your priceless family heirlooms to make this dream a reality, but you who had enough personal faith in me—more, in fact, than I had in myself—to trust me with this job." She paused, looked at the front row. "Clarence, Toni, Gussie—" Her voice shook. "Thank you all, from the bottom of my heart.

"I'd also like to give special thanks to my husband, Jean Broussard, for working so tirelessly on nearly every phase of this restoration," she went on. "In many cases, he knew better than I what to do."

Blackie nodded graciously, but not before he drew another laugh from the crowd by looking around and pretending not to know who Jean Broussard was.

"And my thanks also go to my husband's uncle, Jean Baptiste Charpiot, for so generously sharing his family treasures and his knowledge of Acadian lore with us." She looked at Uncle Bat, sitting solemnly beside Gussie and Alain in the front row, then glanced toward the corner of the porch, where a young *mamou* plant already flourished.

"I may have come to town with a couple of degrees," she went on, "but you—all of you—are the ones who've taught me how to live, and how to love. In fact, I'd like to quote to you the phrase that's enriched my life—that's taught me more than any college course I've ever had." She paused. The audience waited expectantly.

She spread her hands, and her mouth slowly widened into an unerring imitation of Blackie's grin. *"Laissez les bon temps rouler,"* she said, in a perfect Cajun accent.

There was a moment of astonished silence, then the crowd laughed, cheered, clapped, whistled. But Catherine heard only her husband's shout of rich baritone laughter as, in his delight, he jumped to his feet, threw his arms around her and lifted her off her feet in a joyous embrace.

Dear Readers,

We are fortunate to possess a very special heritage. When the Acadian French, among them our ancestors, were evicted from L'Acadie in the Grand Dérangement of 1755 and came to settle in South Louisiana, they were forced to leave behind them nearly all their worldly goods. But they brought with them some things no one could ever take away—their love of life, of family, of God, and of the music that is at the very heart of the Cajun consciousness.

Unfortunately, as often happens, the French language passed out of our own family a few generations after our ancestors crossed the Sabine River into Texas. But other priceless gifts were handed down, such as strong family ties. At every possible opportunity, we all came together to eat, talk, laugh and sing. Even funerals reunited us, and on every occasion we were surrounded with loving closeness.

As children, we took this closeness for granted. Now, we treasure it. We still gather with cousins to play and sing, and our father tells our children of his own childhood, of the evening *veillées* when he and his *cousins* sat on the *galerie* of the ancestral home and listened to the old folks spin tales in French. We hope our children will always remember, even if they live at the far ends of the earth.

It has given us a special measure of joy and pride that in telling the story of Catherine and Blackie we have rediscovered our own heritage. Love and *joie de vivre*—what more could anyone want?

Laissez les bon temps rouler.

The Authors

CRAWFISH ETOUFFEE

3 ribs celery, chopped
2 cloves garlic, minced
1 or 2 bay leaves
1 stick margarine
1 medium onion, chopped
1 bell pepper, chopped
1 lb cooked, peeled crawfish tails
2 cups water*
2 tbsp catsup
1 tbsp green-onion tops
1 tbsp chopped parsley
1 tbsp paprika
2 tsp Creole seasoning, if available
1 tsp Worcestershire sauce
Tabasco sauce to taste (Carefull!)
Salt and pepper to taste
Cayenne pepper to taste
Crawfish fat (optional)

Melt margarine and crawfish fat in heavy frying pan. Sauté chopped vegetables. Add crawfish and cook 2 to 3 minutes. Add remaining ingredients. Cook slowly about 40 minutes. Stir occasionally. Add more water if needed. (Etouffée should be the consistency of a thick stew.) Serve over hot cooked rice. Serves 4.

*If crawfish tails are packed in their own liquid, omit water and substitute liquid.

SHRIMP GUMBO

Gumbo is a nutritious soup thickened with filé (pow-dered sassafras leaf) or okra and served over a mound of hot rice. There are many variations, but gumbo is most often made with seafood. A popular variety uses both shrimp and oysters, but there is also a chicken gumbo, and chicken and turkey carcasses and ham bones may be boiled for the stock. Some cooks add pureed boiled vegetables. It is a great dish for using leftovers and can be enriched in many creative ways.

Gumbo originated in South Louisiana, and the name is derived, depending on whom you ask, from *kombo*, the Chactaw Indian name for sassafras, or from the Bantu word for okra, *ngumbo*. Both filé and okra gumbos have their devotees.

Almost every Cajun recipe begins with "First make a roux..." and gumbo is no exception. A roux is made by browning flour in butter or oil. Many cooks sauté chopped vegetables such as onions, celery and green peppers and perhaps a clove or two of garlic in the butter or oil until transparent, and then add the flour and stir over medium heat until the flour is well browned before adding a liquid.

This basic recipe for Shrimp Gumbo is from *River Road Recipes*, published by the Junior League of Ba-ton Rouge.

3 pods garlic (optional)
2 onions, chopped
1 bay leaf
2 lbs uncooked shrimp, peeled and deveined
1 can tomatoes

2 qts water
3 cups okra, chopped or 1 tsp filé
4 tbsp oil
2 tbsp flour
1 tsp salt
pepper to taste

In a large skillet, make a dark roux of flour and 2 tbsp oil. Add shrimp and stir constantly for a few minutes. Set aside.

In a 4-quart pot, smother okra and onions in oil. Add tomatoes when okra is nearly cooked. Add water, bay leaf, garlic, salt and pepper. Add shrimp and roux. Cover and cook slowly for 30 minutes.

If okra is not used, remove from heat and add filé.

Serve with rice. Serves 6 to 8.

COUCHE-COUCHE

Couche-couche is like a bread, a starch or a cereal. It may be eaten with fried eggs and sliced tomatoes or with cane syrup as a dessert.

2 cups yellow cornmeal
2 cups milk
5 tbsp cooking oil
1 tsp salt
1 tsp sugar
1 tsp baking powder

In a heavy iron skillet with tight-fitting lid, heat 4 tbsp cooking oil. Mix together, in order, cornmeal, salt, sugar, baking powder and remaining oil. Pour mixture into skillet. Lower heat to medium and cover tightly. Stir every few minutes and scrape bottom of skillet. Cook for about 20 minutes or until Couche-couche reaches consistency of crumbled-up corn bread.

PECAN PRALINES

3 cups sugar
3 cups shelled pecans
1 cup milk or cream
1 tbsp butter
1 tsp vanilla
salt (dash)

Cook milk and sugar until mixture forms soft ball when dropped in cold water. Add pecans and continue cooking until mixture forms a firm ball. Add salt, butter and vanilla. Mix well. Pour praline mixture by spoonfuls onto waxed paper or buttered dish to form patties. Allow to cook completely.

Harlequin Superromance.

COMING NEXT MONTH

#394 ALWAYS SAY YES • Anne Laurence
Dusty Landry knew John Taggert was the finest man
she'd ever meet . . . and would make the worst
husband. He was just like her father—totally
committed to the police force. Was it hopeless? Not
if Dusty could help it.

#395 ABOVE SUSPICION • Eleanor Woods
Celebrated by the townsfolk of Jefferson City,
Louisiana, for her sunny disposition, innkeeper
Jenny Castle was suddenly acting like a bear with a
sore paw. No one would ever have suspected that the
reason for Jenny's ire was private investigator Jonah
McCai, who was convinced she was the brains
behind a dognapping ring, of all things!

#396 IN THE CARDS • Julie Meyers
Rachel Locke was shocked to learn that her elderly
aunt had taken in a motley group of boarders. But
the shock turned to gratitude when she met Sandor
Pulneshti, a devastatingly handsome architect with a
mysterious Gypsy past. . . .

#397 JESSICA'S SONG • Virginia Nielsen
CAJUN MELODIES BOOK THREE
The Louisiana bayous were home to fisherman
Armand LeBlanc who could read the tides and the
stars, but not the written word. Professor Jessica
Owen wanted to teach him everything she knew. Yet
it was Armand who taught her about love. . . .

HARLEQUIN
American Romance®

Join in the

Rocky Mountain Magic

Experience the charm and magic of The Stanley Hotel in the Colorado Rockies with #329 BEST WISHES this month, and don't miss out on further adventures to take place there in the next two months.

In March 1990 look for #333 SIGHT UNSEEN by Kathy Clark and find out what psychic visions lie ahead for Hayley Austin's friend Nicki Chandler. In April 1990 read #337 RETURN TO SUMMER by Emma Merritt and travel back in time with their friend Kate Douglas.

ROCKY MOUNTAIN MAGIC—All it takes is an open heart. Only from Harlequin American Romance

All the Rocky Mountain Magic Romances take place at the beautiful Stanley Hotel.

RMM2-1